THREE GRAVES FULL

JAMIE MASON

AN IMPRINT OF PUSHKIN PRESS

ONE
an imprint of Pushkin Press
71–75 Shelton Street, London WC2H 9JQ

Copyright © 2013 by Jamie Mason

First published in the United States by Gallery Books in 2013

First published in Great Britain by ONE in 2013

ISBN 978 0 957548 80 0

Printed in Great Britain by
TJ International Ltd, Padstow, Cornwall

www.pushkinpress.com

for Art, Julia, and Rianne—always
and
for the finest practitioner of
long-distance brain surgery in all the world,
Graeme Cameron

All places are alike,
and every earth is fit for burial.

—Christopher Marlowe

THERE IS very little peace for a man with a body buried in his backyard. Jason Getty had grown accustomed to the strangling night terrors, the randomly prickling palms, the bright, aching surges of adrenaline at the sight of Mrs. Truesdell's dog trotting across the lawn with some unidentifiable thing clamped in its jaws. It had been seventeen months since he'd sweated over the narrow trench he'd carved at the back border of his property; since he'd rolled the body out of the real world and into his dreams.

Strangely though, it wasn't recalling the muffled crunch of bone that plagued him, nor the memory of the cleaning afterward, hours of it, all the while marveling that his heart could pound *that* hard for *that* long. No. It was that first shovelful of dark dirt spraying across the white sheet at the bottom of the grave that came to him every time he closed his eyes to sleep. Was it deep enough? He didn't know—he wasn't a gravedigger. Then again, in his mind he wasn't a murderer either, but facts are facts.

No disaster can stay shiny and new forever. No worry has ever been invented that the mind cannot bully down into mere background noise. For the first few days and weeks, Jason thought of nothing else. Every night, sometimes twice a night (and one fretful night, the first time it rained, it was six times), he slipped through the shadows to the margin of evergreen and poplar that marked the end of his acreage to check and recheck the integrity of his secret. To his eyes, the irregular rectangle of disturbed earth might as well have been bordered in neon. It was a gaudy exhibit to the barbaric instinct that lay curled at the core of every tamed human brain. Evolution had brought us out of the trees, then culture had neutered the beast, but even a eunuch can get angry.

To his right, his little rancher offered up a cozy nook that glowed and whirred with modern conveniences. To his left and just beyond the trees, the ground fell away to a cleared swath of municipal land dotted with linked pairs of electrical towers marching off into the civilized distance. But this middle ground called back to him over and over, whispering, chanting in time with his knocking heart, to keep him ever mindful of the one moment he'd lost millennia of breeding and found himself the puppet of a howling primal rage.

Jason didn't sleep. He didn't eat. He filed his reports and managed his client list robotically and correctly, without forgetting for more than a few seconds at a time that a body was moldering under several feet of topsoil and pine needles thirty yards from his back door.

Then one day, Dave from Accounting made a joke and Jason laughed. The sound of it rang sudden and carefree, natural as a lightning strike. His skin stung as a warning blazed though his blood. *You've killed someone, you idiot. You buried him out back. Don't forget!* But by that time, five minutes had already gone by, and he found, as more days came and went, that the spell became a worry, became a niggle, became part of who he was.

The heater blew his own sour breath back in his face as he sped home from the first time he'd allowed himself a break. He'd blurted, "Yeah, sure," at the unexpected invitation to Friday's after-work beers. The glow of good cheer faded with the parting handshakes, and in its place needles of chills played at odds with the sweat running in all his creases. No amount of anxious accelerator stomping made the drive home take less than forever. He'd bypassed the house altogether and fled straight into the woods, knowing he'd find . . . what? Nothing. Just trees and wooded rustling-quiet and the distant, sibilant whisper of freeway traffic.

The ground kept its promise to lie still, and the pines and leafy trees were faithful to sift camouflage over the scene. Jason's thoughts by day took on an uncriminal rhythm, but the burial came back each night to play against the inside of his eyelids, only in more Technicolor than there had actually been on that moonlit October night.

The anniversary of the incident erased much of his progress. Jason imagined the universe contained just enough irony to disallow him the turning of that last calendar page; the one that would symbolically stretch the hundred-odd steps from the back deck to the body, as if day 366 were a magical meridian in time—his own personal New Year's Day. He marked it, survived it, and spent another winter hibernating in a cocoon of fading anxiety. The nightmares, however, they lingered.

That spring, the neglected upkeep of his house snagged his attention and gave rise to a new and improved brand of concern. The shrubs were overgrown and the small front garden bristled with three seasons of vagabond weeds, but somehow the thought of wielding a shovel and hoe turned his spine to putty and made everything in the pantry vaguely nauseating. Three consecutive Saturdays had him bravely facing down the shed door and left him three consecutive Sundays in bed with a fever of uncertain origin.

If home is where the heart is, Jason had lived in his throat for a long time. As such, not a lot of maintenance had been required beyond crunching antacids to cool the pipes. His paranoia resurfaced with the surety that the neighbors, even as spread out as they were, would begin to wonder about the shaggy disarray of his lawn. The nagging cycle of peering over his shoulder and in between the curtains crested again.

In May, the riotous blooming of dandelions and sow thistle left him with little choice: do it yourself or hire out. Dearborn's Landscaping contracted for the lowest bid to aerate and seed the front lawn, prune the bushes, weed and edge the front and side mulch beds, and plant low-maintenance perennials all around the entry and up the driveway. Jason aimed to keep himself from yard work for as long as possible and didn't mind writing off the cost one little bit. A craggy foreman named Calvin brought two young men and an open-mesh trailer full of rusty gadgets for the two-day job of grooming away a year and a half of avoidance.

Jason hovered out front all that first morning: washing his car, chatting up Calvin, making a Broadway production of checking the mail—twice at that, and well before the postman had even made his rounds. By midday, he dared to breathe a little easier, completely convinced that none of them would go one step farther than they had to.

A bold line had been drawn at the edge of their contractual obligation, and obviously no one was headed out back for fear of finding anything more to do.

He made himself a sandwich and watched the work-men from the windows for a while before wandering off to the den. He enjoyed a dog show on television, one ear straining for any out-of-place thump or rustle from the men outside. Hearing no such thing and wrung out from all his chafing, Jason let his head fall back against the easy chair. Just for a moment. The late-afternoon sun slanting in through the window weighed like warm gold coins on his eyelids. He fought the drag of them, but the orange glow was so pretty, so cheerful. The recliner cradled him close while the ceiling fan shushed the thoughts from his head.

In his dream, a young man in Dearborn's coveralls knelt in the grass. He smiled and nodded up to Jason after having just slotted the trowels and handforks back into his toolbox, absently brushing his hands clean of their work. Jason yammered gibberish. He flailed and capered, will-ing to do a bare-naked anything to stall off the inevitable moment when the gardener would look down again to gather up his kit. The young man, his face familiar but somehow not quite recognizable, listened intently as Jason babbled, all the while wiping bloody dirt from his hands onto a corner of white sheet that poked up from a ragged rent in the ground.

Jason tipped the carafe fully upside down to fill the mug beyond common sense's recommended limit. Once he'd added the cream, he realized that no one outside a Zen-tranced surgeon was lifting it from the counter without spilling, and no doubt burning, a sloppy mess all over hand and Formica alike.

"Crap," he muttered, and leaned down to blow steam from the brimming cup. The doorbell startled his pursed upper lip into the scalding coffee, and one flinch later, the imagined mess materialized pretty much as he'd predicted, although it was his lip, not his hand, that stung. "Crap," he said again. At least the spill had left the mug manageably full. He gave it half a turn against the dish towel and brought it with him to the door.

Calvin and crew had arrived shortly after eight, expecting to be done by lunchtime. The front yard was now trim and tidy, and the flower bed's machined edges were well beyond what Jason could have managed on his own with the shovel, even if he had been able to bring himself to touch it.

He'd felt better just watching them unload the trays of flowers. The glow of the colors was contagious, and the sprays of healthy green radiated rightness. Respectability had to be a well-kept garden, and Jason's mood went warm at the sight of it. The workers had been at it for nearly two hours, and Jason expected a blushing request for restroom privileges. What he got instead, at the front door, was an eyeful of an ashen-faced Calvin.

"Mr. Getty—" It was all Calvin could manage.

"Yes?" Jason's mouth answered on autopilot while a roar rose up in his ears, a nearly mechanical hum, as his mind calculated what in his yard could make a suntanned gardener turn white and trembling.

"Mr. Getty, we've found something. We think you'd better come have a look."

"All right, just let me get some shoes." Jason stumbled as he turned, sloshing more coffee out of the cup onto his pants and the floor. But what did it matter? The game was up. *Thank God, I can't do this.* No, you can play dumb. You can run. *Why did they go back there?* Why were you stupid enough to hire a landscaping crew, you worthless, spineless . . . *must think: What the hell am I going to say?*

Somewhere on the way from the closet to the front door, Jason's mind went blank. He stopped berating himself and gave up casting around for canned answers to the inevitable questions awaiting him in the backyard. He simply walked out the door, pulling it shut behind him. Calvin stood, twisting his red baseball cap in his calloused hands. Jason nodded to him and followed him off the front stoop, numbed straight through to the soles of his feet.

The four of them gathered in a cluster, standing closer than men who didn't know each other normally would, staring down into the rich black-brown of newly turned soil. Jason had a number of abandoned ambitions and had once dreamed of being a doctor. He had pored over medical encyclopedias, memorizing words that carried mystery and clout on their convoluted syllables: frontal, parietal, sphenoid, zygomatic—they flooded his mind as he looked at the ground and labeled what he saw, what the other men saw as forehead, crown, temple, and cheek. The skull's eye sockets were filled with peat, but there was no mistaking the contours and ridges. A human being, or part of one at least, had been unearthed on Jason Getty's property.

Four men stood, three in horror and revulsion and one in complete bewilderment. Jason had followed Calvin down the front steps like a man on his way to the gallows. Part of his mind noted, with a pang of regret as they passed, that the living-room windows needed washing. He had turned around the corner of the west wall, past the den window with its closed blinds, his eyes glued to the label jutting up from the collar of Calvin's blue work shirt—itching to reach out, to tuck it in, and make things right. His musings led him to run up Calvin's heels, not having noticed that he'd stopped. Not having expected him to stop nearly so soon. They hadn't even cleared the back of the house.

The foreman and his crew had uncovered a body, but not the body that Jason had interred all those months ago at the back edge of the yard. That body remained tucked into the shade of the trees and was as far away as it could be and still have Jason Getty paying the taxes on its gritty resting place. This skull turned a baleful eye from the mulch bed at the side of the house, directly underneath Jason's bedroom window, and he had no idea who it was.

2

LEAH TAMBLIN hit the garage-door button again. The hinged panels trundled up and shuddered to a halt only a third of the way open. A taunting slice of spring morning reflected in off the driveway. The defeated motor took a moment of silence, reversed itself, and the door rattled back down again, making Leah officially late for work.

"Oh, come on."

The dangling release handle proved a test of her farthest reach, but eventually she flung the door up its tracks and backed the car out of the garage and into her next dilemma. Leah, being five feet and half an inch tall on a poufy-hair day, was too short to bring the door back down without a ladder, and no way she was leaving her garage door opened to the elements, climatic or criminal.

Leah closed her eyes and took a deep, calming breath, which might have worked wonders had she thought to unclench her grinding teeth. If she was going to be late, she could at least have the repair appointment in the works. She stomped back into the house and dialed her office number, pulling the telephone directory from the bottom cupboard. The phone tucked into place between her cheek and shoulder just as her supervisor answered the call.

"Chris, hi. It's Leah." She flipped and rifled the pages of ads in the vicinity of *G* for garage-door repair. "I've got technical difficulties this morning. I'm gonna be a little l—" The flyer slipped out from between the phone book's pages, from somewhere near the end of the alphabet, as she lifted the book for repositioning. The corner of the paper was brittle and wrinkled from having been wet at some point. It slid across the countertop, and she stopped it with a tentative palm to keep it from sailing onto the floor. Reid smiled up at her, frozen in midparty mirth, from under the bold proclamation MISSING. Chris, on the other end of the line, cleared his throat, but out of necessity or impatience she couldn't tell. Truthfully, she barely noticed. "—late," she finished in a whisper.

Reid's face was still around. In the living room, his eyes crinkled over smiles of varying ease in posed school portraits that chronicled the variations in the rock-star hairstyles of his younger years. There were band photos and a few scattered candid shots in easel-backed frames throughout the house. Stuck to the refrigerator, there was even a magnet made from a snapshot of the two of them at the beach, sunny and windblown, grinning at the camera with their arms wound around each other. But these were fixtures, all but invisible to her. In their routineness, they were easier to forget than the jarring holes they left in her peripheral vision when she tried to pack them away.

His clothes had hung in the closet until the dust on the shoulders of his darker shirts was a grim billboard to his absence. But to be rid of the dust, she'd have to wash the clothes, and the thought of doing a load of laundry for a man who would never need it was more macabre than simply leaving everything just as it was. Eventually, she'd packed his things into boxes and, once she'd grown weary of tripping over them, moved the boxes to the attic.

The paraphernalia of the search had been the hardest to gather up for storage. She'd left stacks of papers and bundles of relevant mail spread out over the counter for so long, as if they still had potential; as if the clues and leads were only stubbornly disconnected, waiting to be joined together by a worthy Dr. Frankenstein and jolted awake to finish Reid's rescue. Lowering the lid over the box of police reports, press clippings, and her own notebooks of lists and contacts had sent her running to the bathroom, falling to her knees, and dry heaving over the commode until flashes of light swam across her eyes. Holding this morning's stray reminder of that time in her life, she couldn't remember having stashed one of the flyers in the phone book or why she would ever have done such a thing in the first place.

Reid had gone out with an itinerary: stop by his work for a bar-staff training meeting; hit the music store for guitar strings; Home Depot for an extension cord and lightbulbs; and bring back a late lunch. He had made his meeting and the trip to the music store. Four days later, the police identified the burned-out shell of his car on a gravel road nearly sixty miles away.

The day he disappeared dragged on forever: annoyance first at the inconvenience, suspicion next, culminating in a shouting match with Dean, his brother, when Leah accused him of knowing "exactly where he is and covering for him just like you did the last time." Dean's insistence that they phone the police, once the sun had set and Reid's voice mail registered full, had sent the mistrust cresting over into fear. Dean was never without a joint or two in his pocket, and he was well-known by the authorities for his petty association with the fraternity of usual suspects. He avoided the local police as much as they kept their eyes peeled for him, and nothing short of disaster would have him inviting the cops into his life.

There was no real sleep with Reid missing. Not for the initial few days. Somewhere in the first forty-eight hours, the lights went out at someone else's say-so and Leah's eyelids closed in spite of themselves. She'd lie down, achingly alone, at everyone's insistence, and without her consent her brain would unhook itself from consciousness. But if there was a footfall on the stairs, or a ringing telephone, or headlights sweeping across the bedroom walls, the crashing, pounding awareness of all that was wrong with the world burned away the blankness in an instant.

Leah's waking hours cycled through minutes of fretting; of frantic *doing*, and the marshaling of the troops—friends, relatives, and volunteers—to *do* also; of praying and discovering that she alternately believed in God and loved Him, believed in God and hated Him, and that she was kidding herself and there was no God. Then there were the seconds she forgot that anything was wrong at all.

When she'd gone looking for a recent photo for the flyer, she'd found Reid's AWOL sunglasses in the desk drawer and picked them up with a laugh, turning around to tease him for his forgetfulness. Through the dining room she saw Sheila, Reid's mother, nodding soberly to a police detective at the kitchen counter. For three seconds and one clear, deep breath, Leah had been free of the day. Reality seeped back through her in a slow, sad flood. A rising, cold dread was what spoiled these moments, not the hot collision of panic and urgency that hurled her from sleep. Her brain continued to trick her like this, running for refuge measured in a few calm heartbeats. It happened more and more as the exhaustion set in.

The first three days were a series of battles with the experts over whether there was any real problem at all. By the end of the evening on the first day, Reid's family and closest friends were convinced there had been some sort of an accident. Dean went driving the most likely routes Reid would have taken, and Sheila dialed the closest hospitals with shaking fingers. Leah spoke to the manager of Neptune, the club where Reid tended bar and played most of his gigs. She called the other band members, who dropped everything and came running, as she knew they would. The gravity of phoning the police, with its implied admission of catastrophe, smothered a quiet down over the group as they waited for the patrol cruiser.

The police confirmed that he'd not been arrested and they took a preliminary report, all the while trying to disguise boredom as reassurance. Reid was a young man with a car and a wallet full of credit, and the obvious implication was left to hang in the air. They grilled Leah as to whether they'd argued, which she denied. The next morning dawned, impossibly surreal, as the first day since the eighth grade that Leah didn't know where Reid was.

Of course, plenty of hours had been unaccounted for in the previous sixteen years, lost hours that had always been a point of contention. Reid loved Leah, there was no doubt. And she loved him. They had been a couple since Mrs. Doyle's homeroom class. But his head had, on occasion, been turned. When she had known or suspected, Leah would fume and rant for a few hours, then withdraw into the threat of unending silence. Eventually she would give in to the barrage of honest remorse. Reid was always hugely sorry in proportion to how much he loved her.

Leah was neither weak nor stupid; she was practical. In her mind, relationship was compromise, and compromise was a simple contract. Everyone offers up something as a loss in order to gain a list of must-haves. Constant fidelity was the sacrifice in this transaction, but Reid was affectionate, talented, and celebrated as the life of the party. In all of his faults, what was good was real. He had held her hand on the science-class field trip through the old-growth forest and never let her go. As angry as she ever got with him, she always felt him there in her left hand, a warmth that tingled in her palm and held her back from the uncharted wildness that could (and surely would if given half the chance) gobble her up and erase her as if she'd never existed at all.

Reid on his own, though, was only part of the arrangement he secured for Leah. It was family, and the years of warm belonging she'd felt, that kept her at his side. Ideas and ideals were fine enough, but Reid, with his smile and off-brand devotion, delivered a clan, solidly there, that loved Leah more than her blood ties ever had: an amusing puppy of a brother in Dean and a mother, with all the sweet connotations the word can hold, in Sheila. Sheila, in her terribly fragile health, owned Leah's loyalty and heart more than her son ever had.

And it was Sheila, with her gentle manipulations, who had brought them all to the very threshold of a wedding to keep them together. The police officers had made much of how Reid had vanished thirteen days before he was due to walk down the aisle. Cold feet made such easy work of a missing person's investigation. And indeed, a set of cold feet figured prominently in the goings-on, but they weren't missing. They carried Leah from room to room, trying to stride off the nervous energy of guilt.

She'd walked with Reid into one very real and tangly wood when they were children, and little by little over the years they'd walked right out into another one, a metaphorical snarl of need and obligation. She knew very well the long, swooping drop between playing along with a situation and being legally bound to it. She'd come to the very edge of that bridge and peered between the slats, hesitating at the choice to cross or jump.

With Reid gone, Leah's manic pacing wore flattened tracks into the carpet, the edgy, useless circles run to purge regret from a bride who had been praying for a way out. But the house, she found, was a treadmill, and she couldn't outrun the secret, little thrills of what her life might yet be. She didn't have to back out. She didn't have to crush Sheila. She didn't have to break Reid's heart. These notions sparked without permission between the fits of crying and the pangs of wanting his hand back in hers, and on their heels, she wrestled the knowledge of how awful these thoughts made her.

His mother's pale face shook with rage at the slow track of official involvement in those first few days. The phone never stopped ringing, and the parade of well-wishers and do-gooders kept up an industrious buzz that felt nothing like progress.

When they came with news of Reid's car, the mood

shifted. The civilians retreated in discomfort with hollow offers of "anything we can do," and the police presence increased threefold. No one said it for days, but everyone knew that Reid was dead. The investigation flowered in false leads, then collapsed under the ponderous weight of nothing to go on.

The milestones of time accumulated—a week, and the crying was still rampant, as were the kind prompts not to lose hope; a month, and the phone rang much less, but still occasionally with callers who didn't realize that he was gone; a year, and a picture of Reid went into the casket with Sheila and rested in a marked grave in a churchyard. His smiling likeness was tucked away in the crook of a dead woman's arm, and also at some point into the back of the telephone book, then finally into a cupboard drawer in the kitchen, while his body lay under hastily strewn and unconsecrated ground, tapped into place with a garden shovel on a moonlit night by a man that none of the rest of them knew.

3

THEY SAY God gives us no more than we can handle. That is either an horrendous lie or the loosest possible definition of the word *handle*. Looking down the length of himself, Jason couldn't understand how everything still appeared attached. His mind had jittered his fingers off his hands and his hands off his wrists a dozen times since he'd stalled over making the call, the undialed phone going warm and heavy in his palm. He did it anyway, of course. A few extra minutes of anonymity wasn't worth the stage fright, trembling there under Calvin's mournful encouragement to involve the authorities. "Call the police, Mr. Getty. They'll know what to do."

So he sat alone at the table, watching through the dining-room window for the unavoidable squad car to turn down the street and ruin his life.

The fever flush that had seeped all the way into his collar still burned in his cheeks. Jason hated blushing; hated that he couldn't keep from doing it; and, most of all, hated that it made him five years old again—every time—for just an instant.

The first blush he could ever remember had lit him up in the lobby of his parents' bank. His feet had dangled well above the floor as he sat in a row of waiting chairs, watching through the glass panels in the door opposite him. His mother's stiff back and the manager's bald head, nodding, then shaking, held him transfixed like the TV westerns he watched with his father, but didn't understand.

"Hey there." The pretty teller with the biggest, palest blue eyes he'd ever seen crouched to meet his level. "You're being so good, little guy, waiting out here this long. Want a sucker?" She fanned a rainbow of candy in front of his face. "What color do you like?"

"Red."

"What's your name?" Her eyelids flashed pearlescent blue to match the irises as she blinked.

"Jason Bradford Getty."

"Well, there's a mouthful. Can I just call you 'JB'?" Jason nodded, dumbstruck in the grip of peppermint breath and sparkling arctic eyes. "Swell," she said, and plucked the red one from the bouquet, but offered the rest in her other hand as well. "Hey JB, want to take the rest of these home? Maybe share them with your brothers and sisters when they get home from school?"

"Don't have any."

"Oh yeah? Same here. We match, JB, you and me. I'm an only child, too."

Looking into her smiling eyes, a feeling welled in his chest, a feeling that Jason would remember at intervals for the rest of his life, like a weighted balloon rising up through him and pulling back down all at the same time. A hope on a doubt. A reach and a recoil. Yes, but maybe no.

"Uh-huh." His eyes stung from not blinking out of her spell. His voice went tiny. "*Very* only."

"Very *only*? You mean, very *lonely*?"

"I don't—" He almost understood what he'd got wrong and "almost" itched like the dickens. It blazed in his cheeks and heated up the back of his neck. He buried his face in his mother's coat, which lay draped over the arm of the chair.

"Awwww, you sweet thing." She laughed softly and ruffled his hair.

He felt her there, waiting for him to look up, but he outlasted her. "Okay," she whispered. "Bye, bye, little Mr. Very Only. You take care, now."

The bank teller had left him all the suckers. Jason left them all under the seat cushion.

Now, he blushed when he counted out exact change. He blushed trying to untangle himself from telemarketers. He blushed at the urinal, which was completely stupid. And then sometimes, he wouldn't. There had been times he would have guessed his face would have flat-out ignited that it simply hadn't. The first time he asked Patty for a ride home. The time he'd talked off a speeding ticket after having had three beers and more devotion to the beat of the song on the radio than to the numbers on the road sign.

Sometimes that climbing sense of promise didn't feel lousy. Sometimes it straightened his spine. In those moments, Jason almost understood the mechanism; almost knew what it would take to cut the anchor and rise with the hope.

"Almost," as always, itched like the dickens.

*

Authorities. Even in the midst of his lava-faced personal earthquake, a kernel of anger glowed at the presumption of the word *authority*. What did some smug, barely-able-to-grow-a-mustache infant know about getting pushed and pushed and then pushed just a little too far? Nothing, that's what. They all ducked behind a tin badge and a gun belt as fast as the academy could churn them out. No one harassed them. No one stalked and taunted. No one found their weakest link and nudged and twisted and—

And there it was. The blue-and-white sedan pulled into view with its boxy band of roof lights dormant. Jason was surprised at the lack of fanfare, but then again, no amount of whooping, flashing urgency was going to do the guy in the garden a lick of good. Who was that guy anyway? The only reason Jason's anxious mind hadn't churned itself to butter and his tremors hadn't tipped him right out of his chair was the distraction of the skeleton in the mulch bed.

He rode the slithering waves of horror at the thought of the dead guy—God, what if it was a woman?—rotting away under his bedroom window. He felt tainted and violated, angry that someone would have the audacity to put a body in a place like that, so close to a house, to a guy's bedroom, for God's sake. He'd been sleeping eight feet from a corpse the whole time. Offended in the extreme, his mind skittered around the elephant in the middle of his psyche. Comparing his own attention to detail in these sorts of matters was a bit more than Jason could face at the moment.

The implied insult of Calvin's declining Jason's invitation to wait in the house annoyed him, too. Jason felt abandoned and miffed at the workers' avoidance as they snatched their tools from the lawn and scurried back to the truck to huddle and smoke and flick their eyes in his direction. They had no reason to be suspicious of him. For heaven's sake, the skull they'd found was bare bones. That takes time. A lot of time. He'd only been here . . .

"Almost two years," Jason answered.

"I see." The officer made a makeshift desk of the trunk lid of the cruiser and scribbled the tidbit alongside the rest of the see-Spot-run basics. He straightened up and stretched, then hooked his thumbs over his belt, fingers just brushing his sidearm to the right and his Taser to the left. Jason assumed this stance was taught at the academy to draw attention to the belt of *authority*. The cop sucked his teeth and nodded. "I went ahead and put in a call. All we need is a detective and a crime-scene team since those are human remains you've got there and I'm satisfied that this isn't"—the cop's eyes slid appraisingly over the yard and its owner—"a fresh crime scene."

"Well, I already told them that when I called and they sent you." Jason stifled the bristling indignation at being presumed an idiot.

The responding chuckle was good-natured with an undercurrent of exasperation. The officer nodded to the back of the house, where Mrs. Truesdell's mutt snuffled along the tree line. "With the calls we get? You'd think we ought to send out a SWAT team every time some hound kicks up a bone."

The both of them watched the dog, one of them casually, and the other one not nearly so. Jason's legs doubled in weight and threatened to buckle as his guts twisted into a leaden lump. The cop didn't seem to notice. He opened the trunk and rummaged through a black nylon bag. "Yeah, last fall there was a little kid that went missing and we got a call from some guy in North County just swearin' up and down that he'd found what was left of him. One look and I seen it was a broke fox skull, just as plain as day. I mean, that kid was nine years old, for cripes' sake, and he'd only been gone a week. You'd think anyone could tell the difference between a weathered, old fox skull and a . . . well, anyway . . . it was nothin'. Just a custody thing." Yellow barricade tape in hand, the cop turned back to Jason. "I'm just gonna go seal this off while we wait, okay?"

"Sure." Jason's head bobbled up and down. "Fine. Right." His stride was uneven as he adjusted his speed to keep a reasonable distance from the cop's backside and still maintain the security of having him close, of being able to distract him from any roving curiosity.

At the edge of the mulch bed, the officer stopped in a jangle of keys and creak of leather. Jason stopped, too—about ten inches off the policeman's elbow, practically close enough to kiss. Jason lurched a quick step backward after having been scanned head to toe under a set of raised eyebrows.

"You don't have to stay out here, you know," the officer said with more recommendation than sympathy in his voice. "I'd understand if it's uncomfortable for you." The cop looked down at the skull with its blanket of dirt pulled up to its nose like someone afraid of the dark.

Jason followed his gaze and shuddered. "That's not making me uncomfortable." Mrs. Truesdell's dog trotted through their peripheral vision. Jason shifted his position in front of the taller man and willed himself a wall between the cop and his backyard.

The policeman set to the task of roping off a perimeter

with the blaring yellow plastic strip wound and tied to the odd branch and gutter. Jason watched over him with unseeing eyes as the cop pinched off loop after garish loop of banner tape. Jason's focus had turned inward, viewing in the theater of his mind the scenes that would play out between now and the time that the damned *authorities* would take away these bones and leave him be—or drag him, cuffed and weeping, from his quiet life tarnished with one incident of madness.

A sharp bark wrenched him from his trance and sent barbs of fear pricking into his armpits and groin. Mrs. Truesdell's dog barked a second volley, and Jason flinched again, even though it was only an announcing call at the arrival of a car, not the excited yip of discovery. Another longish blob of a sedan, this one marked by its government-issue blandness, pulled up to the curb behind the patrol car.

Jason evaluated his opponent as the man introduced himself to the members of the Dearborn's crew still sulking in their work truck, glad-handing in a politician's ploy to set them at ease. This was the man to beat. This was the guy who had to believe him or, better yet, give him no consideration at all. Jason was not adept at fielding adversaries, but he was a crackerjack wallflower. Fear made a grim brute of the troll stalking across the front yard, but reality presented a short, trim fellow in a crisp golf shirt and khaki slacks. He extended a hand to Jason, complemented by a perfectly tempered smile to go with it: professional, comforting, not inappropriately friendly given the circumstances. It was the smile of a man with the casual clarity of being right in his purpose, right in his conscience, and right in his "authority." Jason's spine sagged into the space generally reserved for his stomach. The battle felt lost before it had begun.

"Mr. Getty, I'm Tim Bayard." Detective Bayard's hand was warm and dry, and Jason did his best to calculate the correct number of pumps required to convey his innocent-bystander status. The detective somehow fashioned a neutral pleasantry from the worst thing that Jason could currently imagine: "Some day you're having, huh?"

"I'll say." Jason's mouth twitched into an admirable best shot at an agreeable smile.

"Well, why don't you show me around and we'll figure out where to go from there."

"So, what do you know about the previous occupants?" Bayard asked.

"Nothing. I bought the place from a Realtor. She said it had been empty for a little while," said Jason.

"Did they leave anything behind? Boxes, papers, anything?" Back in the kitchen, Detective Bayard sipped from a glass of ice water as Jason shook his head. The detective's eyes roamed his notes, but Jason suspected that it was only for show, a sort of dimming and raising of the lights before the curtain call. Bayard drew a deep, preparatory breath. "Okay. Well. I'm going to call in a team to retrieve the remains. That's the first thing. We need to know who got themselves buried out here." Bayard drank again, but Jason took it as only pacing the pounce. "Mr. Getty, I'd like to get your permission to search the house."

"There's nothing here." It had zipped out too quickly and more than a bit flat, and Jason had to replay it in his head to assess the damage.

"You're likely right. And I am sorry for the intrusion. We'll be as quick as we can."

"I mean . . . it's just . . . It's my house now. And *my* things."

"If you'd feel better about it, I can get a warrant, and, of course, you may certainly involve an attorney at any time."

It was the oldest tableau in police drama. The inevitable question. That it had been made innocent by legal necessity did nothing for the one on the receiving end. All protestations of protocol aside, if an attorney was called for, the unspoken-by-law implication was *What do you have to hide?*

Jason stalled. "The people before me really didn't leave anything. Just dust."

Bayard shrugged. "All the same, I can't say I've checked it out if I haven't checked it out. You know, attics, crawl spaces, loose floorboards. I'm sorry for the intrusion, but there is every good chance we're dealing with a homicide. It may very well have happened in this house." Bayard continued with an I-feel-your-pain smile that was really just tightly pressed lips stretched back into his cheeks. "Bad luck you ended up sitting on a crime scene. We really do appreciate your cooperation."

Cooperation was actually the last thing on Jason Getty's mind. The months of distance from the October night that he'd sweated and ached through didn't exist anymore. He was back in his living room, betrayed, a fool. Very only, indeed. Hollowed out, trembling with rage and humiliation at a torrent of threats and gibes. The taunts rang in his ears, his chest and back throbbed where the heel of a strong hand had slammed him into the doorframe, the aftershock ricocheting through his ribs. There was a blank, red space in his memory and then a sound like a bell wrapped in felt, dully clanking. There were grunts of exertion and a groan of pain cut short. Cracking plastic and cracking—

"Mr. Getty?"

Jason sighed. "Sorry." He swallowed the last of his vision: his knuckles sinking into a wet crimson breach under a tangle of dark hair. He pinched the bridge of his nose. "It's just a lot for a Sunday morning."

"I know. And I am sorry." Bayard stood and gathered his things. "I'm going to head out to the car and call in for the people I need. May I go ahead and get you to sign a consent form, or should I have them start the process for a search warrant?" It felt as if Bayard made sure to catch Jason's eyes dead-on. "Really, it's no problem, either way."

Bayard would have his ramble through Jason's house, and the twinkle in the detective's damned eye was the period on that particular sentence. Pinned in the standoff, neutral and professional as it was, Jason's heart squirmed hard under his breastbone, and the fleeting hope that he was dying of a heart attack elbowed around in the queue of pressing issues at hand. "No, that's okay. You can come in and look around."

Bayard smiled, but his eyes stayed strong on Jason's. "Thanks. And the lawyer? I can give you time to look one up and get him over here."

Jason wasn't sure he could take this. He toyed with the image of falling to his knees, confessing all, and baptizing Bayard's loafers in a flood of contrite tears. Except that would have been a lie and he wasn't quite sure he'd be able to pull it off. He wasn't one bit sorry that he'd killed that son of a bitch.

Mostly he avoided thinking about it—the actual killing and that the world was short one human being because of Jason Getty. The decision to hide the evidence on his property was an enormous regret, of course, especially now.

But when the torture of the rest of the problem fell away, as it occasionally did, and the bottom line stared back at him, Jason tingled with triumph. There was horror and revulsion and a crippling fear of getting caught, but there was also satisfaction. He'd stopped it. He'd shut that vile mouth once and for all and wiped the smug smile off his lousy face. He'd seen that bastard's blood on his own hands.

"Really, if you don't have anyone in mind, or"—Bayard left a bit of important dead air on either side of a good-natured chuckle—"keep a legal eagle on retainer, the phone book's got a whole page of good local lawyers with great reputations for making sure we dot all our *i*'s and everything."

"I don't see that I need a lawyer right now."

Jason had said it without a quiver. He hadn't blinked or swallowed hard. He hadn't shifted his feet and certainly not his eyes from Bayard's. He'd even managed a comfortable smile. He should have been proud of the performance. But something had changed. Maybe the ambient temperature in the space between the two men had dropped a degree or a cloud had passed over the sun. Something was definitely, minutely altered.

"If you're going to have one, Mr. Getty, I'd say better sooner than later."

In for a penny, in for a pound. "There's no reason to, Detective Bayard. I haven't done anything wrong."

4

D ETECTIVE BAYARD pretended not to notice the inch-wide gap in the bedroom curtain that winked shut whenever he turned toward the house. But Tim Bayard noticed everything. It drove his seventeen-year-old daughter nuts. The twitching curtain and the unseen hand that worked it shouldn't have bothered him really. Getty's behavior wasn't all that strange. Anyone with a skeleton in his mulch bed and a crime-scene unit crawling all over his side yard would be drawn, morbidly, to the view. That was probably all there was to it. Probably.

Bayard cornered the lead tech out of sight of the window and its restless draperies. "So, Lyle, what've you got?"

"What do you mean?" Carter County's lead crime-scene investigator was a man of impossible-to-determine age in that his hair was salted to make the pepper incidental, but his face was as unlined as a college freshman's. His sharply pressed collar gleamed against its color-coordinated sport coat, and it all looked much more suited to night-club prowling than it did to crime-scene mucking. Bayard sometimes wondered what excuses played out to Lyle's dry cleaner, foul as his laundry was likely to be.

"I mean, what do you know?" Bayard's eyes tossed an arc of indication over his left shoulder toward the action in the flower bed. "What do you think?"

"You're kidding, right?" Lyle scowled at his watch. "I've only been here, like, forty-four minutes."

"Yeah, and you've spent forty-one of those minutes taking notes and three minutes scratching your arm."

Lyle gaped at Bayard. "What is wrong with you? You don't have anything better to do than to stand around staring at me? I've got a bug bite. It itches. Get a hobby, Tim."

"I just want to know what your first impressions are. What's in your notes?" Bayard craned his neck to peer at what Lyle had been writing.

Lyle slapped his clipboard to safety against his chest. "It's a letter to my girlfriend."

"I'm gonna tell your wife."

Lyle chuckled. "I know we don't get bodies very often, but try not to drool. It's disturbing." Detective Bayard wasn't going away. "Tim, I don't know anything about him yet." He turned back to the site.

"But you *do* know it's a *him*."

"Yeah, I think so. He's got a very manly brow."

"'Manly brow'?" Bayard scratched the back of his head and grinned. "You sounded just a little turned on right then, sport. You know that, right?"

Lyle tucked his tongue into his cheek and nodded in mild agreement. "You caught me. It was a letter to my boyfriend. Can I get back to work now?"

Bayard snagged Lyle's sleeve before he could drift back into the sight line of the window. The idea of Getty peering out from the shadowed bedroom, watching them and straining to lip-read, tickled unpleasantly at the suspicious part of Tim's imagination. "How long has the body been there?"

"Good God!" said Lyle. "I don't know! We haven't even taken the bones out yet."

"Less than two years?"

Lyle's mouth turned down in academic certainty. "Nah, no way."

"Are you sure?"

"No. How can I be sure of anything anytime soon when I'm talking to you instead of doing what I'm supposed to be doing?"

Bayard scanned the taped-off plot. "I'm just thinking out loud here, Lyle."

"Hope that's working out for you. For me? Not so much." Lyle's gaze, however, followed the cop's, and both men's moment of silence whirred with purpose.

Lyle roused first from his musing. "But assuming he went in whole, that skeleton's too clean. I mean, we've got tons of work to do—you know how long these things take. The tests and all that will be out for weeks—but I'm thinking at least three or four years."

Math and the consequences of speculation clicked away in air between them. "Do *not* write that down anywhere," Lyle added.

Bayard pressed his lips together and drifted into a contemplative headspace. "Hmmm."

Lyle watched him slip into distraction, entertained. He leaned in to stage-whisper, "Do you really get paid for that?"

"Huh?"

"All these years, do they really fork out cash for you to look serious and make thinking noises?"

"You know, I'm gonna make sure I'm on your next review panel," Bayard said.

Lyle snorted and turned back to his work.

Bayard called after him, "Hey! Let me know as soon as you find anything."

"As opposed to what? I don't start my reports, 'Dear Diary, I discovered the most interesting thing today . . . ' Gimme a break, Bayard."

The curb was quickly stacking up with an official-looking traffic jam. Bayard trotted over to a monstrous pickup squeezing into the last space that could still loosely be considered "in front" of Jason's house. "You're quick!" Bayard called.

The man behind the wheel filled up the cab a time and a half the allotted driver's space. A sleek-faced dog in the passenger seat flicked attention to every landmark as fast as its head could swivel. But the dog drew even more notice than it normally would because of the pointy, foil party hat on its head. It sent starbursts zinging off through the windshield with every movement.

"What the hell?" Tim cocked his thumb at the dog, wagging its greeting to him. "What did she do to deserve that?"

"What? It's her birthday." The two men watched the dog, which was not minding at all that the sparkling dunce cap had slipped down over one ear. "You caught me just on the way out for party supplies. This better be good."

Such a scene has an excitement that only cops can appreciate; the secret ingredient that separates those who like to watch cop shows from those who want to live them. It comes with a tight smile and a complementary tightening in the gut. "It's good," Tim confirmed. "Body in the mulch bed."

"You peg him for it?" The big man ticked a discreet nod to the front door of the house where Jason stood shuffling, hands squirming deep in his pockets. His brow mimicked his lips in a parallel set of worried crinkles that left him looking lost somewhere between a pout and a dire need for a toilet.

Bayard's flickered glance was equally camouflaged. "Nah. Not unless Lyle is way off."

"That'll be the day."

"Right. Anyway, thanks for not making me wait around, Ford."

Ford Watts climbed out of the truck that perpetuated the corny joke he'd floated for going on fifty years. He'd finagled his driver's training at age fourteen and, ever since, would not be caught behind the wheel of anything other than a namesake vehicle. Not, at the very least, without substantial grousing. When the department had gone turncoat and switched to Chevy for a stint in the eighties, everyone from the receptionist to the chief had reaped an earful from Ford Watts. This year's Ford was a deep-red, double-cab pickup.

And how he loved his cars, buffing and dabbing in devotion to the showroom glow, and always eyeing the sky for birds of ill intent. The truck bounced on its springs as he climbed out, and although the season had been wet and chilly, Ford was as rosy and shiny as the finish on the polished cab. He dwarfed his human company by about the same proportion that his truck made the other cars look like toys.

Bayard briefed him on the basics as they crossed to the house. Jason had slunk back inside at the slamming of the truck door, so they were alone on the stoop while Bayard sketched out the simple strategy. "So, I'm going to take Valerie from Lyle's team with me and we'll have a first look around, while you get the search consent forms signed. You know, ask him all the same stuff I did. Just keep him outta my hair for a little while."

"You brought me out here on a Sunday to babysit?" Ford grumped from his full altitude, an impressive nine inches above Bayard's head, without somehow achieving the intimidation he was trying for.

"I could've called someone else. I thought you'd be interested."

"It's Tessa's birthday," Ford said.

Bayard pulled an inspired face, all high eyebrows and pursed lips. "Oooo! Maybe you should go get her, trot her around a little."

"I do need to get her out of the truck. She'll get lonely. And she'll likely need a wee if I'm gonna be a bit. But either way, uh-uh, Tessa's not working on her birthday."

"Ford, Tessa doesn't know it's her birthday. She's a dog."

"Yeah, well, Maggie surely knows, and she's none too happy with you. That's where we were going. She was sending me out for candles for the cake when you called."

"Oh, God, your wife has finally lost her mind. She baked the dog a birthday cake?"

"Well, meat loaf *is* a cake if you're a dog. It's Tessa's favorite."

Bayard shut his eyes and shook his head as they both chuckled, Ford trailing his laugh behind him as he hustled back to rescue Tessa.

Tim called after him, "And do you think she could lose the doggone hat? It might be nice if we looked just the least little bit legitimate here."

Ford flashed him the middle finger from behind his back with such blinding speed, Bayard would have missed it if he'd been mid-blink. Ford snatched a quick look over his shoulder to see if he'd made his mark and then every which way to see if anyone else had seen him.

In fact, there was no real mystery in Ford Watts's inability to terrify. It seemed that God had simply taken a coffee break once He'd chiseled out the six-foot-five-and-a-half, rawboned frame. And when it came time to breathe life into the giant, the Almighty had reached over one jar too far and added a pinch of eternally ten-year-old boy instead of the helping of tyrant that would have better suited. The damage was done. The resultant creature inspired love and loyalty across the board, from his mother all the way down to the muttly puppy that he and his childless wife had adopted four years earlier—Tessa the wonder dog.

Tessa had, at times, filled the K9 void in Mid-County Division. As a volunteer and occasional recruit, her worth had been proven more often by accident and by being in the right place at the right time than by anything else.

Carter County laid out a sprawling semirural splotch on the map, wedged in between two humming cosmopolitan grids. It was a turmoil sandwich: bustling at both ends with the spillover of drugs, thievery, and the inevitable violence created by too many people crammed into too stingy a square acreage. In between, it was mostly the car-boosting, brawling, mailbox-baseball prankster set. Mid-County boasted only three all-purpose detectives and no frills. But the legroom was more often appreciated than bemoaned, and the workload was just enough to keep everyone complaining more or less good-naturedly. And they had Tessa. Ford was helplessly in love with the animal and figured she was the smartest dog in all the state. As guileless as he was, Ford wasn't often wrong.

Ford was also an excellent choice to sit across from Jason Getty and massage more details from him. Jason chatted, working in his ten-dollar words of nerves and distraction over the big man's slower manner. Jason, apparently, did not watch enough television police drama. Ford shrugged off any offense and accepted the arrangement for the benefit of what he could discover.

He split his attention between Jason's answers and crafting the next question for maximum open-ended options, and also, lastly, to watching Tessa. She had poked her nose into the corners and twitched her ears to the household sounds, but only in mild interest, using up the time in the way dogs do between naps. At first, she seemed mostly content to sit at her master's knee once the two men had taken up their places at the kitchen table. When they were good and settled into their conversation, though, she was anything but at ease in her place.

She fidgeted as if the floor were shifting beneath her and sped urgent looks from Ford to Jason, leaving Ford to wonder what all he was missing in the exchange. She finally cast what could only be a pleading glance back to him, then crept forward the two steps to Jason's side and licked his hand.

Houses were jumbled to the point they were sometimes boring for Tessa. The daily business of the same people pacing lap after lap over their closed-up spaces wore stale paths through the rooms. Traces of any interest stacked up until nothing meant much at all. Sometimes shoes were good, or maybe their clothes if they'd been out, or their hands if they'd been eating, but all the cleaning up and scrubbing down just made perfume soup of anything important.

The only thing newly interesting in this house was the man. Worry pressed out from him, over Tessa, like the tickle of a brewing storm. It roused out the fussy that lived in the pads of her paws and ran up and down the length of her backbone. But she didn't want to bite him and he didn't raise a growl in her throat. She only wanted for him not to fret.

Ford didn't seem to see it, the worry in the man. Ford didn't smile or lean back in his chair to put everyone at ease. He didn't tell the man that everything would be just fine. So she told him herself as best she could with a stroke of her tongue to the back of his hand. He patted kindness into her head, but he wouldn't meet her eye.

The crime-scene investigator's assistant, Valerie, clipped down the hall, hard on her boot heels, stopping at each doorway in her search for Bayard. "Tim? Where are you?"

"Hey, Val! I'm back here." *Back here* was what Jason had referred to as the laundry room during the initial tour, but if honesty were afoot, it would more accurately have been labeled the laundry closet.

She made her way to the last door and leaned on the frame to deliver her findings.

"Bet you go through a lot of shoes," Bayard said with a wink and a smirk before she could start.

"Huh?"

"You don't grind down the heels?"

"Do your job, Tim." She laughed. "Quit analyzing me." She snuck a quick peek at her boots. "Anyway, I talked to the real estate agent. She's amazing—a real busybody. She knows everything, down to the last rumor, going back years. She remembered this place, no problem. Apparently was a young couple living here." Valerie looked to her notes. "Boyd and Katielynn Montgomery. They moved out half a year before she sold it to Mr. Getty."

"Okay." Tim grunted and squeezed between the washer and dryer and shone a flashlight through the grille of a tall access vent in the wall behind the washing machine.

"She said she only dealt with Mr. Montgomery. Nice enough guy, very country-proper and polite; always quick with the 'ma'am' and the—"

"Val." Bayard leaned in and squinted into the murky recess. "Can you hand me a screwdriver from that case, please?" He held out his hand, a gumshoe-surgeon waiting for his sleuth-scalpel. She delivered the tool having barely looked away from her notebook. Bayard unfastened the panel and jiggled the bright beam deeper into the unobstructed hole in the wall.

"Anyway, she said she'd be happy to bring copies—"

"Val."

"Yeah?"

"I'm gonna need a pair of gloves and an evidence bag."

Valerie handed over the requested items, all chatter extinguished. The louvered panel had covered a hole cut into the wall, a foot and a half off the floor, giving access to the plumbing behind the washing machine. For a man of Ford's size, it would have been the biblical eye of the needle, but Bayard hooked one arm into the drywall and ducked a shoulder into the narrow space. He reached behind a tangle of pipes and slid a small bag over years of accumulated dust and laundry powder. He chewed at his lips as the flashlight bobbed over his grim prize: a woman's purse, the canvas darkly stained. Tim ran his gloved thumb across a plastic photo sleeve dangling off a ball-chain key ring. A young blond woman beamed from behind the clouded cover, a brindle, box-headed puppy under each arm, crushed against her cheeks in a gleeful cuddle.

"Val"—Tim's tone had changed in discovery—"I need you to go find Lyle for me. Tell him I need him to look at something."

Just as a magnetic compass points north, a cop's compass swivels toward the indelible stain of trespass. Detectives live for the hidden clue, the evidence that marks the next turn on the path. The thrill of following a hunch and of having been right about it often outshines the paycheck. But there is always a moment of regret, too, when the thing turns up, proclaiming the deed, unmistakably testifying that someone has done something terrible.

Lyle and Bayard squared off on the concrete walk that bisected Jason Getty's front lawn.

"Everyone always says that you're so smart," Bayard started.

"Well, everyone is lovely. Remind me to send them a fruit basket," said Lyle.

"Yeah, but you were wrong."

"Unlikely, as I haven't done anything yet."

Bayard extended a paper bag toward the crime-scene specialist. "You said it was a *he*. I'm pretty sure that body is Katielynn Montgomery's. She used to live here and I have her purse. It appears to be covered in blood." Tim gave the bag a little shake for emphasis.

Lyle extended his own paper bag. "Tell me, when you're sitting on my review panel and it's shown that I've done all your work for you, do I get your raise as well as my own?"

Bayard considered both paper bags. "Mine's bigger."

Lyle ground his teeth over a laugh. "It's a him. And I know who *he* is, unless *he* was carrying someone else's wallet and shopping. Bow before the gods of nylon and plastic, the downfall of worms, bugs, and grave-juice everywhere." He gave his own bag an imitative shake. "And I'm pretty sure I know just about when he died, too."

Bayard thought back to the hidden handbag, dark with ruddy stains. "Well then, what the hell happened to Katielynn? And why's her stuff hidden in the wall when his is out here with him?"

There was an odd symmetry to the scene. Two men in latex gloves clutching brown paper bags in the middle of a sidewalk that cleaved the front yard in equal halves and ran plumb perpendicular from the street to the front door. The door was centered smack under the peak of the simple A-line roof. Two windows to the west, two to the east. Three small shrubs under each set of windows, planted in identical mulch beds that ran around their adjacent corners. Only one thing weighted the tableau; one thing ponderous enough to tilt the picture to the right: the body in the west flower bed.

The slant seemed to occur to both men simultaneously. Tim narrowed his eyes at the matched frown playing over Lyle's face. Their eyes met in an instant of grim realization, and together, they turned and looked to the east, to the side the Dearborn's crew hadn't yet had the chance to dig up.

"Lyle."

"I'm on it."

5

S OME DAYS deserve a toast for their sheer aesthetic perfection. Mostly, this happens in the springtime, when the memory of the long winter is still sharp in the bones. Leah made a strong drink and settled into the deck hammock with a novel, but the buzz soon outpaced the prose. She stared into the swirls dancing in the bottom third of her drink while a circle of cold seeped through her shirt where the glass rested on her belly. Her fingers drummed along the rim of the glass, testing and daring its balance. She admired the sunlight glittering in the condensation, a miniature, flameproof fireworks display in her hand. She wondered if it was the alcohol or the ice that set the ghostly ripples waving in the booze and juice. Booze and juice. And how did that happen anyway? She smiled at the ingredients at odds in her glass. Like welcoming a tattooed carny strongman through your door because he was holding the hand of a little girl all done up in pink bows. Or cranberry-colored ones in this case.

Her thoughts were thinned enough to slide through the smaller gaps in reason, and she rode the drowsy flow. She smiled at the notion of motes and molecules weathering their silent tempest in her late-afternoon cocktail. What did *they* do to take the edge off after all that whirling? she wondered.

"Ms. Tamblin?"

Surprise zapped the sweetly blurred day back into sharp focus. But her heart tapped again in easy rhythm after a quick once-over of her visitor.

"Hello, Detective." She smiled and struggled out of the hammock. "Did they transfer his case file *again*?"

The man gaped and stammered, "Aah—buh—umm."

"If you're not a cop, then I've really had too much to drink." Leah laughed. "I lived and breathed cops for months. You guys will never be able to sneak up on me again." Down the steps and onto the grass, Leah's bare toes telegraphed to her brain that it wasn't actually quite warm enough to go without shoes. "Usually they just send me a letter. What's up?"

The man wasn't tall, but Leah, so accustomed to peering from a disadvantaged height, looked up into his face as she took his friendly-but-down-to-business handshake. No salesman here. She knew she was right.

"Ms. Tamblin, I'm Tim Bayard with the Carter County Sheriff's Department out in Stillwater."

"Then you're not here about Reid?" she asked, all self-assurance draining at the mention of another jurisdiction.

"Yes, ma'am." He nodded quickly at the ground. "I'm sorry to say, I'm here because a body was discovered a few days ago in Stillwater. He's been identified through dental records. It's Mr. Reynolds, I'm afraid."

"Oh." Leah pinned her upper lip between her teeth, then gasped in a wounded breath. "Oh."

"I'm very sorry."

"No, it's—I mean—" Her lower teeth raked and kneaded her lip. Her fluttering eyelids lost their rhythm and were overrun with tears. "I knew, but I didn't . . ." She sucked in another breath. "I'm sorry. I need—I'll be right back."

Bayard nodded. "Of course."

Leah Tamblin, over three years removed from Reid's loss and, in fact, never married, stumbled back into the house on widow-weighted feet.

Bayard's wife often shook a sad head over what a burden it must be, bearing that kind of news. Most people assumed that this sort of thing was the worst part of the job. But it wasn't and he didn't hate it. It was always a profound moment, though, painful and heavy. Tim had seen grown men faint and teenagers throw up on their shoes at being told that their circle had been broken and diminished. He didn't enjoy it any more than a doctor likes telling a patient he has cancer, but just as the oncologist didn't order that first cell to replicate rampant, neither did Bayard set the fuse on a disaster that resulted in a death.

His calling was to forge a way to continue, to repair the structure and the balance. Broken spirits and the universal meaning of loss were elements to be attended to by priests and therapists, but the framework of society was order, and law. Damage to these components required expert repair. It always began with a revelation, a dry-eyed statement of facts. Bayard knew that his face would be etched indelible on the memories of those he felled with such terrible news. He respected that role and was determined to do right by it. It was easy, really, compared to failure. Destroying a perfect stranger and not being able to follow up with some sort of resolution—*that* was the worst part of the job. By far.

He watched the screen door seal Leah into the safety of her home with a bang, and he nodded a silent acknowledgment to the only thing that ever left him stranded on the hard side of his duty: the looming possibility of a dead end. Time and the elements were against him on this one. The bones were dry; the players scattered. The game was on.

This one seemed straightforward enough. That should have felt like good news. But somehow this particular little gem of reason inspired no confidence at all. Instead, in its rightful place, he noted a chill of misgiving.

He strolled a course around the neat, whitewash-over-brick bungalow. The file he'd received from the local police had, through dental X-rays, confirmed the identity of the skeleton in Jason Getty's westernmost garden plot. Along with the medical records, it had included some sketchy notes and, for some reason, a photograph of Reid Reynolds's last residence. Bayard oriented himself and stared back at the little house from the same vantage point the police photographer had used for his exterior shots.

It had been a flimsy thing, that file. You shouldn't judge a book by its cover, but we do. Guys who wear glasses and pocket protectors are automatically smarter than the rest. Beautiful people must be happy. And a nice dense case file means an investigation that's going somewhere. None of these are strictly true, of course, but the tendency is to start there and be proven wrong.

The facts in the file added up to no conclusions. A reasonably well-liked young man with modest debts, apathetic detractors, and an upcoming wedding to his childhood sweetheart had vanished without a trace. Dismissed at first as any sort of suspicion-worthy event, Tim could see by the call log that Leah and Reid's mother had been almost rudely ignored. The car, the only piece of physical evidence that would turn up before the man himself did three years later, was emptied of everything but a few bucketfuls of ash. And none of this had anything to do with the slight, pale man who lived where Reid Reynolds had apparently died, but that didn't stop Jason Getty from tugging inappropriately at Bayard's thoughts just the same.

"Detective?" Leah had put on a sweatshirt and cross-trainers and looked even smaller for the added padding. "Sorry about that."

"Please don't apologize."

"It's pretty stupid. I mean, I've known since they found the car." She blew a stray lock of hair from her face. "That's a lie. I knew that first night when he didn't turn up at any of the hospitals. He wouldn't have cut and run. He would never have done that to his mother." She winced, pricked guilty and embarrassed. "He would never have done that to me."

Bayard joined her on the deck. "I'm sure you have a lot of questions. And, of course, I have a few things I need to ask you."

"Sure. Let's go inside. Can I make you some coffee?"

"Actually, I'd love a glass of ice water." It was always good to let them serve you something if they offered. People needed to touch something civil, something normal, in the wake of catastrophe. It smoothed the way for a productive interview and it was a kindness to let them gather their bearings. But, a delicate gut and years of experience had taught him to decline coffee brewed in bereavement.

*

Leah crawled into bed a stranger to herself. For years she had been the one whose fiancé had gone missing, presumed dead. Presumed dead was dead enough. Presumed dead was a picture on an easel at the memorial service and boxes of things stored away in remembrance. Presumed dead was a coupon book of sympathetic looks to be cashed in for years and years, and a stash of melancholy to use whenever a grim day needed to be grayer.

Take away the *presumed* and it was a skeleton in a bag on a morgue slab. It was a murder investigation and a checklist of questions; an order of operations that would attempt to advance the cause of justice. It was an expectation of cooperation and an invasion of privacy. Dead-for-sure was a fact, or the capital variety Fact even, and a call to action. It was a responsibility of the living to a timetable of denial, anger, grief, and all that nonsense mapped out by authorities with diplomas on their walls and letters after their names. It was the boxing bell to announce a round with answers, which was all she'd ever wanted when the loss was fresh, but not so much after three years' time had padded her pain. This kind of dead was a burden, heavy and exhausting.

She pulled the covers close around her, but her eyes stayed open, fixed to the shadows wrestling on the ceiling. The trees and wind played a creaking, clicking tag outside her window. It was anchoring, that confirmation of solid forms around her, because when she closed her eyes, she felt adrift in a swooning seasickness of unfamiliarity.

But something was recognizable in all of it. The one habitual hurt she would have bet a paycheck that Reid could not have inflicted on her again: the mortified burn of disloyalty. It was somehow pathetically predictable that Reid wouldn't have died alone. When Detective Bayard had pulled out the photo of Katielynn Montgomery, Leah had bitten back on the urge to crawl under the table. Katielynn was just Reid's other type: all legs and long, blond hair. Everything Leah wasn't. If he'd been there, she would have wrung his faithless neck for putting her up in comparison to the icon of American beauty once again. She'd managed a straight face, however, as she always had under the scrutiny that weighed her feminine worth against that of one of Reid's diversions.

But, of course, Reid wasn't there. He was dead, and not just presumed. He'd been chewed by time and the elements alongside the last Barbie doll to have caught his eye. She shrank away from the cold cruelty of that thought. She tried to conjure the image of Reid's face, so handsome in concentration and so utterly goofy in animation. *Think of the good things, Leah. Think of why you put up with all that crap.*

Which brought her around to that alien solitude again, that space walk of isolation that stole the comfort of sleep. When they had fought, Leah had always been welcomed by the rest of Reid's family as the wronged party. They'd shut out their lovable scoundrel in favor of his long-suffering victim. They'd always loved her best when Reid had acted his worst.

Over the years, she'd sulked for hours with his brother, Dean, and his young friends. They plied her into sunnier moods with Dr Peppers and endless games of pool when they were of a certain age, and then with tequila shots and bong hits when they were older. She'd made dozens of pots of spaghetti with his mother, an exercise each time that lasted the entire afternoon and produced gallons of rich, red sauce. Served up in company, it was a balm to the betrayed edges that had left everyone on eggshells. At the end of the ritual feast, always taken in a silence that still echoed with Leah's cursing and crying, Sheila would request, with an imperative flick of her head toward the kitchen, that Dean and whoever else was there help her with the dishes—*right now*. Reid and Leah would be left alone, plucking awkwardly at their napkins, until one of them, usually Reid, suggested they catch a late show at the movies or bowl a couple of games at the West End Lanes.

But now, Sheila had been dead for more than two years and Dean had followed his girlfriend to Seattle at Christmastime and she hadn't yet been able to reach him. Leah was alone with her knowledge and her memories. The first night in her new role as the girl with no presumptions was long and fitful.

Jason Getty and Leah Tamblin, miles apart, but with overlapping worries, dropped off to sleep at almost exactly the same moment. While Leah's musing spanned the better part of two decades, Jason's preoccupation was more immediate, more tactile, closer to home as it were. The two bodies that had flanked the house on either side had been taken away, but Jason couldn't shake the dread of having hovered all this time in a Bermuda Triangle of sorts, and of his own making. He had closed his world into a wedge of hidden misdeeds with an uncanny mathematical precision. And he'd slept in the eye of this wicked geometry for more than a year and a half.

What he had learned of the case, however, eased his mind, at least a little. It looked like a simple soap opera of a cuckolded husband with a rifle and a reasonably steady aim. Once they found the man who had lived here before him, the case would be closed. Jason would be your average citizen again, with only an invisible psychic chain to tether him to the undiscovered corpse he'd planted at the back of the plot. He'd come to terms with the secret months ago, had only just finally been able to manage it. Once the police had their man, Detective Bayard would have no reason to wonder about Jason. As it stood even now, there wasn't any good reason for the detective to give Jason a second thought.

But the policeman did give him that second thought; Jason knew it. And he feared that it had even maybe strayed into third- or fourth-thought territory.

The first seeds of a plan B took root that night. Jason dozed, and the dream of the burial, so worn with use, played again. But that night it played in reverse. The black dirt flew in the moonlight, out of the hole this time, instead of into it. Jason's mind remembered the deep sting in the muscles of his back and he moaned out loud into his pillow. The glow of the exposed white sheet grew rather than dwindled, and in his dream, Jason gathered the corners and gave a mighty heave.

6

"WHERE the heck have you been?" Over his big feet crossed atop a stack of papers on his desk, Ford glared at Tim.

"You know, I thought I'd dodged a bullet, finding a wife who didn't nag," Bayard said, as a smile tugged up one corner of his mouth. "But the universe just has this way of balancing itself, doesn't it?"

"I've been trying to reach you for almost three hours. I found your radio in your desk drawer. What, is it too heavy for you?"

"It was taking up too much space in the spare-change dish at home, of course." Bayard laughed and shoved Ford's feet off the desk, then rummaged through the flotsam. "I'm hungry." Tim waved his find, a well-worn Chinese menu liberated from a folder of interoffice memos. "What? I told you I had some things to do this morning. You could have—oh, crap."

"Yeah."

Bayard covered the empty space on his belt where his phone clip should have been. "We went to the movies last night. I switched it over to vibrate. Then I forgot it on the floor of the car and I didn't hear it."

Ford sighed. "You're not supposed to hear it. You're supposed to feel it. That's why normal people wear their phones."

"I know, the clip broke. But I can't say I miss it. It bugs me."

"It bugs me if I can't get ahold of you."

Bayard slid a tower of files aside to make a space on the corner of Ford's desk and sat in a contrite slump. "Sorry. What's up?"

"Ooooh, nothing," Ford said with a grand display of hand waving and head shaking. "Obviously, speaking with your flower-bed-burial guy, the one who used to live there, Boyd Montgomery? Guess chatting with him isn't so high on your to-do list today."

Open wonder blanked Tim's expression. "Today? You found him already?"

"Nope. I found him last night. Didn't want to disturb your evening." Ford's pleasure in needling his partner sparkled under a mask of long-suffering. "I thought it could wait till this morning." Ford sucked his teeth ruefully. "Guess the joke was on me."

"Where is he?"

"Ah, don't worry about it. Let's just order ourselves some lunch." Ford hmmmed over the menu, eyes shining with mischief. "General Tso's chicken, isn't that the stuff you like?"

"Ford."

"It's okay. The guys over in East County can handle it."

At that, Tim bolted from his perch, tipping the uppermost folders off their ledge to break open and spill their

reams of paper across the floor. "He's here? I thought he
went to Texas. El Paso or something."

"He came back. Last known address"—Ford pulled the
relevant memo from the mess with a flourish—"Branson
Heights."

"Son of a bitch."

"Yep." Ford squared the remnants of his filing system
even with the edge of the desk. "Still hungry?"

The name Branson Heights slapped an overly ornamental
tag on a shaggy, gray area of the map where suburbia fiz-
zled to unkempt and unkempt transitioned to middle-of-
nowhere. It was high neither in altitude nor in splendor,
and the whole thing ignited suspicions that whoever had
named the place intended, in some vague future, to tack a
premium on the lots and tracts for sale. The overall effect
was weedy, rusted neglect, dotted with the tacky efforts
of a few cheery homesteaders by way of spinning plastic
sunflowers and garish garden gnomes.

Winter had reached forward into spring for one last
tug at the change of seasons, sending all but the hardi-
est folk back to their attics, basements, and top shelves
for the warm clothes that had been stowed away in
optimism. The sooty sky and cold gusts did nothing to
improve the view through the truck's windshield. Dog
breath did nothing for the atmosphere inside. Tessa
fogged the cab from her custom-fitted seat on the back
bench, her wide dog-smile pivoting under alert eyes
that could never take in everything that interested her,
not even if she'd been allotted all of the nine lives of
her feline foes.

"Good God! What have you been feeding her?" Tim asked.

Ford laughed. "Garlic!"

"You're insane."

"It's good for her coat and eyes."

"Well, it's making *my* eyes water," Tim said.

Tessa, knowing full well she was the topic of discussion, turned to him expectantly for more, blasting him with tongue-lolling humidity. He nudged her snout to a more neutral compass point. "Come on, Tessa, give me a break."

For Bayard, the ride to a confrontation was always too short. Even the long trips. Tim was thoroughly rehearsed, but the suspects never knew their lines. Of course, that was the entire point, but it also made it one of the most dangerous aspects of the job. Squirmers were fun. Stonewallers were annoying and predictable. But this deck was always stacked with wild cards, and it wouldn't do to walk into these situations looking nervous. So every ride was spent in meditation, in the plastering over of any giveaway that didn't project complete competence and the shine of integrity. From several turns into the labyrinth of his own mind, Tim heard Ford's voice, but not the words that formed the question. "What?"

"What do you want to do about East County?" Ford asked again.

Navigating interrogations, tricky as they were, was much simpler than balancing interdepartmental etiquette. Deputized toes, once stepped upon, were kinked for an unreasonable amount of time, and no one holds a grudge better than a spurned cop.

"I say we call them just as we get there. That way, they're invited—we just get first crack at him."

Ford's attention flicked to a tilting road sign. "Well, get your phone out then, if you think you can find it, 'cause we're just about there."

The two lanes of crumbling blacktop were a snug fit between the borders of bracken just into its full greenery. The gloom was permanent down this lane, no matter what the weather. Even vigorous sunshine would be snuffed out by the heavy canopy of oak and hemlock.

Ford eased the truck to a stop next to a dented mailbox leaning sentry at the mouth of a long gravel drive. "Ready?"

"I can't believe he'd come back here," Bayard said, his eyes drilling the kudzu twilight ahead. "Arrogant prick."

"No telling. Let's go hear what he's got to say, then." Ford let off the brake and the wheels crunched over the graveled ruts toward the clearing and the house.

Tessa began whining even before Ford killed the engine. She strained over the seatback and thrust her nose deep into his face space.

"It's okay. We'll be right back. Watch the truck." Ford kissed her sleek brow. "You're in charge."

Tessa's worried whine went up an octave, but her tail wagged devotion in spite of itself.

Ford came around and joined Bayard on the passenger side as he leaned in to gather up his notepad and phone. The two men watched Tessa's frantic tap dance on the leather seat. Bayard said, "What's with her?" At the same instant, Tessa brayed a chorus of sharp barks over the low warning growl of the lead dog in a pack of three, rounding the truck's back end. Tessa lunged at the open door, but Ford intervened and slammed it shut before she could bolt into the fray.

With heads slung low from thick necks, the three advancing animals were of indeterminate breed, but obvious purpose. Two of them bared teeth, and all three forced their ears flat against their blocky heads in a show of intensity.

Tim pressed himself against the side of the truck. "Oh, shit."

Tessa bellowed threats through the passenger window as the other dogs pinned Ford and Tim to their places with growls and spring-loaded menace. The dogs spaced themselves across the path to the house and bristled hungry aggression. Their concentration spoke to training, but instinct had them flitting anxious glances at Tessa, thrashing berserk in the truck. Tim stretched a tentative hand for the door handle, and their grumbling erupted into a soul-shriveling racket, backed up by a frenzy of impotent protective calls from Tessa, imprisoned behind the men. She banged her muzzle against the window, splaying her lips from her fangs and smearing the glass with distraught foam.

"Don't move," said Ford, taking his own advice by barely moving his lips to say it.

"Best have yer dog go quiet," said a man from the splintered and sagging front porch. "It's workin' up my gang too much." He leaned against the roof support, eating a bowl of cereal.

The crazy notion that the bright white milk dripping from the spoon would be the last random thing he'd ever notice streaked through Tim's mind, but it was better than watching the pulse pounding in his own eyeballs. A primal panic pinholed his throat, and thinking past the vision of curved, yellow teeth tearing the meat from his leg was a struggle. He knew he'd probably been this scared before, but he just couldn't think of when that might have been.

Ford rapped the glass with a knuckle and hissed an urgent command. "Tessa! Quiet!"

Tessa bit back on the next bay with a jerk of her head. The fur over her throat rippled as if she were swallowing something too large, and she rolled her terrified eyes to Ford for acknowledgment of her great effort. The other dogs relaxed back into their sullen, toothy vigil.

"Good girl." Ford turned back to the man on the porch. "Call them off, Mr. Montgomery."

The man took another lazy, slurping spoonful. His vowels were wide in a mellow twang. "One word either way. We'll see. I'm not big on unannounced comp'ny."

Tim found his voice. "This is Ford Watts and I'm Tim Bayard. We're with the Carter County Sheriff's Department." Tim eyed the animals a foot and a half off his knee. "A patrol car from East County Division will be here shortly."

If he was impressed, the man didn't let on. "What do you want?"

"We want to ask you about your wife."

"I ain't got a wife."

"I'll bet you don't," Ford muttered under his breath.

Tim took the lead. "Where is Katielynn, Mr. Montgomery?"

The man startled hard and set the bowl on the slivered railing board. "Oh, good God. You want to talk to Boyd." He gave an ear-piercing whistle, then called to the dogs, "George, Ringo, Yoko! Back!"

Impressively, all three animals did exactly that. They backed up, all six eyes never leaving the two men, until they drew even with the porch and their master's blue-jeaned legs.

"You're a couple of Beatles short," Tim offered.

The man grinned. "Well, as it happens, John ran off, and I shot Paul for bein' ornery."

With the immediate danger at least a few strides away,

Tim turned his full focus to the man's face. He and Ford had studied Boyd's picture from an old mug shot taken after a tailgate party gone ugly at the local high school some years earlier. Same yellow-blond hair; same dimpled chin.

Their scrutiny was not lost on the man on the porch. "Look just like him, don't I?" He walked past them to Ford's truck, Tessa's agitation growing with every foot of ground he covered, until her lather was frothed nearly as badly as it had been moments before. With no hesitation at all, the stranger yanked open the door. Tessa readied her legs to lunge and snapped her teeth at him. "Now hush," he commanded. Tessa cocked her head and pitched to sitting instantly, but still growled.

"Hush, 'n' I mean it."

Tessa stopped the noise immediately, looked past the man to Ford, and stamped her indecision.

"Cookie?" the man asked.

Tessa pawed the air and woofed, unsure. Her tail decided earlier than her head and started a slow sweep of the seat. The man pulled a dog treat from his shirt pocket and smiled back to a gaping Ford and Bayard.

"I like dogs." He shrugged. "And mostly they like me. 'Cept for Paul." As if to prove his prowess, he pointed at his own three. "Y'all, go say hi." Released from the spell, the three transformed directly into smiling, wagging mutts. The tan one licked Bayard's hand.

"Neat trick," Bayard said. He didn't like being humbled at the outset.

The man sighed. "Boyd's my brother. My twin. Least he was. He's been dead a year and change. I'm Bart Montgomery." He patted his thigh, and Tessa leaped from the cab, but straightway pledged allegiance to her master's knee. "Let's all go inside," Bart said. "I guess I got a story to tell."

The East County patrol arrived halfway through the interview, scrambling the balance of the room, though to no real consequence. All official opinion came quickly to the same conclusion: as far as homicides and their fallout go, the case of Reid Reynolds, Katielynn Montgomery, and her husband, Boyd, was as neatly sewn up as they come.

Boyd, and everyone presumed Katielynn, had packed up and moved from Stillwater three years before. Never reliable to anything but his own interests, and more than a little disinclined to explain himself, Boyd's pulling up stakes didn't make much of a ripple through the small circle of folks who even noticed he was gone.

Katielynn had been clear of her dirt-floor-and-outhouse kin for more than a decade by then, and it had been a good handful of years since any of them had even asked after her at Christmastime.

A year later Boyd appeared on his brother's doorstep, disheveled and morose, claiming that Katielynn had run off with another man. After a fashion, it was the truth, although well after the fact and only if the Great Beyond could be agreed upon as a place a young couple could indeed run off to.

Eight months droned on in his self-imposed seclusion, and Boyd drank his government disability checks. Then one day, Bart came home to a confession scrawled into a suicide note on the back of the telephone bill and an ungodly mess of splattered Boyd. Bart saw no need to tarnish his brother's already smallish reputation. What was done was done, and done thoroughly. A load of official ugliness stamped to Boyd's name wasn't going to bring any of them back, so Bart cleaned the linoleum and buried his brother in the woods. He also hadn't seen any reason to stem the cash flow.

It was an easy scam. Apparently not overburdened by a diligent conscience, Bart already had Boyd's face by virtue of being his twin, and he held his paperwork by having not buried his brother's wallet in the ground with the rest of him. The checks just kept coming, and that was reason enough, in his mind, to keep cashing them. Bart had, however, possessed the foresight to keep the suicide note handy lest his brother's sin, at some point, become his own problem.

Bart retrieved it and presented the note to the detectives. The indulgent mix of self-pity and blame cleared away all doubt as to the motive and culpability behind the murders of Reid and Katielynn, and in admirable detail for such a small scrap of paper. It was well speckled with flecks of long-dried blood and the braille of a few more substantial bits of the man, which gave Bayard, as case-hardened as he was, a shiver. Suicide pinched him in a place other deaths couldn't reach.

Of course, Bart was now in his own bog of felonies and misdemeanors, but Bayard and Ford had got what they needed from the interview. They left the remainders for East County, all laid out and orderly to downplay that it was really only table scraps. With much ceremony and fraternal back-patting, Tim and Ford turned him over to the sheriffs who'd showed up after the meat of the case had already been eaten.

Back in the truck, Tim massaged the bridge of his nose. "What, is it just fashionable now to dig your own holes?

Who needs funerals? Who needs cemeteries? Just plant 'em yourself—no fuss, no muss. Jesus."

Ford puffed out his cheeks in a restrained sigh. "Well, that is about as tidy and easy a case as we've ever had." He cut his eyes at Tessa and Bayard. "Except for the dog part. I almost needed a change of shorts."

This gave both men a brief case of the snorting chuckles. The residue of fear that had been gumming up their thought processes fell away behind the funny. In its wake, a peaceful silence settled. Tessa dozed in the back, while, in his mind, Tim batted questions over the net. The answers bounced back, neat and quick, off Bart Montgomery's tight story. The resolution was simple, but dismal. East County would inherit the task of exhuming Boyd Montgomery and prosecuting Bart for his fraud and for the do-it-yourself funeral he'd staged for his brother. A couple of death notifications and a few hours' worth of paperwork would wrap it up for Bayard and he'd be on to the next thing.

"Guess we can call off our own dogs, so to speak," Ford broke into Bayard's trance. "No sense in Lyle and his team destroying Mr. Getty's place. I think it's safe to call this one closed."

"Yeah. I suppose."

They rode on for miles without further comment, the road noise whooshing a lullaby in the wake of such a hard adrenaline burn.

"You can't hear that?" Ford was both amused and annoyed.

"Hear what?"

Ford thrust an accusatory finger at the floorboards on Tim's side. His cell phone quivered and buzzed like an angry bumblebee.

"Oh!" He snatched it up and looked at the screen and grinned. "Well, speak of the devil and name him Lyle," he said after flipping it open to take the call. His eyes traced the horizon, unseeing in concentration as the crime-scene investigator chattered into his ear. Tim's replies and their tone chipped away at the calm. "Where'd you find it?" "And the others?" "That's just weird." "Okay, Lyle. Thanks. I'll have a look. Bye."

Tim chewed the inside of his cheek for a moment. "Ford, if you were distressed enough to kill yourself over feeling *so* guilty about murdering your wife and her lover—so upset that you had to get it all out on the back of a phone bill, in gory detail, before you ate a bullet—would you leave one out?"

"One what?"

"Another murder."

Ford risked a glance from the road. "What are you talking about?"

Tim frowned at the landscape rushing by. "I don't know. Lyle's got something to show me. I know you need to get home, but drop me at Getty's place first, if you don't mind."

7

JASON had been one turn away from home when he noticed the bulky red pickup truck up ahead of him. The bobbing, overlong aerials brought the realization full circle. He'd eased off the gas and let the distance accumulate between the detectives and himself.

The day had been horrible enough, being dismissed from his own home knowing the police would be there for hours, excavating the mulch beds and poking around. His lie had forced him into a pretense of alliance, and he'd had to smile while handing over the keys with hands that he willed not to tremble. His fingers obeyed well enough, but the giblets took on all the flutter instead. He was hot and cold with a belly full of brimstone, but the tech never looked twice at Jason.

He'd hidden, scared rigid, all day behind an industrious calm. Pins and needles sparked in his toes before his feet finally went numb because Jason never once moved from his chair. He remained blindly bent over his work, clamping his desk phone's stealthily disconnected handset to his ear. No one bothered the busy bee, so the only thing Jason heard all that day was his own pulse and the voice inside his head promising his jelly heart that the technicians, like the landscaping crew, would find only what they were paid to look for.

The craving to be alone in the woods had been lit in him even before he was positive that the two cops were en route to his house. Once their turn gave them away, Jason knew more than ever that he needed the time alone to steel himself for another face-to-face with Detective Bayard.

Jason was navigationally challenged. He always had been. And it made him feel less of a man. He wore the cliché too easily, the reluctance to stop for directions, but stereotypes are often thick, ugly plaster over a framework of truth. Sometimes it took him a dozen passes at a route before he was comfortable enough to risk the distraction of the radio. If his concentration slid at the wrong time, he might as well write off the next hour for putting himself back on course. And let him make a wrong turn, even once, and it was branded for the foreseeable future in the panic center of his brain. On approach to the offending fork in the road, Jason's attention would flail in a squirrel-in-the-intersection zigzag, trying to recall whether he remembered it because it was the right way to go, or if he remembered it because that was where he'd gone wrong the last time.

That's how he'd found his haven, more than two years before he'd ever imagined he could kill a person, by twice taking an accidental turn onto a road that led nowhere.

The Realtor had been overzealous when Jason had asked what was available in small properties with a fair bit of green space and a whole lot of quiet on the outskirts of Stillwater.

She had sent him off with a stack of listings to preview, each with the dreaded miniature map that might as well have been a squirming knot of worms for all the dismay it caused Jason. On both trips to the house that eventually became his own, he'd overshot the red x that he'd drawn and, without knowing it, substituted the next one for his turn. He trundled along a narrowing, winding trail that he came to realize didn't look to be dancing to the same song that the road shown on the map was playing.

The first time, after several minutes of brow furrowing and mental rummaging for his bearings, Jason had to concede that, once again, he'd missed his mark. Of course, there was nowhere to turn around. Just as the maddening tingle in his bladder had worked around to an honest debate on the merits of using the ditch for a quick pit stop, a confident swath of fresh asphalt branched off to the right and back, more or less, in the direction he had come.

He'd cranked the steering wheel over with hope, only to dead-end in befuddlement. Farther into the woods, the blacktop blunted off as cleanly as a diving board. Jason was at a loss and staring down an eleven-point turn. But nature prevailed, both as a twiggy, green roadblock outside, and also as an urgent, relentless distraction on the inside. He jerked the gearshift into park and paced off much farther than modesty required to relieve himself behind the largest screening oak he could find. A glimpse deeper into the trees explained the road's abrupt surrender. A sinkhole, sixty feet across, and probably more than twice as deep, had yawned a halt to the pavement's progress.

The next bout of disorientation in the same part of town stranded Jason once again at the lip of the sinkhole in the woods. Although this time, it wasn't as worrisome to him.

Lost in the same place twice is a little less lost the second time around. The memory of the breezy green and gold dappling the forest floor was more than enough incentive to kill the engine and wander once again into the trees. This time, he sat against a broken stump and considered the rim of the chasm. How had it happened? All around, the land was a firm platform holding up a grove and a road and then, all of a sudden, *whump!*

He finished his diet cola, ears-deep in the twitter-quiet of the thick woods, and concluded that Chicken Little had feared the wrong thing. The sky falling on your head was Providence and you were blameless. But the ground falling out from under your feet was something you should have felt coming.

The word *twist* would not begin to cover the contortions ol' fate had performed to arrange that Jason found himself a face-saved widower. Heartbroken twice by his wife in a quick succession of painful words and then her sudden death, he'd been stranded, almost out-of-body, as an observer over the chaos that spilled a new life at his feet.

Patty had by all accounts been healthy when she told him, dry-eyed and as kindly as she could, that she no longer loved him, wasn't sure she'd ever really loved him at all, and hoped he understood it was habit that had kept her at his side for seven years, but that it couldn't make the distance until death do us part. Except that it had. Less than seventy-two hours after the bombshell, and before she could pack up her things and their friends and sign him off her bank books, death intervened the first time to make Jason's problems go away.

Pleasant, lovely, and more than a little spoiled, Patty had possessed a unique dedication to getting her own way. But her vision of how things ought to be was undermined by a lazy lack of bark and bite. A rhythm was spawned the first time Jason had brought his class notes to her, without her having asked, when she'd missed an early-morning lecture in Intro to Income Taxation. She sparkled and he held up the candle to her automatically. He'd always known that her attachment to him was founded, in part, on the recognition that they were very much alike, in all the feeblest ways. But to him, that was as good a defense against being alone as any he could think of.

His father-in-law had detested him on sight, and his mother-in-law had never really looked at him at all until they were forced into a stiff, obligatory embrace in front of the casket. He was almost sure he'd seen a sneer behind the tears. The two inches of powder, though, and the softening juniper fog of gin fumes, made it hard to tell for certain.

It's often said that dead people look as if they were sleeping. Jason didn't find this to be true. Patty's expression, backlit with the glow from the white satin coffin pillow, held none of the slack-faced stupor of sleep. The morticians had done a masterful job in setting her features and rouging her cheeks. In fact, he'd had to rein in the fear that she was faking it and was, at any moment, ready to spring from the box and proclaim him the fraud that he was, standing there being lauded as her beloved husband. The cat had been more beloved, and it was going home with her parents.

The softer side of Jason knew she didn't belong there. The dentist's chair, although often unpleasant, wasn't expected to be the executioner's recliner. No one died that way. But her heart had spilled more than one secret that week. A dearth of real affection for him was one; an intolerance for Versed and Fentanyl was another.

Somewhere along the line, perhaps in infantile trauma or schoolyard bullying, Jason had suffered a courage-ectomy. He'd withstood his father-in-law's bristling analysis during the finalizing of Patty's not insubstantial estate. It passed clear, but unspoken, between the two men that her father knew very well of his daughter's intent to start anew. Tact and decorum were encoded into Jason's father-in-law, so there was no ugly scene. Jason matched the silence with a passivity that was indivisibly a part of his skin, even more restricting than his father-in-law's armor of pride. It prevented Jason from rising to the challenge of that sober glare, to argue that he would have fought for his marriage if he'd had the chance. He even thought, in the hours he didn't sleep, of ways that he might have done just that. He hosted dialogues in the dark with his dead wife and convinced her on the stage of his imagination that they were good together, that she should stay. But in the end, a shame-pink face in the mirror was all his one-man shows earned him, and he took the money and ran—out of the frying pan and into the fire, as would be his hapless habit.

He'd adopted the trek to the sinkhole as a good omen and also a cleansing ritual. He came back often, especially once the trouble with Harris started, taking great pains to ensure that the smug, prying bastard hadn't followed him there and didn't know all of his secrets. Occasionally he was disappointed to find his seat taken by kids playing hooky or lighting séance bonfires in the glade, but not often enough for him to give up trying.

He had boosted himself off the usual tenterhooks one afternoon, shortly after he'd moved to Stillwater, relaxing against a tree and watching the light and shadows make kaleidoscope patterns on his closed eyelids. The blank bliss had been deep, so the commanding and not entirely friendly "Howdy" simply scared the shit out of him.

A county sheriff, decked out in starch and polished leather, stood over him, conjured out of God knew where. Jason hadn't heard a thing.

"Oh. Hello." Jason jumped to his feet and immediately wished he'd been more casual about it.

"Can I see some ID, sir?"

Jason scrabbled at his back pocket for his wallet. "Of course, Officer. Is there a problem? I mean, it's okay for me to be out here, right? I just like looking at it." Jason glanced over his shoulder at the hole, brimming with the golden light that fell through the gap it left in the trees. "It's quiet here."

"Oh, it's something, isn't it? The Public Works Department don't care for it too much, but no problem, really, for you to sit here, if you like. It's not private property, but it is dangerous. I know you'll keep mind of the risks. We've just had kids hanging out here when they're s'posed to be in school, or lighting fires at night and general hubbub. That sort of thing."

"Well"—Jason pushed a chuckle to an awkward spot in his mouth—"I'm no kid."

The cop nodded over Jason's driver's license. "I can see that, Mr.—ah—Getty. You haven't been drinking, have you?"

"Oh, no, sir. Not a big drinker," Jason stammered, then flinched at the obvious omission. "I mean, I did bring a drink out with me, but it's just diet soda, sir." He swept a hand at the can on a nearby stump. "Oh, and I always take my trash with me."

"That's fine." The policeman jabbed his tongue into the side of his smirk and craned a look through the immediate trees and slid himself another quick once-over of Jason, head to toe. "Well, you have a nice day."

"Thank you," Jason said, knowing that it wasn't likely. The shiny finish to his nice day was all fingerprinty now. "Uh, you, too." But he said it to the cop's back and didn't really mean it anyway.

Beyond that one encounter, it had always been a peaceful place for him. Sanctuary. There, in the rustling jade cocoon, he allowed himself to dismiss the constant company of guilt and cringing. When he was alone there, no mirrors nervously ogled him, measuring him against the next guy. It was the one place to find a rare peace with his naked thoughts.

The forest grows ferns and trees; it cultivates mushrooms and spores; it fosters its creatures from nothingness to more of the mulchy same. And for Jason, the seeds of backbone, of entitlement, were nurtured in the fertile hollow that had dropped the bottom out of civilized advancement. The forest insisted. It pushed back. At some sudden swell of that's-enough, it emphatically refused to be overrun by bullying machinery and someone else's idea of what it should be. Jason had taken the lesson to heart without necessarily meaning to, and in some ways, the forest, with its reassuring murmuring and nodding boughs, was as much to blame for Jason's ultimate predicament as anything else.

*

Pulling into the driveway almost two hours after he'd first spotted the detectives in their truck, Jason was not entirely surprised, nor pleased, to see Bayard still there, pacing at the front door, cell phone pressed to his ear.

"Mr. Getty." The detective snapped closed his phone and took the front stoop in a loose-jointed, limber spring that made Jason's skin crawl with annoyance and envy. "I'm glad I didn't miss you."

Jason heard it as *I would have sat here until next week for the chance to give you the hairy eyeball*, but he forced an agreeable smile. "How are things going, Detective? Any developments?"

"And how."

A day spent trying not to die of anxiety had left Jason raw, and he could feel the prickling on his skin of the policeman's predatory interest.

Bayard continued, "And the good news is, Lyle and his team are the neatest forensic crew I've ever seen, so if it looks bad, please know it could have been a lot worse." He stepped aside to allow Jason to and through his own front door.

Had he been able to imagine their thoroughness, Jason would never have made it through his pantomimed work act. Dark paper covered the windows where the shades and curtains had been inadequate, and a flat, alien darkness stole any sense of home from the rooms. In the gloom, Jason could see traces of black powder smeared into the grooves on the doorframes and pick out a faint chemical smell still lingering in the air, but all in all, the place was reasonably in order.

"I need to show you something," Bayard said. "If you think you're up for it."

In answer, Jason swallowed hard.

Bayard nodded acknowledgment to the unspoken misgiving. "I wouldn't normally. I thought we were all done." He let it hang for an important second. "But now I'm not sure that we are."

Jason felt the air turn to molasses, and Bayard, close enough to touch, was hogging it effortlessly. The darkness helped, though. For the first time in his life, Jason found breathing a distant secondary concern to something else. In this case, to retaining his composure. "Of course." He barely even stammered.

"Boyd Montgomery confessed to the two killings."

Relief punctured Jason's bubble of held breath and a grateful sigh rushed out of him. He wouldn't even have noticed it at all but for Bayard's steady appraisal, motivating a hard stop to his contented deflation. Bayard peered another few seconds off the clock, at Jason's face in particular. "Let me show you what we've got."

A psychologist's dream, Jason had chosen the smaller of the two back rooms for himself, and Bayard headed toward what anyone else would have claimed for the master bedroom. Ultraviolet lamp and spray bottle in hand, he led the way. Jason made an effort not to drag his feet or breathe too loudly or do anything that would cause Bayard to look back or, God forbid, turn on the overhead light. Under well-lit examination, Jason knew his pulse would play on his skin for Bayard to see. Jason's ears were hot enough to have him pray they weren't glowing in the gloom.

Bayard stopped in the doorway and waggled the unmarked bottle. "We sprayed the rooms with luminol. When I turn on this light"—he waved the flattened cylinder between them—"it'll glow where there was blood."

In the murk of the close hallway, Jason couldn't be sure the walls weren't leaning in to the tipping point, poised to crush him. "Do we have to do this?"

"No." Bayard loved his dramatic pauses. "But it will go a long way to understanding what comes next. I know this is awful, but you have to remember, there's nothing in this room that you haven't lived with the whole time. It's not pleasant, but it doesn't change anything. It just makes it make sense."

There was a logic there that granted permission to the part of Jason's mind that desperately wanted to peek between its fingers. "Okay."

Bayard stepped into the room and spritzed the floor in wide arcs. The pump squawked dry plastic rasps into the darkness, then went quiet. Bayard switched on the hand lamp.

Jason groaned.

"Yeah," Bayard agreed softly.

The room in natural lighting was bare but for some unpacked boxes and a few odds and ends that hadn't found a place elsewhere in the house. Dust grayed the brown carpet. Jason, not having any use for a guest room, used it for storage more than anything else. As the outlet to the darkened hallway, it had been a black hole of apprehension. But in the eye-aching glow of the black light, it was a shrieking disaster. The lustrous ghost of spilled blood marked out two sprawling stains, but it was the trickles and splashes and stray splatters that sang of struggle and panic. A fragile, incandescent handprint, clear and lonely on its own, was stranded in a blank patch between the two larger stains.

Jason's eyes rolled, fighting to take it in and flit away at the same time. A seashell roar rose up in his ears and gave a hollow voice to the echo of ruin mapped out in the luminous swirls on the floor. He swayed and threw a hand out to the wall for reinforcement.

Bayard had a point to make, which didn't seem to include Jason losing it in the spare room. He took Jason's arm and steered him out, shutting off the lamp as they cleared the threshold. He spoke quickly in the dark, over Jason's raw breathing. "I know. Montgomery didn't even do all that great of a job of cleaning up, once you know what to look for. Lyle got samples from the baseboards. There were even flecks of blood on the window glass that no one would have noticed." Bayard gave Jason's shoulder a bolstering pat. "We're almost done."

After another burst of hisses from the spray bottle, Bayard flicked the switch on the UV bar again and extended his arm down the hallway. Jason, on cue, grunted dismay. Two stuttering, twining, luminescent tracks faded down the carpet toward the front entryway.

Bayard continued, "Yeah, it's pretty obvious what happened." He turned the lamp off again and Jason's eyes stung with afterglow. He reeled in the wake of the shock of having to accept that this ghost-scene had been under his feet and in between his walls all day, every day, since the moment he'd moved in. He had decided to buy the place standing in this very hallway. Standing on their blood. The dark and the quiet that Bayard allowed was a kindness.

Jason's personal worries had been flashbulb eclipsed, stunned into the background. His mental screen was blank except for the wailing smears and strokes of blue green that he tried hard not to know had once been red and wet. His ears rang, but for himself and his own wheelbarrowful of troubles, he was afforded a break from the tension. The selfish fear that had been zinging through him for days trickled out on gratitude once that cruel light had been extinguished. He found he could breathe again once the darkness had fallen like a curtain and hidden the evidence that begged for reconstruction in the mind; insisted on the pictures that led backward in time to a room where furtive lovers were caught unguarded.

They'd stopped in the foyer and Bayard resumed, unruffled, "Lyle has confirmed that the size and intensity of those stains in the bedroom are consistent with what he called 'grievous' blood loss. So, he was a little surprised to find this."

The click of the button on the lamp crashed like cymbals in Jason's ears with the simultaneous realization that Bayard had sidestepped him and had aimed the luminol into the living room, talking calmly over the slyly fizzing spout. The coffee table had been moved against the sofa, and the dark field of open floor bloomed in a vivid lightning-on-storm-cloud flash.

"Neither of those people should have lived long enough to leave another stain like that, and anyway"—Bayard's light-holding hand swung away toward the far end of the room, where faint glowing traces in the fibers streaked off toward the kitchen and, ultimately, as Jason well knew, the back door—"this goes off in an entirely different direction." Bayard let the lamp dangle on its lanyard, swinging the stark shadows around the room as it swayed. He spoke into the tilting, jumping darkness between them. "This scene is very different, too. Much cleaner. Lyle thought he was going to have to pull up the carpet to get anything, but he's thorough." Light as a dancer, Bayard hopped onto the coffee table and waved his lamp at arm's length. Three short bands, tightly spaced, flared from a blade on the ceiling fan.

Jason's legs wouldn't buckle and he didn't know why. His muscles turned to granite, his bones fused to steel. The bellows of his lungs worked against every effort of his brain to unplug them, and even the knocking of his heart was muted against the solid rock that he'd become under this Medusa's spell. He was a stone and his eyes would only leave the fan blade with its three succinct, tattling marks to scan the mantel and his collection of solid, sturdy, clanking antique telephones, their coiled cords looping and dipping off the edge of the varnished plank.

No one but Jason knew that the parade line of interesting old phones was one short. The missing one lay wrapped in an old newspaper, tied in a plastic grocery bag, and fussily layered in with household refuse in the precise middle of a large trash bag, under a year and some months of garbage at the landfill. It was safe and gone and somehow still having the last word.

Lock-jointed and rooted to the floor as he was, Jason's mind was still loose and fluid. His thoughts weren't a train, but a river, rushing, slipping and eddying over memories that had brought him to this moment. He saw Harris facedown, bleeding into the living-room carpet. He saw himself disengage from the straddling perch over Harris's back, blind with triumph and horror, clutching at the mangled phone. The broken pieces dangled and defied him as he struggled to his feet, and with the clarity of hindsight, Jason saw himself yank the pieces from the floor and could almost feel the whistle of displaced air past his cheek as the springy cord whipped toward the ceiling, just clipping the edge of the fan blade. He'd barely registered it then and had certainly never thought about it since.

During the cleanup, Jason had toyed with the notion of burning the place to the ground. Standing next to Tim Bayard in his living room, admiring the black-lit glow of the white stripes in his handsome golf shirt, never had a man so dearly wished for a time machine and a match.

8

EVERY EVENT is boxed in by a set of facts; the truth as it were. There's the *what* and the *when* of a deed; there's *where* it happened and *how* it was done. But it's at the *why* that the liar's margin begins. It's from this border that we launch the justifications for everything we do, and for all that we allow to be done to us. Only our distance from the hard truth and the direction of our push—toward or away from it—is the measure of our virtue.

Gary Harris was killed by Jason Getty on the carpet of Jason's living-room floor by repeated blows to the head from the base of an antique telephone. That's the story. The End.

The naked reality of this case is that one man took another man's life, and we all know, regardless of creed, *thou shalt not kill*. The straight truth would have had Jason convicted and sentenced in a court of law. But even the law resides in that sloping space between truth and lies. It strives heroically for justice, the margin's most noble construct, by allowing for the heat of passion. The law also marks, in shades of gray, the difference between reasons and excuses. So, Jason would likely have earned some small reprieve for having been shoved that night, for having been taunted and bullied in the weeks leading up to it. Maybe second-degree would have fit what he'd done, and why he'd done it.

Perhaps most important, though, we store our memories in the liar's margin, to cushion our conscience and to safeguard our self-esteem. Jason had been pushed, as he recalled it, well past the point that second-degree and its mandatory punishments felt in any way fair. He felt justified, and if he could have deleted that night from his life's history, he wouldn't have. If he'd been allowed a purge, it would have had to start back at the beginning. It would have rearranged a summer's afternoon by three minutes.

Jason had not been all the way happy that day, but it had been close. Warm sun with a slightly less warm breeze set to ruffling his hair and rippling his shirt so that it tickled pleasantly against his chest and arms. This sort of day erased the memory of ever having been cold, the kind that made winter more of a concept, an abstraction, like something once read about in a book. It left him nibbling the corners off a random smile, so as not to look like an utter simpleton standing at the gas pump, grinning at the sky.

It had taken months, but he'd come back around to a kind of contentment in his new hometown of Stillwater. It was a feat after boiling in the shame of being told that he hadn't enough zest to him, hadn't owned enough basic appeal to keep his wife satisfied in their life together. He'd loved Patty, loved the ease of their routine, and the radiant heat from another body in the bed with him at night. At least it had felt like love. They didn't quarrel often. They regularly shared a laugh, and in company their conversations were stocked with private jokes. They'd always breakfasted together, with their heads behind their respective bookbindings, and, to him, their silences had been companionable, not desolate. But she'd been only hours to days from writing him off as time wasted, stranding him in shame in front of everyone.

With her death and the consolation prize of skipping the king-size serving of humiliation, Jason wrestled a new conflict. His reaction to this sudden tragedy needed to present as pure grief. It was the only proper thing. It's what everyone expected. He felt their eyes watching him for a performance of suffering. They leaned into his space, all ears for arias of weeping. They watched him, and he watched them as each person plucked up one of Patty's funeral cards to hold as a souvenir to remember her by and a talisman against any misfortune of their own.

All the attention embarrassed him. He knew, privately, that his feelings were a tad overseasoned with relief, and he couldn't stand the thought that it might show. He didn't enjoy the money, not that it was even all that much after the government got its bite of things, but he couldn't entirely beat back the surges of lightness at being free to box it up and drive his life out from underneath the sympathy that he wasn't at all sure he deserved. It felt like a win, being able to afford to leave his job and move away from his in-laws' disapproval.

But no one should win like that. It subtracted something from his soul and left him an amputee of sorts, very alone in the world. He was most comfortable when he was hiding his deformity from others, knowing that regular people would never feel the way he did.

There'd been no outright confrontation, just one excru-ciating episode at his father-in-law's grand banquet table two weeks after the funeral. Naturally, Patty's father had sat at the head of the table, with the family lawyer directly to his right. When Jason had arrived, the housekeeper had inexplicably set his glass of iced tea one seat over from the first chair to the left, stranding Jason at loose ends over whether to sit there, dangling off to the side all by himself, or to slide his drink to the empty seat next to his father-in-law. He couldn't shake the feeling that they'd left an empty space for effect, and that to fill it would leave him sitting on the ghost of his late wife's lap.

"What do you think she would have wanted done with her money?" her father had asked, spearing Jason straight through with eyes that sparked under sleekly combed salt-and-pepper brows.

"What do you mean?" Jason bought a few empty beats with a useless question, but instead of stealing constructive time to think, it only afforded him a chance to plumb the depths of his discomfort.

"She had the hospital charity that she supported here in town. And the ASPCA, maybe. She cared about animals. She had always said"—her father swallowed some hard emotion that made his cheeks burn and his eyes shine—"that she wanted one day to look into a Peace Corps tour. Maybe you could arrange a sponsorship donation in her name. That would be in line with what she would have wanted."

Jason was skeptical that any of these suggestions represented actual facts about his wife, but didn't doubt for a second that she'd mentioned some or all of this to stay in the good graces of her civically minded father. She'd not been stingy, just very much a willing victim of inertia. The truth of it was that Patty, like Jason, had been content to let the clock wind circles over her intentions. That she'd let the two of them drift along for seven years before leveling with her own husband was plenty well testament to that.

"We left everything to each other," Jason had replied.

"I understand that. I just wondered if you'd given any thought to what she would have wanted under the circumstances." Her father didn't say what those circumstances were. Nor did he need to.

The aggressive silence flung at Jason by both other men at the table probably backfired. Their stony stares and throbbing jaw muscles scared him right out of answering them properly. Had they been less intimidating, Jason would likely have made a fool of himself, bumbling out a lame argument that their threat-sharpened legalese would have gutted. But instead, he froze, thankful that the tablecloth hid the knocking of his knees.

"But I'm her husband," he blurted.

The other two men mistook his clipped succinctness for deep resolve, and knowing full well that they came from a position of statutory weakness, they wrote Jason his checks, signed him from their ranks, and all but shoved him out the door. He stood blinking on the mat, bewildered at how easy it had all actually turned out to be.

And so he came to Stillwater. It could have been called Backwater by contrast to what he'd known, and its lack of grandeur made him feel safe because it put him comfortably out of path-crossing distance of his in-laws' snobbery. He needn't have worried that his erstwhile father-in-law would have sought him out. He wouldn't have and, in fact, undertook a thorough effort to erase Jason Getty from every detail of his life, right to the threshold of where the memories of his daughter would allow.

Ultimately, it would have been better for Jason to have

undone, rather than simply lengthen, the apron strings to his original hometown. He stayed within an hour's drive of the house he'd grown up in, the church he'd been married in, and his in-laws' grand Tudor, which had always underscored his own meagerness.

All on his own for the first time in almost a decade, cycles of numbness and loneliness were shot through with manic industry and giddy freedom until Jason took a job just to parcel out his time for him. Routine settled his nerves, and predictable human contact forced his loneliness into the darker corners of the night when he'd run out of interesting television and munchies. He'd thought about getting a dog.

That's what he'd been thinking about at the gas pump that day: What breed would suit him? He imagined unlikely strings of days just like this one, getting fit and tanned through hours of romping on the lawn or in the park. A big, loping hound, maybe. Or a small, feisty one with an aura of energy to draw on. Definitely one that would lie snuffling at his feet in the forlorn space in the evening between being tired, but not yet asleep. A dog for whom Jason would always be enough.

He hadn't paid much notice to the motorcycle that pulled up to the opposite pump, but couldn't help noting the avid "Fuck!" coming from the dismounted rider. Craning his eyes to their limits in order to gawk without looking like he was gawking, Jason watched the man strut a perimeter of rage around the bike. He ripped at the catches on the saddlebags and scrabbled up to the elbow through the odds and ends inside them.

The man yanked a cell phone from one pouch and, after dialing, yelled a blue streak into it. "It's unfuckingbelievable!

My wallet must have fallen out at Heather's. . . . She's at fucking work now. . . . No, I don't know . . . and I've got seventeen fucking cents! . . . I'm on fumes, man. I'm never going to make it. . . . Don't give me shit! Like I need that right now. . . . Well, don't sell it without me . . . do not . . . I'm fucking serious, man . . . I'll kick your ass. . . . Okay. . . . Fine. . . . Yeah, I'll figure it out." Then he laughed like the sun jumping out suddenly, as it sometimes does, from behind black storm clouds. "Shut the fuck up. . . . I'll be there as soon as I can." Another laugh. "You're a prick."

He snapped the cover down over the keypad and sighed hugely, raking his hands through his dark, Hollywood mane. It takes a very particular type of hair to make light of helmet-head. Straight hair gets bent. Curly hair gets molded into hilarity. And the sort of man who relies on sticky products to keep him looking potent will be outed for a fraud once the brain-bucket comes off. This man's hair was mussed perfect, and it took more than Jason had in him to leave off admiring it. Not even noticing as he did it, he ran his fingers through his own wispy hair as he sized up the stranger's predicament.

Jason was in a good mood that was just cresting over to full-on glad, having decided right then and there that a dog would chase off the last of the demons. And Jason had, earlier that day, read an e-mail, one of those stupid chain letters that promised sad times if you didn't replicate its viral cheer to five people within the next five minutes. Ten people promised an orgasm of good fortune, and fifteen would make your head explode in a shower of gold ducats to be replaced by a fresh new mind-set enclosed in a better-looking face than you'd had before. Probably topped with hair like this guy's. The body of the message touted random acts of kindness as the cure for all the ills of the world. A couple of trite poems and a series of improbably lit photos positively purred with serenity.

Jason hadn't had fifteen or even five people he felt chummy enough with to spread the love to, but that was okay. He didn't believe in good luck. Or bad luck. But maybe, just for today, at the gas pump, he did believe what the e-mail had preached.

"Excuse me!" Jason called out to the man, bent over the saddlebag once again.

"Yeah?" The man looked over his shoulder, a neutral appraisal roaming Jason from head to shoes and back again.

"I couldn't help but hear your phone conversation."

The man straightened around to face Jason. "I'm sorry, man. Cut me some slack. I didn't mean to cuss a cloud over your sunshine."

Jason bloomed in heat. He'd already gotten it wrong, reaping confrontation where he'd hoped only to sow good-will. "No, no, that's fine. That's not what I meant. I was just going to say that I'd be happy to buy you a tank of gas."

"No shit? I mean, really?"

"Yeah." Jason smiled. He felt nobler already.

"You don't have to buy a whole tank. Just a splash would get me where I'm headed."

"No, it's okay. Might as well get some mileage out of a 'random act of kindness,' right?"

Something in the younger man's easy smile and slack shoulders made Jason feel bold. Some of it was envy and the guy knew it, was accustomed to it even. But he carried such an excess of confidence that he could afford to make a magic mirror of it. You looked into his face and he gave it back to you. For a moment, you were the one at ease in your own skin; you smiled and showed big, white, all-the-better-to-eat-you-with teeth; you felt your hair curling at its robust tips and your eyebrows cocking humor into everything. And when the young man looked away, it was as if a lamp had been snapped off, and suddenly you were the size you'd always been, your borders shrunk back to the contours of your place in the food chain.

Jason extended his hand. "Jason Getty."

The smirking man took the offer with a grip and a deeper smile. "Jason Getty, you saved my life. I will make it up to you, man. I'm Gary Harris."

Harris convinced Jason to give him his address, insisting that he be allowed to reimburse Jason for the gas when he was next in the area. The glow of camaraderie lasted hours. The pride of having been the nice guy boosted Jason along for a week. As the days from the encounter marched into double digits, though, a faint annoyance at Harris for not showing up as he'd promised was a fly in the ointment. No, a gnat really. It was okay. Jason honestly hadn't wanted to be paid back.

But if he would only have admitted it, although not having anyone handy to admit it to, he very much wanted to look into that mirror again, into that face that made him so sure he could mimic it all, *have* it all, with a wink and a swagger.

The Saturday that Jason had set aside to shop for dogs in earnest was ripped to soaking gray shreds by a thunderstorm that clattered at the windows. Jason bent over the newspaper, circling the classified ads showing dogs for sale and looking up breed information on the Internet. He ticked addresses on the opened map with a highlighter. Peals of thunder pressed in close behind the lightning, making him jump, and the rain splatted the glass in startling bursts.

One rumble lasted well past the overhead rolling, and it took Jason a moment to realize that the banging was picking up tempo and rattling his front doorframe. He opened the door to find Gary Harris, holding a soggy pizza coupon over his head. Water dripped from the tip of his nose.

"Jesus, man, it's fuckin' pouring. You gonna make me stand out here all day?" He stepped in as Jason moved aside.

Jason made the invitation official with a sweep of his hand. "Wow! No. Sorry, I didn't hear you with all that thunder." But by the end of his sentence, he was already speaking to Harris's back as he'd continued on down the hall, peering into Jason's rooms as he went.

"Heh. Well, look at you," Harris crooned, admiring the big plasma television in the den. "Nice digs." He looked Jason up and down. "Who'da thunk it?"

Jason smiled, pleased with being pleasing.

Harris clapped him on the back. "Gotta beer?"

9

H E WAS "Gary" to Jason at first. Calling someone by his last name was the province of bullies and hateful phys ed teachers and the drill instructors Jason had seen in films. He had never once been called out by his last name that it hadn't felt like a rolled-up newspaper to the snout. And he wasn't inclined to be combative. In fact, with Gary, Jason wasn't inclined to be anything at all. He nearly forgot himself completely. No cringing, no nerves, no self-consciousness, no *self*. For those hours he was only the expression on Gary's face. He fed out stories and was rewarded with the interest, amusement, agreement, and outrage reflected back to him in Gary's lively reactions. It was good to be lost. It felt like freedom.

Gary was mostly everything Jason was not. He was good-looking, with broad shoulders tapering to small hips, and annoyingly it was as a result of good genes, not endless hours in the gym. Jason wasn't homely, only pale and soft, and even more so on the inside. Gary had big teeth and wore his clothes with ease. Jason's shirts always came untucked and his smile flickered uneasily in the lower wattages.

Jason started stocking beer after that first visit, having been set to blushing at not having a drop of anything festive in the house. Gary played like a party on two feet or two wheels and liked to keep his good mood lubricated. An endless supply kept the magic mirror in place, so Jason ran out and bought beer. Lots of beer.

They'd talked that first afternoon. Harris rode to the store with Jason for the first case of domestic he'd ever bought, and afterward, they sat at the kitchen table and just jawed, a thing Jason hadn't done since college. "So where'd you grow up?" rolled easily into deeper waters. The cans piled up and the stories came out—of Jason anyway. In retrospect, he could only recall Gary doing a lot of nodding and smiling.

The end of that first evening came too quickly for Jason, although in actuality hours had passed and the thunderstorms had blown themselves out without his noticing. By then, he was exhausted, wrung out, and happily empty of stories for the moment, head humming where it wasn't numb from more drink than he was used to. Gary, looking far less worn by the marathon, promised they'd "do it again soon." Jason hadn't believed it for a second.

But to his delight, Gary showed up again. And again. The number of days in between would vary, and Gary wouldn't allow himself to be cornered into a schedule. But he always came back.

He had balked when Jason asked for a phone number. "You're not my girlfriend."

"I didn't mean it like that," Jason pouted.

"Don't get sore. There are just like four people in the whole world who have my phone number. It's nothing personal."

"Well, how do people get in touch with you?"

"They don't. If I keep it low, I keep it sane. I don't want

people thinking they can have a piece of me at the push of some buttons."

"But everyone gets phone calls. It's normal," Jason said. "I never know when the heck you're coming over."

Gary squinted his irritation at Jason. "Tell you what. If I ring the bell too many times that you don't answer, I'll manage to get over it somehow." There was more he could say. Jason saw something hateful and, worse, something possibly true straining against Gary's tightened lips. But the insult stayed caged, wrestled silent by a brutish diplomacy for the win. Gary's patience wasn't much more than a look he wore part of the time, but it would always be for the win.

Jason backed up a step, then two. "No, it's fine. I was just asking. Forget it."

Gary shook off the cloud and, with it, the muzzle. "Don't worry about it. Seriously. Like I said, it's nothing personal. Look, I've learned to avoid hassles. And believe me, anyone can turn into a hassle—at any time. I don't give out my number and I don't give out my schedule. Besides, my ex and her family, they've got it in for me. If I don't get any calls, then I always know it's not them."

"Pffffft. I know how that is." In every hope of steering them back to placid waters, Jason unknowingly baited a hook. The conversation veered to complaining about in-laws, and according to Gary's face, Jason had never been so fascinating.

Jason found himself cramming errands into the afternoon commute only to end up twiddling his thumbs through the evening hours and going off to bed grumpy, unable even to gripe over botched plans. There were never any plans.

The day that Gary showed up with his own drinks, he smiled more than usual and brought along something else as well: a bedraggled girl called Bella. Her waist-long hair was a few tousles shy of starting dreadlocks and was the color of a rust stain in a dirty sink. Fifteen additional pounds would have had her healthy-looking, but her face was a perfect porcelain heart, set with misty blue eyes and a tiny, impossibly pink mouth. Her laughter slid as easily up her throat as the booze slid down. It was fairy dust, her laugh, and it softened Jason's attention to keeping count of his own drinks. He was almost sure he'd sipped at number seven more than once. By the time Gary was inclined to leave, rather earlier than was his usual habit, Bella was too woozy to be trusted to hang on for the motorcycle ride back, and Jason was too far gone to drive her home in his own car.

Gary pulled him aside once Jason's fidgety discomfort had made even the twirling and giggling Bella concerned for her welcome. "Just let her crash here, man. What difference does it make?"

Jason wasn't so sure, but he was, at this point, so readable that Gary only laughed at him. "God, you're a freak. A cute girl—a cute, *wasted* girl—needs to sleep on your sofa, and you look like you're about to shit your pants." Gary grabbed Jason by the shoulders and gave him a bolstering shake. "Just don't give her any more to drink or she'll puke on the carpet, son. Take her home in the morning. Easy peasy."

"Okay."

"Don't do anything I wouldn't do, big guy." And with a wink and a nod, like some skinny, sardonic Santa, Gary was gone.

They didn't drink more, but Bella didn't sleep on the sofa either. Jason woke up to her staring at him. The soft glow of her eyes turned out to be a natural asset, not a by-product of too much alcohol. She smiled at him, unself-conscious in her nakedness. The sheet, only a few shades brighter than her milk-white hip, was scrunched out of the way of everything important. Her radiance, at odds with her crazy hair, was plenty searing to Jason's already burning eyes. He blinked and they watered up as he gaped at her, trying too hard not to appear to be gaping. Jason's head pounded, a very few clear-ish thoughts sneaking out between the pulses that boomed from somewhere deep behind his ears. Each surge seemed just a fraction bigger than the last one, as if both halves of his tenderized brain were lunging to meet in the middle for some evil brand of fission.

He remembered making her laugh, a bona fide sparkle that anointed him with courage. He batted at the cobwebs between him and the memory of feeling charming. She'd called him sweet. He'd called her beautiful.

It was several moments before he realized that he, too, was bare under the covers, without so much as a pair of socks on. Sheets and skin and a naked girl. Bella. Right. And he needed to pee. Desperately.

"I, um, I need to get up and, well, um, go, you know, out there." Jason pointed toward the hall.

"Go ahead," she cooed.

Jason circled his finger in the air, dialing his blush brighter as much as pantomiming his request. "Do you mind turning around?"

She shifted around in a rustle of bedclothes, a sound Jason hadn't noticed that he'd been missing. His bed had been so quiet since Patty had last turned beside him, whenever that last time had been. In the swish and crinkle of sheets, the sound of a woman twisting away from him sparked a twinge-memory—the bewilderment of rejection. But it was also the background music of not being alone. He wished he had known it was going away, the sound of his wife. He wished he had known to remember it.

He nearly reached for Bella then, wanting to know soberly what her skin felt like under his hand, but he didn't. Bella's silvery chuckle, as she faced the wall, was more embarrassing than her watching his naked butt hustling out the door would ever have been.

A week later, Gary, for the first time, invited Jason along for an outing.

"Out where?"

"I don't know. It's a party. We'll hang out. Drink somebody else's beer for a change. Trust me. You *need* to get out."

Jason assumed he'd be the designated driver, but Gary stopped him with a nod to his motorcycle.

"Leave it. Let's take my bike."

The gathering was a noisy, smoky clutch of people too old to look right at a house party and too rough to be less than an intimidating nuisance out in public. Gary didn't seem to know anyone in the fray. He kept leaving Jason alone, dropped in the middle of the room like forgotten luggage. Jason seemed unable to get out of his own way, much less anyone else's. He tightrope-walked Gary's absences, dancing forward and back to accommodate the flow of leather and stubble and too snug tank tops as they slipped behind him or pinballed off the front of him. Gary was making calls, he said, looking for better fun, but it never presented itself. So they wandered laps of the grubby house, bumping shoulders and going deaf under the constant babble and bass.

"Let's get out of here," Gary said after a long hour had overshot Jason's last hope for a nice evening.

Back home, at the landing, Jason clearly didn't need his key. The front door, to his dismay, showed an inch of foyer in its distance from the jamb. He pushed it wide, but looked to Gary for agreement before stepping in. "I know this door was locked. I never leave the door unlocked."

"No. You wouldn't, would you?"

"Should we go in first or just call the police?"

Gary held a smirk at bay and looked up and down the street. "Let's just go in."

The house looked as it should have, more or less, but the walls rang with the stealthy echo of trespass. The nap of the carpet didn't quite match up to the way Jason thought he'd left it, and everything looked ogled. Then there was the dust-bordered clean spot on the credenza, a shrieking blank spot in the space between the shelves of his music and movie collections. His television was quite gone.

"Come on, quick! We've got to get out of here," cried Jason.

"Relax," said Gary. "There's no one here."

"How do you know that?"

"Well, they're awful quiet if they are." Gary strolled down the hall, unbothered, Jason trailing after him. Gary crouched at every doorway and pounced through, yelling, "Boo!," and waggling his eyebrows at Jason with each discovery that a room was indeed unoccupied except for the two of them.

In the bedroom, Gary flipped back the bedclothes, crowing, "Come out, come out, wherever you are!" Meanwhile, Jason discovered that his dress watch, an engraved present from Patty, was the only item missing from the scattered contents of the catchall dish on the dresser.

"Oh my God. I don't believe this. You're right, I don't think they're still here. But don't touch anything. I gotta call the police." Jason dashed for the phone with Gary closing fast on his heels.

"Hang on, hang on." Gary's gentle pressure on Jason's arm wouldn't have been enough to keep Jason from raising the phone to his ear, but the smile that played on Gary's lips most certainly was.

"What's going on?"

"You can't call the police," said Gary.

"What do you mean?"

"Take it easy. You can replace the television. And a watch? Pffffft!"

"What? I have to make a police report."

Gary was laughing now. "No, honestly, you really don't." He held Jason's arm harder.

"What are you talking about? Why wouldn't I?"

"Because you just won't. Look, let's go crack a beer and I'll spell it out for you. You're probably going to be pissed, but if you can look at it a certain way, it's pretty fuckin' funny. And I promise, at the end of the day, you're not out anything. Could even be karma at work, my man. You may just feel like the cat that ate the father-in-law's canary."

So it was at his own kitchen table, watching Gary swill the beer that Jason kept on hand expressly for his visits, that the con was detailed for him.

A surgeon needs steady hands. A teacher needs patience. A garbage collector needs a strong stomach and a wandering mind to put him elsewhere in his drudgery. As in all endeavors, a swindler needs a skill set. Gary Harris was an ace at snatching relevant facts from casual conversation. Names, dates, places, habits, and appetites, they all stacked up in neat columns and rows in a corner of his head until an equation presented itself. The solution to the math usually involved larceny, and it always resulted in a net profit.

Until Gary's attention, Jason had never allowed himself an outlet for the dislike of his father-in-law. Such men were enviable—successful and bold all the way to the diamond cuff links—whereas Jason had never done anything except inherit the dirt that the meek were promised in the Bible. The wishful thinkers had always transcribed it as if Jesus had said that they would earn the Earth, but Earth and earth are apportioned by strength, not by mildness, as every mild man knows.

Jason's father-in-law was righteous: generous, scholarly, sleek, fit, and far too much for Jason to take head-on. Jason wasn't without pride, but had always confined his snappy comebacks to the bathroom mirror.

The privacy of his own home had been no release either. Jason couldn't very well have complained to Patty about her dear daddy. She'd been at once the spoiled favorite and the unproductive black sheep and was clever enough not to tip the balance out of her favor. She had no qualms about letting Jason have the sharp end of her temper if he complained. And he simply wasn't at ease enough at the office watercooler to let the gossip fly. So he'd swallowed the slights, choked them down, and let them eat their way through his guts to turn him yellow and cringing.

Gary had cared. He had wanted to hear what had happened to Jason at the hands of his highbrow in-laws. He'd asked him for more, for how he'd felt, deserted there on the drafty side of their cold shoulders, and he asked for a full account of what Jason had done about it. Gary had got angry on Jason's behalf as the tales of the snubbings poured out. Molehills rose to their indignant height and in the process, the Coates family's location, assets, and patterns were detailed, often at Gary's urging. He always wanted Jason to set the scene clearly—just for authenticity, of course.

The setup was simple. All the best ones are.

It was the biggest job Gary had ever managed. He'd done deals as meager as lifting food stamps from trailer-park mailboxes, but the opportunity to hit something more than a house and just less than an estate was flush with challenges and payoff.

And Gary was good at what he did, albeit small-time. He arranged and conducted the hits from a distance, perched out of reach, both literally and figuratively, from the action as it happened. His ties to the capable hands-on thieves he worked with were kept thin for everyone's peace of mind. He had been sincere when he'd told Jason that only four people in the whole world knew how to get him on the telephone, a rolling series of noncontract, pay-as-you-go numbers that were never in his name. And one of those people was his mother, who could rarely be bothered. The rest of them had every interest in keeping to as much radio silence as their business allowed.

For Gary, alone was better. He slept like the dead, but only when he'd spent days on his own, away from people. Sometimes it depressed him that he couldn't just enjoy a chat or a friendly gathering, but no matter the occasion, a part of him was always circling for the most advantageous angle, looking for a weak spot in the fence. He couldn't help himself. It was exhausting and it never switched off, although he had actually tried a little for the sake of Jason Getty.

"It's the biggest haul we've ever made. Your father-in-law won't know whether to shit or go dancing," Gary cackled. "We got a Mercedes, man. A fuckin' Merc!"

"You took his car?" Jason had lost even the color to his lips, all his blood pulling maximum distance from the story as it crashed into him.

"Dude, we took everything. I haven't seen it yet, but the haul was epic. Shit, the old bastard deserved it. You know that. Besides his insurance will cover it."

"Just like mine will," Jason said, head down.

Gary clucked and shifted in his seat. "Um. No. Your case is a little bit different. Don't be sore at me, man. Your TV and watch and stuff—"

"Stuff? What stuff? There's more?"

"Just a few little things. Don't get your panties in a wad. Your stuff is *my* insurance. And yours, too, really. We don't hit with a third party unless they get tapped, too. Your stuff will be held and eventually sold off with the other things. It's all mixed in together. Cops find us, they find you."

"That's bullshit." The curse slipped out of Jason's mouth without clearing his head, but hearing it in his own voice made him bold. "I'll just tell them you robbed us both."

Gary raised his eyebrows, irritatingly mild in his amusement. "Well, that won't go very far in explaining the thirty-five hundred dollars cash you deposited at the bank drop tonight."

"What? I haven't made any deposit," Jason spluttered and stammered. "And if you think I'm going to, you can just forget it."

"I wouldn't ask it of you." Gary had grown tired of Jason's new tone in seconds. "You'd probably just fuck it up, anyway." Gary sucked his teeth. "And look at you growing all kinds of balls now. Anyway, it's your car that's on the surveillance tape. Your jacket. Your ball cap. Your deposit ticket from your checkbook in the desk drawer in the other room. We paid a guy about your size to keep his head down and drop the envelope in the slot. He did it for twenty bucks." Gary loosed a laugh, a jolly warning laugh, by way of a last invitation for them to make light of it all. "Course, that meant we had to find a fourteen-year-old who could drive. But what I'm telling you is—the camera saw *you*."

Jason didn't laugh back.

"Christ man, don't be such a tight ass. That money will cover anything you lost. It's no big deal! I protected you. You're not out anything. I made sure of it. I'm trying to be a friend, here. This is how it works. My guys will work with me no questions asked, no hassle, no danger to you at all, because they know I put a rubber on these things so as no one catches preggers with problems. I can trust you now, and you can trust me—hey!—I'm being straight with you, ain't I? And now I'm protected. Everybody gets paid and your asshole father-in-law gets screwed out of one big shock and a few days' trouble putting his castle back together. So what? Get a grip."

Jason spared a groping second to search his conscience for remorse for his father-in-law's hardship, but there wasn't much. It was well overshadowed by a brighter shame than Patty's father had ever caused him. Jason raged in layers. At the core was a dizzy cold spot, spinning, impossible to pin down. His stomach burned, bearing down and dragging a heavy heat inward, bending his spine. Over that, his muscles crackled with lightning, itching to strike out in quickly fading flashes. On top of it all, humiliation pricked his skin. It stung his cheeks, his palms, his neck, the backs of his legs as they trembled against the chair, but most especially, it stabbed into his eyes.

"Are you crying?" Gary asked. "Tell me you're not crying. Jesus, what a puss." Although he'd started the comment in laughter, in only a few short words Gary was hit full in the instinct with alpha-male bloodlust. "Look, Jason, your chicken's been plucked. It's not like I can cram the feathers back in. And just because I don't care doesn't mean we can't be friends. But you sitting there crying like that is straining my last fucking nerve. I'm not your girlfriend."

"Get out. Get out of my house." Jason kept his voice low to tighten down on the quaking that welled up through him.

"Oh ho! Is that how it is, is it?"

"I mean it, Harris." Jason bit the words off to good effect, managing to sound stern over crushed.

Gary sat bolt rigid in his chair. "Harris? Did you just call me Harris?"

The fight, ill at ease to begin with, whooshed from Jason in a hurry. "I'm—I'm—I'm sorry, Gary. I'm just upset—"

"No. Stop right there. You think you're man enough to bark me out by my last name? Do you?" Gary slapped the tabletop and launched out of his seat. "Then that's what you call me. All the time. From now on. Fuck that. I was trying to work this out, trying to make you see that it wasn't a bad deal for anyone except some rich asshole who deserved it. I went to a lot of trouble for you. You think I bother explaining myself to the other shitheads? You think I do? Fuck you. I'll knock your goddamned teeth down your throat the next time you call me Gary like we're friends."

Jason was left stammering, an ache and a panic zinging between his ears, scrambling everything he wanted to say. He followed Harris to the door. "Listen, don't go like this. We'll work it out. You've been drinking anyway and—"

Harris put a finger over his lips. "Shhhh! Just say, 'Good night, Harris.'"

The part of Jason that was still angry despised the pleading bleat that squeaked out. "Gar—"

Harris pulled back his fist so fast Jason could only flinch and clamp his lips down over a squeal. Harris stopped the blow an inch off Jason's cheekbone.

"Say, 'Good night, Harris.'"

"Good night, Harris."

A sneer crumpled Harris's good looks into a gargoyle's leer. His breath was sour and yeasty in Jason's face. Jason tried to pull his eyes to meet Harris's close inspection of him, but they wouldn't stay put to take in the change that had come over his erstwhile friend, his magic mirror. And then, of all the odd things, Gary Harris took Jason's face between his two hands.

"See you around, Jase."

Then he leaned in and kissed Jason's cheek. A warm, lingering, utterly terrifying sensation. Excruciatingly slowly, Jason felt every millimeter of Harris's soft lips lifting, tickling his skin. Harris pulled back from the embrace, and before a blink could fall, he slapped a cupped hand hard over the spot on Jason's face. There was more noise than pain, and the tears held until Jason could throw the lock over with trembling fingers and stumble back into the first of many sleepless nights.

10

J ASON left the living-room light on all night, every night, after the burglary. It burned as a beacon, an invitation to parley, just in case Harris rode by. That was the more noble posture of it at any rate, when Jason was able to convince himself that the light wasn't just a shield against being caught alone in the dark. It didn't much explain why he left the hallway, the closet, and the bathroom lit up like the Las Vegas Strip.

Rolling the lamp's switch to its startling little click each night also served as a ritual, a votive lit for a dead opportunity. It marked off a penance for that one moment he'd chosen to flex his temper and lower his horns at Harris; the moment he'd have back if only he could. Turning into his driveway each afternoon was an exercise in unrelieved tension. It wasn't as relaxing as it could have been, letting out the held breath each time he found his house *not* tossed over. He knew there was always tomorrow. Jason's too quiet evenings were wasted on wishing he could flip the choice he'd made that night, change things back so that Harris's dark side still lurked, semisafely, below the surface.

Jason daydreamed, in replay, the whole event and its aftermath spooling out differently: his mild acceptance of what had been done, of replacing the lost items and the door locks without a fuss, and then of Harris's attention drying up, his interest in Jason waning in a few weeks or months just as Jason had always known it would have done sooner or later. Jason wanted the footnote, the whole business fading into a diary entry to be read by someone packing up his things long after it mattered anymore. In those daydreams, his life was gifted back to him. He was bitten and twice shy to be sure, in those fantasies, but no worse for the wear—exactly as Harris had said it would be. Jason hated himself mostly for that tweak of insult, that Harris had been right. The one time Jason hadn't played along as the butt end of a joke resulted in a pissing contest that left him with nothing but wet shoes. That and an unrelenting paranoia inside his own house.

When Harris did resurface, on a late-summer evening, he came with a six-pack. As he stood there under the porch light flickering inside a whirlwind of moths, it was hard to tell if it was challenge or good fun that radiated under his smirk and arched eyebrow. Jason's blood slushed in his veins, and all the speeches he'd rehearsed vanished from their sentry posts.

"You gonna let me in?" But the question was only a line out of a script with none of the blocking. Harris took the threshold as if he owned it and closed the door behind him. "Wouldn't be good to have unwanted guests, now would it?" He laughed at Jason's startle. "Relax. I meant the bugs."

Jason's head was empty, buzzing a hollow alarm. The only thing that tumbled from his lips was a tremulous "Everything all right?"

"Let's have a beer" was all the answer he got.

Harris's brand of manipulation was in that nearly every-thing he said was delivered tone-neutral. It wasn't an affectation. He didn't need to try to mask his intentions, because quite often he didn't have any. The desire to con-nect with another human being weights the conversations of most people. To make themselves known, they work their opinions and desires out of the best-fitting words and truest inflections they can manage. Harris, by nature, wasn't concerned with being understood. He only looked for an angle. Almost anything he said could be plied as a joke, a threat, or, most maddening, like indifference. His targets marked themselves by how they translated.

To his great discomfort, Jason could map his own com-plicity in all their exchanges. He'd betrayed himself over and over by wringing exactly what he'd wanted to hear from the next to nothing Harris had actually said. The jarring contrast of Harris's fury during their last confrontation was made all the more pointed by the way it couldn't, unlike nearly everything else Harris had ever said, be played back as anything other than menace.

His "How've ya been?" was accompanied by the happy whoosh of air rushing up from under the twisted bottle cap. It scanned as "friendly" in the mind's ear, but really, it was only three words and a bit of carbonation.

"I'm okay," said Jason.

"Still sore at me?"

Yes. "No!" Jason's pride splintered off and refused to participate beyond grumbling in the corner of his mind. "It was just a shock, you know, that whole night. I wasn't expecting it. I mean, you don't expect that sort of thing, do you? You were very . . . What would you call it? Cool and everything. I just didn't have a clue. My house was robbed. I wasn't really hearing you. I didn't mean to upset you." *He set you up and you're apologizing. Outstanding.*

"I see you didn't get a new TV yet," Harris said as he handed Jason a beer.

"Well, I have the little set in the bedroom. And"—Jason swallowed a painful knot of his drink—"I didn't know if you'd want the money back."

Harris laughed over the rim of his bottle, watching Jason with too steady eyes, his lips just brushing the rolled-glass edge. Jason locked his shoulders against a shudder at the unwelcome memory of the feel of those lips. "Jase, you really are a piece of work." Harris flopped into his usual chair at the table. "But it does so happen that I actually *do* need a little money."

Jason's offer of a check was rejected on practical grounds, so he drove, against a tirade of abuse from his kneecapped self-esteem, to an ATM. It was only $300. Harris was being nice. *Harris isn't being anything. His visit is an olive branch, a threat, a scam, an honest need—face it, it is anything your jelly spine makes of it.* Jason let the argument ricochet inside his skull, tearing him a headache. But he spoke to Harris of only inconsequential things and laughed whenever he thought he heard a joke.

They stood in the foyer in the same positions they'd taken at their last showdown. Jason was damp in his uncertainty, knowing he'd played along as best he could, cautiously hopeful that he'd eased the lid back over Pandora's box. It wasn't the sort of hope that could boast firm footing, though.

"Well, Jase, you came through for me." Harris clapped him on the shoulder. "I thought you might. Good man."

"Look, Gary, the other night, I never meant to—"

The slap rocked him to the right and burned like hot pavement against his cheek.

"You think everything's all right? Think again, *Getty*. Pissing your pants and kissing my ass all night doesn't put us back as good buddies. I tried to be a friend to you and got *Harris* for the fucking hassle. So *Harris* it is. And if I have to tell you again, you'll wake up on the goddamned floor."

"Why are you so mad about that?" Jason held a cooling hand to his face, but his eyes burned. Pain, shame, and anger brewed stinging tears.

"Because you're ungrateful. And you just need to believe me, I am not about second chances."

Harris became regular in his attentions after that. At least regular in that rarely more than three or four days separated his appearances at the door. Sometimes he'd hang out as if nothing were wrong: drinking beer, cracking jokes, and complaining about mundane things across the table from a stiff-backed Jason. Other visits were short, taunting episodes of ringing the bell in the small hours of the morning, waking Jason for a loan or a chat. Harris seemed to get a kick out of telling Jason that he looked like stir-fried shit, so Harris kept him good and tired. Harris always returned the money he borrowed, though. On his next visit he never once failed to settle their account in full.

Harris started bringing things for Jason to hold for short spans: boxes of loose jewelry, computers, a case of new cell phones, and, once, an Acura with a smashed passenger window.

"What if it has one of those tracking things on it?" Jason

tried to rein in his pout, as it always sparked up the bully in Harris.

"Well then," he'd replied, but had to stop for a short fit of mocking giggles, "you'll just have to tell them that you're holding it for your good friend Gary Harris. See how that works out for you."

Jason remembered his sanctuary in the woods by the sinkhole. At first he went on sunny days, sweating in the low-hanging summer shade, sometimes reading, but always whittling time from the hours in each day that Harris could use against him. A forecast of rain would make him nearly despondent, stealing his options, until he realized that umbrellas were as fully functional in the woods as they were on the sidewalk. It turned out, rain on the skin wasn't so bad either. He learned to clear his mind and feel nothing but the drops tickling through the maze of his hair, turning to little rivers that slipped over his cheeks, rushing to merge and cascade off his chin. He felt the fabric of his clothes swell and grow heavy, chilling his skin at first, but losing the battle to his own radiant heat, ending up all musty and warm. The rain meditation took the place of untroubled sleep and left him restored, and slightly distanced from his problems.

Harris met him on the stoop, waiting for him one stormy afternoon. He looked Jason over with a sneer. "What the fuck happened to you?"

"It's raining," answered Jason, still dripping, but relaxed in every muscle and able to meet Harris's eyes in a singular moment of unbothered confidence.

"Never heard of an umbrella?"

Jason only smiled and, in it, took a slice from Harris's satisfaction. He looked, for once, distinctly ill at ease in his needling. He didn't stay long that day.

He showed up the next night with four sealed boxes for "storage." He'd also brought Bella. Bella, it seemed, had forgotten to bring her laugh. She kept her eyes downcast and bloomed crimson while Harris made a show of nuzzling her neck and tonguing her earlobe in front of Jason.

"Okay, Har—, Harris." Jason rued the day each time he faltered at the name. "I get the point." He whispered to Gary in the hallway to safeguard Bella's embarrassment, looking back over his shoulder to test the distance to her, hunched over a drink at the kitchen table. "You're making her cry."

"Oh, what?" Harris hissed back. "You think she's something you need to act like a big hero over? That she's your girlfriend?"

"No. It's just you don't need to do this. She didn't do anything."

"She'll sleep with anybody. You know that, right? For some blow, some weed, a few drinks . . . It doesn't matter to her. What, did you think you were special? Pffffft. I got you laid."

"I know that."

Harris studied Jason from an aggressive few inches away and shook his head. "So ungrateful."

Harris had stayed away the full four nights' length of his tether, and Jason had settled into a nearly peaceful sleep when the irksome triple ring of the bell announced his return. Jason slapped his hands against the bedspread and ground his teeth. But he also didn't get up. It chimed again and Jason threw himself over and pulled the pillow down to block his ears. The bell rang on at intervals throughout the night, and Jason's startled heart scorched his blood every time, but he would not get up. In the lulls of up to an hour, Jason dozed, but only once did Harris beat a barrage of blows on the door with his fists and his feet. Jason's breath congealed in his throat, locked solidly out of his lungs by the memory of Harris at his angriest and then magnifying that picture to imagine what shape his temper might take to match this random act of defiance. Jason's stomach boiled his dinner into something caustic, and his guts sizzled in it all night.

And still he would not answer the door.

In the morning, before his shower, Jason tiptoed to the windows and surveyed the street for a man or a motorcycle out of place. He checked again after he'd dressed, and then once more before breakfast. Behind the wheel of his car, Jason dared enjoy a touch of satisfaction, if not buoyancy, until just as he pulled the lever into reverse, the flat of Harris's hand whacked down on the windshield, his body suddenly blocking the gold and green light that had been filtering in through the trees.

A clatter of thrown keys grated on the hood of Jason's car.

Harris nodded at them and crouched to get his face close enough to the driver's-side window to be heard through the glass without shouting.

"Your boss's keys. I left everything else, but I scratched the shit out of his ride. You pull a stunt like that again and somebody's going to get hurt." Harris slapped the glass over Jason's face again and was gone.

*

All of these things Jason endured. He fled to the rim of the crater in the woods whenever he could. He stole time away from work for it if he had to. He minced words and strides everywhere else, trying to be small and ignored. He calculated that he could outlast him, that Harris would get bored and drift off to a new diversion. Jason certainly didn't count himself as interesting enough to earn lifelong harassment for using a last name, one time, in a moment of heat.

In hindsight, it was funny that he expected Harris to change while never sparing a thought for his own limitations. It never occurred to him what sort of man might split out of his own brittle composure if it ever lost its glue.

Harris brought a monkey. Of all the things Jason never expected, a monkey would have been right up there with a volcano and the ashes of Albert Einstein.

"It's a chimpanzee, not a monkey," Harris offered. "Help me carry the cage in. The little bastard's heavy. Watch your fingers. He bites."

"You can't leave it here," Jason said, huffing big breaths to wrestle the heavy cage inside.

"Yeah, I can. I have to."

"What am I supposed to do with it?"

"Feed it. And keep it hidden. You can't tell anybody it's here."

"Feed it what?" Jason pleaded. "And who am I going to tell?"

Harris smiled. "Exactly."

He promised to come back for it within three days. By the fifth day, Jason was as frantic as the boxed monkey. The creature screamed and shook the wire mesh of its pen with terrifying strength. Jason locked his bedroom door, listening for the chimp's coop to finally give way under its frustration. It hissed at him when he shoved food through the slot, baring its teeth and tensing for an attack if Jason wasn't quick enough at banging the food dish into the sliding tray with his trembling hands. Other times, it waved its fingers through the gaps and whimpered like a human child until Jason felt moans of sympathy aching in his own throat.

Jason sealed up all the windows in the house and pulled the drapes and still worried that the sound would carry. He bought some hours of ease by lugging his small television from the bedroom into the kitchen. The monkey seemed to like cartoons and commercials, but some random images would set it to screeching, frantically rocking until Jason was sure the entire cage would tip over and the poor thing would be trapped on its side until Harris came back.

If Harris came back. Jason had often fantasized about Harris's motorcycle launching him over the handlebars, headfirst into something hard. Preferably brick. Before Patty died, Jason had never thought of someone else's death as an escape hatch. He'd never seen the possibility of an upside to a tragedy before, and he considered it the darkest thing his mind had ever drummed up. He had shamed himself with his relief that no one knew she was going to leave him; doubted that he could be a decent human being if he could see anything about her untimely death as fortunate for him. But now, with the practice for it laid, he couldn't help imagining the freedom he'd feel if Harris met with an accident.

Until then, he'd never thought it through very well. He'd fantasized about liberty and the private celebration he'd stage. He'd find a bar and buy a drink for every sad sack sitting there, then leave with an enigmatic smile. He'd plant a tree in the clearing by the sinkhole and record its progress in pictures. He'd buy himself that dog.

But he forgot to calculate into the scenario the fact that he'd never know. If Harris tripped down a well or got eaten by a bear, Jason would be none the wiser. His first problem would be that he'd find himself stuck with a miserable, and likely illegal, primate. But beyond that, he'd sit in angst for God knew how long before he'd dare breathe easy again. He'd look over his shoulder, flinching for that wicked grin, for years. Maybe forever. He didn't know a thing about Gary Harris—where he lived or what he did with the time he wasn't tormenting or burgling. He didn't know Bella's last name, or if she knew any more about Harris than he did himself. He didn't even know the make of the motorcycle that he'd been wishing a malevolent malfunction on.

But Harris did return—after nine of the longest days that Jason had ever suffered through. He was exhausted. He'd missed a week of work. The house reeked like a zoo; the floor and walls were grim with the dried and drying muck the chimp would splash and fling to amuse itself or when it lapsed into one of its frequent rages.

"Jesus." Harris looked Jason over as part of the trashed landscape. "You need to open a window in here."

Jason's face was numb with fatigue, eyes expressionless, and his voice a dazed monotone. "I would, except there's a screeching monkey in the kitchen."

Harris wiped his clean hands down the legs of his jeans. "Look, I appreciate it. I'm sorry it took me so long. This one was complicated." He sounded, for a change, infused with sincerity.

"Get out."

"I said I appreciated it. What the fuck's your problem?"

"Get the cage and get out of here."

"Fuck you, man. You pick the goddamnedest times to get ballsy. I'd punch your lights out if you smelled any better than that fuckin' monkey."

Jason ignored him, only reached down to grip his fists around the carrying bar of the cage. The chimp's wet eyes locked onto Jason's; they burned with accusation and welled deep with hatred and desperation and a heartbreaking understanding of its plight. Jason clamped his lips over the sob that pressed hard against the roof of his mouth. He kept his head down, face averted, while they huffed over the strain of loading the blanket-covered box into the van that Harris had borrowed for the errand. Jason stomped back into the house, banging the door shut and slamming the lock into place without another word.

The doorbell rang over the next days, but never so insistently as it had that one night. The phone racked up scores of calls from blocked or unknown IDs, but Jason wasn't answering any of them. Through the office window across the hall from his desk, he thought, on several occasions, that he saw Harris's bike on the far side of the filmy floor-to-ceiling glass, but it barely raised his pulse. Harris wouldn't risk being seen. Jason knew that.

Since meeting Harris, the weather had lingered over summer, drawing it out through a golden September and into a brass October. The mornings and evenings bookended warm days with a bracing chill. Jason left a jacket in his car for his treks into the woods. He felt nothing. He would have called it calm, except that in its anticipation of a storm, it would have been too clichéd. He was a blank. He bought a new television just for something to do, but he wouldn't have minded sitting in his chair staring at the plain white wall.

Inevitably, a night came when a few rings of the doorbell wasn't the last of it. Jason heard a key scrape in the lock. Harris pushed open the door and they faced each other over the threshold.

"What? You think I couldn't get a key?" Harris stepped past him, making sure it was far enough into Jason's space to cuff his shoulder. "Little brother, I don't care how pissed off you get at me, this bullshit isn't an option. Shut the door."

Jason did.

Harris laughed. "God, you're easier to play than my grandmother."

But Jason wasn't listening well enough to take any offense. Seeing Harris in the doorway had pulled his mind back into a dream he'd had just that day. He wasn't sure he would ever have remembered the details until he'd been reminded of them with that exceptional sneer that only Harris could pull.

Jason had fallen asleep outside after tidying the glen by the sinkhole. He'd taken to keeping a box of trash bags in his car, now the self-appointed caretaker of the wooded chapel. The other parishioners had obviously held a service with cheap cigarettes, cheaper beer, and campfires. The frequent visits from the cops had discouraged their irreverence, but not eliminated it.

Jason had shivered with disgust after forking a used condom into the bag with a stick, and he worked out the lingering picture of it by kicking a thick bed of fresh leaves over the clearing. Contented and out of breath, he slid down against the trunk of his favorite tree, maybe three yards from the edge of the drop-off. It was the last large oak to have dug in its toes and remained. Everything else close by was small, scrubby pines or spindly new elms. Jason had leaned over once and seen a basket of his oak's roots jutting out from the wall of the abyss. It was anyone's guess if it would last in its precarious disobedience. The hole wanted it. That much was clear.

But for now its notched side was the perfect place for Jason to wedge his back against and snooze. In the dream, he'd been cradled in a strangling cage of boughs and vines. He wasn't comfortable, indeed it was crushingly claustro-phobic, but at least it held him out of Harris's reach. Harris harangued him from the base of the tree. The wind rocked Jason's twiggy hammock, and although he knew he was safe, fear sizzled through him whenever he'd tip far enough to see Harris still down there, waiting, smirking.

Suddenly, as dreams do, the scene turned and Jason wasn't in the tree, although he could still see a version of himself, his back reclining in the webbing of laced branches. He was on the ground, face-to-face with Harris, who grinned and snapped his teeth at him. Jason looked up, longing to be reunited with the part of himself sway-ing above, safe and imprisoned in the stranglehold of the tree, but each time he'd bent his head back to his present view, Harris was closer to him and the tree was nearer to his back, pressing him forward.

Harris, Jason, and the oak were inched to the lip of the sinkhole until they were essentially all taking up the same space. The bole of the tree was cold against Jason's back, Harris's breath hot in his face. In a roar and gray-brown blur, the oak opened to pull them in. They were wailing inside the tree, mauled, ground together. High above, the roil and rumble shuddered up through the cradle of branches holding the rest of Jason as the tree chewed its Harris-Jason meal.

Jason had woken with a start, a cool, misty rain sweetening the sweat on his skin. A jet plane roared overhead, a pale echo of the racket in the dream. Jason had already forgotten the details before the contrail faded from the sky. He took the garbage with him and tut-tutted over the thoughtlessness of others, hating just a bit that there were others at all.

Now backing through the hallway, Jason was sweating again, tripping over his own feet, shuffling away from Harris, and cringing at his fury. Lost in the memory of his dream, he'd not heard a single thing Harris was saying.

"Are you even listening to me, you faggot? I'm talking to you. No, you know what? I own you. I'd kick your ass, but I don't know if I can stop myself from killing you." Harris shoved Jason hard in the sternum, knocking him against the sharp molding that framed the living-room doorway.

"Don't push me," Jason said, a plea with an edge to it.

"Why not, Jason? Huh?" Harris hit him in the chest again, harder this time. The doorframe bit into his back. "Why not? You're pushing me—not answering the door, not taking my calls, moping around every time I ask you to do one little goddamned thing." Harris sidled up too close, his nose beaking down into Jason's. "I've been easy on you. You have no idea. But you're so ungrateful."

Jason felt the waves of rising temper thumping from Harris until it seemed the room itself had a heartbeat booming into the air. But with a tingling, cold surge, he felt a countering strength climbing the rungs of his own spine. His back muscles cramped around the wood poking into it. "Back off me, Harris."

"Well, look at that. It finally suits you." Harris pinned him against the wall, his shoulder and hip pressing, grinding Jason into submission. "Say it again," he purred through gritted teeth. "Call me Harris like you mean it."

The pressure of Harris's body revolted Jason. The dominance that wanted him to shrivel, to invert and receive, lit the last length of Jason's fuse. He bent his knees and Harris relaxed a fraction, thinking he'd buckled Jason's will. But it was only for purchase. Jason drove all his strength down through his legs and locked his arms against Harris's chest.

The two men stumbled together, grappling and swinging at each other through the small living room, cracking their shins against the coffee table and toppling the lamp from its stand. Jason latched onto Harris, scrabbling for every hold and lock he could keep, his hands slipping against sweating skin and shifting clothing. Harris was stronger, faster, and more experienced, but he couldn't draw any distance from Jason for leverage or for swinging room.

Near the fireplace, Harris had twisted around, so that Jason was left clinging to his back, one arm crooked in a choke hold on his neck.

". . . fucking kill you . . . fucking kill you . . . ," gagged Harris, over and over, thrashing to dislodge his passenger. He spun and lost his feet to the raised hearth. Harris spilled out onto the floor. What little air he had left was forced from him as Jason crashed down onto his back.

In the fall, Jason had thrown out a saving arm and, in the motion, snagged the drooping cord of one of the antique phones that lined the mantel. It thumped and clattered onto the carpet beside them, rapping Jason's knuckles hard as it settled over their sprawl.

Everything seemed too soft for a good grip: Harris's smooth back, flexing and bucking under him, the short nap of the rug, sliding away wherever his fist searched for a handhold. And then there was the solid, angled density of the phone. Jason's right hand closed around its sturdy weight. He raised it over his head in the time it took Harris to crane around to see it come hurtling down.

11

H OW LONG would it take to dig him up? Jason stood at the open shed door and wondered why his mind made that question sound like *How many lawyers does it take to screw in a lightbulb?* Bayard had said it would take a few days to process his request to the State Investigative Unit for corpse-sniffing dogs and ground-penetrating radar, and Jason hadn't trusted his voice enough to ask for anything more specific.

But now he wondered.

Pre-Harris Jason would never even have made it out the back door, across the yard, and through the plank door of the shed to take stock of his tools. It was crazy.

He marveled that a good percentage of his reluctance to take up the shovel was purely physical. After he'd put Harris in the ground, his muscles had shrieked for days—every movement pulling hot, barbed threads through places in his body he hadn't even imagined could hurt. And for reasons he had not cataloged, he'd denied himself the comfort of an aspirin or an hour against the heating pad. The last of the soreness had faded after a fortnight, but the memory of it was still sharp enough to factor into the plan.

The plan. How long would it take? How long had it taken going the other way? The timeline of that night was fuzzy at best. Jason was fairly certain that Harris had died (*Harris didn't die . . . you killed him*) sometime near 9:00 p.m. He recalled looking at his watch over and over afterward, but that somehow the time refused to imprint over the squelchy sounds slithering into his ears and the glistening reds, grays, and ivories he was seeing. He knew he'd only just stretched out under the covers, a barely breathing slab of cold and ache, when the dawn began seeping through the curtains in the tiniest increments of blue.

He'd meant to take Harris to the sinkhole, to throw him in and never look back. That had presented at least two problems. Jason had already been noted in the woods by one of the county's uniformed finest and, should Harris be found, that encounter might come back to haunt Jason. The car was the other issue. Jason knew himself well enough to predict it would become his albatross. His home was already tainted, the living room doomed to gather dust and cobwebs from now on, but that couldn't be helped. If he would never again be able to load groceries into the trunk or drive Dave from Accounting to lunch in it for the sheer horror of the forensic ghost riding shotgun, he was going to need new wheels. In the interim, while he waited for the invisible smoke to clear the barrel of his metaphorical gun, he'd be sure to drive himself straight into a tree out of pure distraction.

But losing the sinkhole as his sanctuary bothered him out of proportion to any logistical problems. To deliver Harris's body to the one place Jason loved most would have been to surrender the single little victory he'd managed throughout the whole ordeal. He wouldn't do it. After all, he had a shovel, and the big pie-wedge lot was more than he needed. He rarely went out back anyway. He figured he could better control what happened if he just kept the whole thing close and tidy.

That he was only adding a grave to the veritable cemetery already there was a punch line well beyond the reach of his inner comedian.

Certain elements of that night stood out in inexplicably lively detail. He remembered wanting to eat the sandwich he'd been about to enjoy just before his dinner was knocked out of priority by Harris's arrival. He had imagined the bread growing drier each time he'd had to hustle through the kitchen for towels, bags, spray cleaner, gloves. Insane tears had stung the corners of his eyes as he tipped it into the trash before turning in for what was left of the night. And a fat, brown spider had flinched and brandished its forelegs at him in the shed as the shovel handle pulled through its web. From that night on, he couldn't see a spider without thinking of it.

He'd been unusually aware of his nakedness under the sputtering showerhead once it was all done and everything—plus one—was in its rightful place. He'd watched in fascination as the grime lifted from the sparse trail of hair tracking down his belly. It wound down along his leg and swirled onto the porcelain in a sooty stream, dragging his gaze to the drain as it swallowed his secret. He'd showered until the water ran cold and the goose bumps raced over his skin in sweeping surges.

While dressing for bed, his reflection had mocked him, withholding the transformation that should have been apparent. He looked just as he always had. Tired, for sure. A little stressed. But doughy, and familiar, and very, very Jason.

He'd felt absurd to the point of disgust, all bound up in his flannel pajamas, and in a fit of manic vitality, he'd clawed at the faded plaid, sending buttons pinging off the dresser mirror. Thready, little rips filled the silences between his sobs. And with a longing that seemed perverse in context, Jason still remembered too clearly the cool thrill of bedsheets sliding over his skin that night; skin so well scrubbed that it was more naked than a simple lack of clothing could account for.

No red and blue lights whirled into his window as he lay there, and no militant pounding came at the front door, nor any pulsating chop of helicopter blades with a SWAT team dangling from underneath. No one was coming for Harris. And no one ever would.

Where there should have been relief, there were two needling pains. One poked home the thought that he probably knew Harris better than most anyone else. No one knew where he went or whom he met. Harris iced his trail as he went along because he was smart enough to know that it was the only way for him. With this stab of insight, Jason realized that there may have been just the feeblest attempt at connection, if not exactly friendship, in the details Harris had shared about his solitary habits. He had tried to explain himself, and what that pale generosity had meant, Jason would never know.

The other hurt scraped a bold, burning underscore to Jason's default station in life: more than ever, now and for always with this impossible secret, he was alone.

The radio alarm startled him most days, but that morning, as his stare pulled the blank, white ceiling down through his eyes to smother his thoughts, the sudden surge of some castrated boy band in midwhine goosed a scream from Jason. He had dressed quickly, stifling the thought that the man he was covering up was not the same man he'd disrobed in a frenzy just a little while earlier. He'd not been nude for longer than eight minutes at a stretch ever since.

Working at the math now, his calculations put the actual digging and planting at seven or eight hours. His idea, however reckless, was to buy a couple of evergreen saplings and place them into the hole that he'd dig Harris out of. A few to the left and right of the pit would hopefully stand in for some authenticity. He'd ply the excuse that it was a good time of year for planting and explain that once they'd gained some height, the new trees would improve the winter view from the house. There was truth there. It really *had* bothered him that the closest electrical tower was just barely visible, November to April, through the leafless trees. Mrs. Truesdell had done something similar, screening the borders of her property with fast-growing cypress trees, and she seemed pleased enough with the effect.

But the success of the whole thing was contingent on the result of a day's (or night's) worth of gardening, and he was perfectly prepared to admit, even from the outset, that it might not work. And then what? If it didn't look good enough, or his resolve wobbled when it came time to face Bayard with a laundry list of new lies, what was left? As soon as he put shovel to soil, he was committed to play it out or run.

It would be easiest to go to Mexico, but the thought of himself south of the border amid the cacti—a man who turned pink if he even looked out on a sunny day for too long—was enough to make him laugh, even while staring into his musty garden shed in about the worst fix he could imagine. But at least he could drive there. He wondered if he could beat Bayard's intuition to the airport, to try a neutral European sanctuary and a gentler climate. His passport would betray him, though. Bayard would know exactly where he went, and something about his ease and his golf shirts told Jason that he'd pack lightly and come looking for him. A man could get lost in Mexico or points farther, especially if he had a head start. So it was south, if he had to run.

Regardless, he had no margin to dally. His reticence was a birth defect, but as such, he'd also learned to live with it, like congenital blindness. He had already proved he could work around it. His courage was best stored for when he'd need it most—for seeing Harris again, what was left of him anyway, and then for looking Bayard straight in the eye and defending another hole in his lawn as the most natural thing in the world.

Leah couldn't keep her eyes from falling out of focus. After all those years together, the white noise of thinking of Reid was so automatic it was like not thinking about him at all. That wasn't the problem. He was there at every corner and every doorway. It seemed at some point they'd marked every inch of that town with a kiss or a fight, a tire track or a footprint. Over all their years together, they'd probably filled every cinema seat and sat at nearly every table in every restaurant, except for the Tuscany Terrace, which had mostly been out of their budget save for birthdays, anniversaries, and the inevitable, and somehow depressing, marriage proposal.

Leah's mouth had been dry that night no matter how much water or wine she took in, because for good or bad, Reid had never been able to keep a secret. His brother had known. Their heads together then lurching apart, merry and red-faced, when she'd stepped into the room was clue enough. Reid's gathering up his hair into a semirespectable ponytail and his fidgeting encouragement for her to dress up could hardly have been ruled subtle. The meandering route he drove was meant to manufacture surprise, but it merely drew out the dread.

The reward for "yes" was a beaming Sheila and a loving family legally bound to her; the price of it was the folding of a corner of her self-respect and the flowering of a strangling vine of resentment. She'd known this before she'd stretched a close-lipped smile over her dismay. She memorized the feel of it for future use, knowing she'd likely need it again, and said the word anyway.

But Reid *had* managed to hold on to a secret—his final one—for more than three years, and the not knowing had put Leah on edge. And it had left her there, to her unrelenting distraction. With Reid, the only thing that had kept her in possession of the upper hand was that, by confession or discovery, she always found out the truth. She was a sleuth, a hound dog, a nosy reporter, and utterly tireless in the race to the platform of superiority. She reigned benevolent from that podium of facts from which she couldn't be lied to. Leah positioned herself as the Queen of Long-Suffering to hear his petitions for pardon. She'd extracted details from him in the same way you compulsively bend a hangnail and marvel at the odd satisfaction of the pain.

Not this time, though. She didn't know how often Reid had stolen off to a place almost an hour from home, or if he would have kept up the long round-trip after the wedding. He'd no doubt lolled in a bed there. Someone had seen to it that he'd kept that last posture under a patch of dirt, and she'd never be able to squeeze one bitter drop of gratification from the story of it. She didn't even have a picture of the place in her mind, and the dot on the map that showed her the town of Stillwater was wearing a bit thin as an anchor for her fixation.

The detective had played it coy when they'd last spoken; talked around it so deftly, she'd only realized he'd revealed nothing of importance after she'd hung up the phone. She'd wanted specifics but had been left with a kind and professional echo of "ongoing investigation," "private property," "protocol," and "we'll be in touch as developments occur." And that just wasn't going to cut it. She couldn't concentrate, and although it would change nothing, just as it had always changed nothing, the details were the lid. Her own version of the story, complete with names, dates, and pictures, was what she screwed down tight over every unpleasant event in her life before she put it on the memory shelf. A pantry of poisoned preserves.

She pushed back from her desk and let the tears polish her eyes. How far removed was "sad" from "frustrated" or "adrift," and would anyone be able to spot the difference? She was glad that tears for any of these were just as wet, and just as valuable a coin among her coworkers, who already gossiped over the discovery of Reid's bones in Stillwater. She needed to trade in the tears for some time away from work.

"Chris?" Leah leaned in over the threshold to his office.

Her supervisor lifted his shaggy, graying head from his task. "Hiya, kiddo." He bent immediately back to peering at his work, his nose inches from the computer screen. Leah waited for his brain to process the image of her pinked nose and too shiny eyes. He shot up tall in his seat and really looked at her. "Hey! Come in, come in. Shut the door."

"I'm sorry to do this," Leah said, as the door rattled into its frame. "It's just with everything that's happened, I can't think straight."

"What do you need?"

"A day or two. I thought I'd be okay." She caught even herself off guard with a fresh torrent of hot tears.

"Hey." Chris bumped his chair against the wall and hustled his paunch sideways into the tight passage around his desk. "You know you don't have to ask. Do what you need to do." Standing next to her, he seemed at a loss for purpose, his hand tapping out of any rhythm on her shoulder. "Grab your stuff and don't even call until Monday, okay? I mean, unless you need something."

Leah rubbed away the tears with the backs of her hands. "Thank you, Chris. You're the best."

"Get outta here." He smiled, his eyebrows imploring a return of the same.

Leah obliged through the prism of new tears and set out to clamp a cover over the last story Reid would ever tell.

Reid's mystery would likely remain sketchy forever. Everyone who knew anything firsthand was already long dead, which was a strange thing to say about a group of such young people. It felt as if there should have been a disaster: an earthquake, a twister, or at least a road accident, to lose a trio so flush in their prime. What had happened was sordid and theatrical, and without the specifics, it was all too thick for Leah to properly absorb. Whatever details were to be had rested in the files and the guesswork of the detective, Bayard. He was the only one who could help her put it together, so that she could then put it away. She explained this, as best she could, to his voice mail on her way to corner him at his office.

If nothing else, a minor mystery of the universe *would* be solved that afternoon. Leah now knew how to make a room, crammed to the edges with file cabinets, computers, and cheap office furniture, look like a wasteland. You just paint it tan. Whoever had mixed the paint had overshot the nuance of neutral and condemned everything slimed in its supergloss to a pasty tribute to nausea. Slap a few bars of flickering fluorescent overhead, and it was no wonder that the three desks were empty. The look of the place weighed on the back of her throat like a spoonful of cod-liver oil.

"Can I help you?"

Leah whirled around to stare at the midchest buttons of a starched oxford-cloth shirt. Her gaze tracked upward as her feet backpedaled for some distance.

The giant smiled down at her. "Sorry. I didn't mean to scare you."

"It's okay. I was just looking for Detective Bayard. I tried calling him a couple of times on my way over here."

"That was you, huh? I heard his phone ringing in the drawer." He pointed at the uncluttered desk to their left.

"Well, the only reason I came on was that they told me he was here when I called the main number."

"Well, *they* would have been right, if he hadn't ducked out the back door a little bit ago." The giant passed her and set a can of orange soda on the desk wedged into the farthest corner by the window. Leah stayed by the door. A little perspective was necessary to make a man that size manifest in one frame. "I'm Ford Watts. I work with Tim a good bit. Can I maybe help you with something?"

Leah's speech had been rehearsed for Bayard alone. With that script in the wastebasket, she lost her prefab confidence and went red in the face. "My name is Leah Tamblin. He found my fiancé, I mean, found his—you know. On Sunday. He was buried in someone's flower bed. I just wanted . . ."

"Ah. Please." Ford swept his hand at the spare chair in front of his desk, and Leah took the offered ease. "Can I get you anything? Coffee? Soda?" He tilted his own unopened can toward her.

"No, thank you."

"What can I do for you, Ms. Tamblin?"

The view was tailor-fit for the room. The window overlooked the parking lot and a Dumpster. The sun lobbed headachy splashes of light off the windshields, and Leah felt suddenly foolish, and on its heels, angry that she'd been driven to this. "I just want to know what happened. For three years, all I've known was that somebody burned up his car and that he was gone."

"Tim told you about Boyd Montgomery, right? His confession in his suicide note—"

"Not that stuff. He told me all that." Leah swatted away the official tone of what she already knew. "I'm sorry. That was rude. I'm not trying to be difficult. I just want to see. I just want to have it make sense."

"Ms. Tamblin, there will be a time for more complete disclosure, but there are still things from that scene which are under investigation. Everything is sealed until we've got it all sorted out. The evidence is pretty degraded, and being handled very carefully to preserve it. His effects will be turned over—"

Leah pressed her shaking fingers against her temples. "I just want to see. Can't you understand that?"

Ford sighed into the quiet that had crowded into their shared space. Leah held hard against another storm of crying. "Listen," he said. "Lyle Mosby is our chief forensic investigator. His office is about forty minutes from here. He's a good guy. I can call him; get him to get you into the morgue and give you a moment. He'll understand. He'll let you see him."

"See him?" Leah's struggle with the offer played over her face. "See Reid?" Before she could weigh the effect of her outrage in all its bad form, the wave of frustration crested and Ford Watts took it full in the face. "I don't want to see him! I want to know what *happened*! I don't *care* about Reid!" Her eyes snapped wide, not at the revelation, but at having said it out loud. And very loudly at that.

Composure is a wily thing and, in the absence of physical danger, can sometimes attempt a comeback without express permission. Automatically, she sat up straight and folded her hands into her lap. The color receded to the expected borders of her cheeks, and her eyelids pulled the shades over her glare. "I mean, of course I care about Reid. It's just that's not what I was talking about. It's not what I meant. That sounded terrible."

Ford looked down at the papers spread over the desktop to grant her another moment to regroup in as much privacy as the setting allowed. "It sounded true." Before she could protest beyond an urgent squeak, he smiled and leaned in on his elbows toward her. "It's okay. I've long since stopped guessing at people's stories. You do that after being wrong a couple hundred times. Everyone has their reasons. I know you have yours and it's none of my business."

She searched his open face for judgment and found none.

Ford leaned back and his chair squealed its effort. "So, let's start over, shall we? What can I do for you, Ms. Tamblin?"

She stared at her hands gripped together in her lap. "He died with another man's wife. He died in their house. He was buried there. I just want to see it. I just want to know what it looks like."

"Mind if I ask why?"

"Once I've seen it, I've seen it. I don't need to keep trying to make it up in my head."

Ford gathered a stack of papers and tapped them into alignment against the desktop. He squared the corners on a pile of files. "I'm sure Detective Bayard has mentioned that someone else lives there now. Someone who has nothing to do with what happened to your—what happened to Mr. Reynolds."

"Yes. He told me that."

"He also told you that there is still an investigation in progress on that property?"

"Yes, but—"

Ford held her to a midsentence stop with an extended palm. "In a case like this we'd be risking trespassing, harassment, and maybe even crime-scene contamination. I can't have that. It'd put me, and everyone else, in a heap of trouble."

"But I wouldn't—"

"I can't endorse you troubling Jason Getty. He's a nice enough fellow, but if he were to lodge a complaint . . ."

"But—"

"I know there'd be no way for me to prevent you from taking a drive down Old Green Valley Road when none of us are there working. I will trust that you understand my position on this."

Leah closed her mouth and blinked at the information still charging the air between them. "Where's Old Green Valley Road?"

Ford stood up and offered his hand to shake by way of dismissing her, but not without a kind smile and a wink. "Now that would be telling, wouldn't it? Good day, Ms. Tamblin."

"You're gonna love this," Tim said, squaring the shoulders of his jacket over the back of his desk chair. "Kyle from East County is downstairs. He tried to call me earlier, but—"

"Well, he's not the only one," said Ford. "You had a visitor."

"Hang on, hang on. You have to hear this." Tim dropped into his chair and scooted back to prop his feet on the bottom drawer he'd opened as a footrest. "So Kyle's dropping off some stuff for court, but he was trying to get ahold of me anyway. Seems after we left, all hell broke loose over at the Montgomery compound."

"What happened?"

"Well, he didn't know exactly how it all went down. Either that or he didn't want to tell it *exactly* as it happened, so as not to make his colleagues look like a choir of jackasses. Apparently, good Mr. Montgomery didn't realize how big a heap he'd gotten himself into by cashing his brother's checks. When they started making arresting noises, he flipped. Those damned dogs, it turns out, work on hand signals, too. However it played out, it ended up with three impounded dogs, at least one East County detective missing a chunk of his ass, and Bart Montgomery flying out the back door, never to be seen again—as yet."

"Holy Moses. Did a runner?" said Ford.

"Yep."

"It's getting to be the mess that just won't go away. That's what I was going to tell you—"

"Detective Watts?" The intercom snapped to life from the speaker of Ford's phone. "Your four o'clock appointment's here. He's waiting for you in conference room one."

Tim's cell phone rang from the desk drawer. He caught it before it connected to voice mail. "Hey, sweetie."

And as with so many conversations started between them, their work pulled Ford and Tim in opposite directions. The workday closed over the unfinished business of Leah Tamblin's tenacity.

12

I T WAS ALREADY late in the day when she'd set out
to find the place. The big detective had given her nothing but a name and a street and the strong counsel not to
be noticed. Searching for *Getty* in the phone book turned
up a blank, and the information operator confirmed a J.
Getty in Stillwater, but that the number and address were
unlisted by request. The map showed Old Green Valley
Road as the winding, three-and-a-quarter-mile crossbar
of an *H* of state roads.

On her first pass, the sky had been coral pink in the
twilight, damping everything below the tree line into a soft
gray-blue haze. She'd been looking left when she should
have been looking right and had missed the house entirely.
On the way back, she would have missed it again but for
the glow of neon-yellow police tape winking at her in the
rearview mirror. She marked out an ill-advised *U* in rubber
on the asphalt to get back and get it over with. Her hands
trembled as she slid the gearshift to park, across from the
house where Reid had died.

The plain, little house was set far enough back from

the road and deeply enough into its sickle of trees that the dusk ate the details. Her eyes strained in the gloom, while the now pink-and-lavender sky pulled up all the remaining light for its finale.

The anger that had sometimes diminished Reid in her mind slid away at the sight of the last place he'd been. The best of him came back to her without warning. She faced Jason Getty's house, but she saw only Reid smiling, all dimples and carelessness and too long hair. She saw him at thirteen, taking her trembling hand in his in the dark of the trees. She heard his halting humming, and his fingers plucking out chords as he worked out a song on their sunken sofa. She thought of how many, many of those songs had been written for her: love songs, complaints, promises. An ache expanded in her throat as she remembered how the last thing she'd felt every night for so many years was the heat of the circle of Reid's arms and kisses in her hair as she drifted off.

Awash in belated panic, Leah wondered if he'd been afraid, if he'd hurt and fought to live. Without a trace of jealousy, she weighed Reid's sense of gallantry and knew full well that he would have tried to save her, the other woman, from her own husband's fury. She would never know if he'd got half the chance to fight for that girl.

Leah didn't realize until she was across the street that she meant to do just exactly what the detective had cautioned her against—intrude upon a stranger's property and disrupt a crime scene. She wanted the dirt in her hands. She craved to sink to the wrists in it and hold handfuls of it to her eyes, to see the truth of it, and to forgive it. She wanted to offer her own remorse to whatever echo of Reid remained there. Leah was sorry, too; so sorry that she had ever imagined he'd deserved it; sorry that she'd been such a coward to take comfort in playing the martyr. The lawn shimmered through her tears as she strode toward the house, but two things brought her up short. In the last of the light, she saw two yellow-taped plots, one on either side of the house. She hadn't thought about that, and there was no way to know which one had been Reid's. As this puzzle stemmed the flow of grief in favor of analysis, she heard a screen door at the back of the house creak open and slap shut.

Her heart leaped up and scattered a wild, jumping pulse into her eyes and throat. Her trespassing feet backed up without consulting her brain, so that Leah kicked her own ankles in the struggle to get them back under her command, and she stumbled back to the car. She cranked it to life and forced the pedal down in a tire-screaming hurry. Glancing into her mirrors as she swept out of sight, relief shuddered through her and faded to hot embarrassment. No one had rounded to the front yard. She hadn't been seen.

Leah's retreat was only temporary. She fled to an overlit delicatessen and let a cup of coffee go cold between her hands. Even calmed, she knew she still had to have her moment at the house on Old Green Valley Road. That's just the way she was. She'd wring what little bit of a story there was to be had from the scene, and then she'd be done with the town of Stillwater forever. What did it matter which grave had been his? She'd sift the dirt of both of them through her hands and cry for him and for *her*, and for herself, too. But she'd do it late and she'd do it quietly. And the poor man who lived there now would never even know she'd been there.

So, Leah bought a romance novel at the bookstore next to the deli. She tried to check her voice mail to see if either of the detectives had called back to scold her off her errand, but the battery was stone dead. She double-checked herself for any craving to be talked out of it anyway. The ceremony was bound to be a flimsy stand-in for knowing the whole truth. But instead of bitter complaint for what she wouldn't know, she found the first green shoot of acceptance, which made her smile. Perhaps she'd managed the first rung of maturity in the few years she'd been all on her own. Could be.

For now, though, she would do this thing and take whatever peace it brought her. Leah sat in her car, in the town-square park, and watched the skateboarders bedevil the last few ambling couples under the streetlamps. Once they'd all drifted away to the things that called to them, hearth and home or petty vandalism, she read by the dome light of her car, until her eyelids first begged, then demanded, to fall closed. Then she switched it off.

"Daddy, telephone. Think fast." Bayard's daughter tossed the handset over the book he had propped on his thighs. His reflexes beat the phone to impact, and he caught it just short of manly injury. He goggled at her as if she were crazy. She stuck her tongue out at him.

"Mr. Mosby. What can I do for you at this fine off-peak hour?" he said after checking the caller ID and waving his daughter away.

"Heh. Sorry about that," said Lyle. "I'm going to be in court probably all day tomorrow, but thought you might want a little extra time to chew on this bit of weirdness."

"And who doesn't like a little bit of weirdness before bed?"

"Please. Let's keep your sex life out of this, shall we?" Lyle waited for his due laugh before clearing his throat back to business. "It's that suicide note you sent over."

"Weirdness *and* suicide. Charming. Sweet dreams to you, too, Lyle. What have you got?"

"Didn't even need to put it under the microscope to see it. It's the ink. It's on *top* of the blood. You can see it with just a magnifying glass and a strong light."

"I don't carry a magnifying glass in my pocket, Lyle. I'm not Sherlock Holmes," said Bayard.

"So I see. So. I. See. Anyway, unless you're suggesting the guy shot himself and *then* wrote this weepy note, there's something off about your story."

"It's not my story. It's his brother's."

"Oh, hang on, I gotta hand something off to this guy here before he's gone for the night." Lyle thunked down the phone, and the background noise blurred into a conversation Tim couldn't make out.

Bayard watched his daughter twist gracefully into her jacket and reach for her purse, which hung on a peg by the front door. Megan looked so much like her mother in certain postures and lighting that he sometimes felt as if he lived in a time machine. They were alike in other ways as well and enjoyed a closeness he didn't like to admit envying. Megan never asked to use his car, only her mother's. They shared clothes, iPods, shoes, and hairbrushes. They went shopping separately and came home with half a carload of the same things. He feared for his wife when their girl headed off to college.

"That's your mother's bag," he called.

"No, it's not. It's—oh, wait. It is. How did you—? They look exactly the same." Megan glared and smiled in astonished appreciation.

"Hey, it's me!" He pinned the phone between his cheek and shoulder and spread his arms wide, grinning at his gaping daughter.

She pulled aside a wool coat that was hiding her own identical bag and replaced her mother's on its hook. "Yeah, and you're a freak of nature. Be back soon." At the door she turned away before she'd pulled it open and trotted back to kiss his head. Then she was gone.

Tim pinched his bottom lip, and his concentration drifted to blend into the indistinct hum flowing from the earpiece. Christine's purse always bulged with an extra pair of glasses, with tissues, with a paperback, and a diet soda and a snack for later, while Megan's identical bag sagged loose, the bare necessities weighing down the bottom, always hanging wide with plenty of room for hauling her impulse buys. What they carried whispered of a catalog of differences that other people didn't see in any light.

He'd always been intrigued by what you could guess about a woman in the arrangement of her handbag—in how she carried it, and where she laid it. His thoughts lit on the subtleties to be read in the size of the purse, the material it was cut from, the order of it, or the disorder, the little flairs and extras that younger women often clipped to their sides . . . Katielynn Montgomery's purse sprang to mind, and how it came to be ruined.

And, anyway, just how many people in a single family, or in all of Carter County for that matter, would have the stomach to bury their own messy dead? The likely percentages seemed to be off in this saga.

A scrape and a rattle preceded Lyle's return. "Sorry about that."

"Did you run any fingerprints?" Bayard asked.

"Fingerprints?" Papers shuffled noisily on the other end of the line. "Nope. Bart Montgomery wasn't arrested. He ran first, right? There's no booking card."

"Can you lift some from somewhere?"

"Sure. What are we looking for? What do you want me to check?"

"It doesn't matter. Anything from that house that he would have touched recently will do just fine, you know— the sink taps, the doorknobs, whatever. Then run them and see if they hit," said Bayard.

"I thought this guy didn't have any priors."

"He doesn't."

Lyle left a beat open for a better explanation, but when none was forthcoming, he asked, "So you just like tasking me with Chinese fire drills?"

"Well, that, too. But fingerprints will be faster than finding that body out there at the Montgomery place. *Bart* Montgomery shouldn't show up in the system. Up until he lost his mind and started burying bodies and cashing checks that weren't his, he'd been an angel. Neither should Boyd Montgomery show up off those doorknobs, strictly speaking, since by all reports he's been dead a good long while. But somehow, I'm thinking he just might."

13

MARKING the moment when a bland man goes mad is an exercise in not blinking at the wrong instant. With the exception of one notable scuffle in his living room, there wasn't usually much to see when watching Jason Getty go about his business. His enthusiasms and upsets rarely played on the outside, and his wedding-picture face didn't look all that different from his driver's-license photo. Jason's gestures were generally mild, his voice pitched to match, and his handling of conflicts nearly always deferential. So the true snap in his psyche, the rip cord that yanked him free of reality, didn't roll out on a terrified scream or rise to heaven on a cry of despair. It limped out on a whimper, wriggling past waxen lips in a face greased with sweat and grave dirt. It launched Jason into an inner space well out of the reach of reason at a time when reason was mostly likely his only hope.

He'd waited until ten o'clock to get started, and a fat, lopsided moon took away the risk of a full border of camp lanterns. As it was, he got by with only two. And it was probably better that way. Some things are better left in the half-light.

Once Harris had turned the corner from trifling mean to cunningly cruel and had taken to showing up whenever it amused him, Jason had started wishing him dead. He had some guilt in thinking it and a little bit of a twinge for wanting it. But the true wrestling with the shoulder-devil came when he began picturing it. There were your basic single-vehicle crashes, lightning strikes, and aneurysms that kept all but Harris out of the soup. But then Jason watched more elaborate scenarios develop in his imagination: a rogue neighbor cut free of conscience and flaunting his right to bear arms; a bar fight with a good old boy the size and temperament of a B-movie Cyclops all done up in flannel and denim; a hit-and-run as Harris strutted unheedingly outside the crosswalk as if he owned the whole goddamned street. The unsettling detail to this brand of daydreaming was that Jason could always see the hands holding the shotgun, balling the fists, gripping the wheel, and he had to resist the urge to examine his own knuckles for comparison.

Once it had been done, the violence realized, and the stream of abuse cut off in mid-harangue, Jason couldn't get Harris out of his sight fast enough. It had taken two layers of extra large garbage bags, overwound in an old bedsheet, to hide Harris's loose joints and broken head. The need to erase him from the foreground had ignited a vigor in Jason's limbs. The shovel had felt weightless in his grip, the soil parting like the righteous Red Sea.

The scent hounds that Detective Bayard had threatened to bring down on Jason's land were far more tangible than the demons that had whipped him to bury Harris as fast as he could, but they were no more real. The plain, bloody fact of the dead body had spawned a troop of shadow imps that rode Jason's kidneys all that night and howled inside his head until he'd smothered the evidence under a literal ton of dirt.

He absolutely did not want to dig Harris up. But here he was.

He'd raked aside the accumulated leaf litter to the shock of a clearly marked, though sloppily executed, rectangle. The ground had settled in a full inch since he'd last peeked. It would have taken Bayard no time at all to find the anomaly he sought. If it hadn't occurred to Jason to move the body, if he hadn't prodded himself into actually gathering up the rake and the shovel and the tarp, it would have been a sealed fate for him in one pass of the experts, with their radar and their cadaver dogs. There was no guarantee that this tap dance on a minefield would work at all, but now he knew he had to at least try.

Every move was weighted ten times what it would have been if he'd only had the guts to mow his own lawn, and that he couldn't even sell his soul to unmake that call to Dearborn's Landscaping brought him right to the wobbly edge of despair. Jason lugged the needed tools from the shed, more committed than ever, but mired in dread up to his windpipe. Before he'd even started, his neck ached from throwing desperate looks over his shoulder, and his heart kept forgetting that it wasn't a fish flopping pointlessly in the cramped bucket of his chest. His eyes watered from the lack of blinking, peeled to flit to every crackle and night murmur in the trees.

The monotony of digging soothed the worst of the jitters for a while. The rhythm of set-push-scrape-toss forced a hypnotic competence, and the progress was steady. He worked in silence, with only the occasional grunt, for going

on three hours before the blade of his shovel finally trans-
mitted the denser tone of having found something other
than rasping topsoil. He yanked the handle back, scalded
anew in every nerve, and he gagged, his body trembling at
the slanting edge of the pit.

From there, he worked in tightening ovals until he
couldn't deny that the remaining layer of dirt was finer
than could be answered with a shovel. It was time to get
his hands dirty—so to speak. It's beyond absurd to don
a pair of yellow rubber house gloves to slip a ripe corpse
from its clod of muck, but Jason did it anyway and cinched
the ends down to his wrists with wide rubber bands. His
hands went instantly hot and heavy, but he flexed away
the tingles and carried on. The heat of fear stewed with
the heat of exertion in his grave-robbing getup, and the
sweat ran down his sides in tickling tracks under his layered shirts. The bike shorts with jeans over them offered
a two-ply barrier against the damp dirt, while tucking the
cuffs of his pants into his socks and boots assured him of
unsoiled feet. He'd have worn a suit of armor had it been
handy, clanking be damned. Jason was sharply aware of,
and grateful *for*, every millimeter of separation he could
contrive as he pulled at the heap.

The sheet was rotted, the lawn bags slick and yielding,
and his efforts served more to unveil Harris than they did to
move him. In a goal-line attempt to avoid deshrouding the
very last thing on earth he wanted to see in the moonlight,
Jason knelt in the hole and wrapped his arms around the
man he'd hated more than anything that had ever drawn
a breath near him.

He braced his back against the stubborn pull of the
bundle that was so bogged down in the trench it felt glued

and stapled there, and he hoisted it to his chest. The clay
sucked at the plastic and dragged against Jason's labor. For
every increment he gained, the floppy weight countered. In
his concentration, he ignored gravity just long enough to
let the tipping point drift beyond his control. Realization
dawned, buggy-eyed and a heartbeat too late. Even a flailing
slew of adjustments couldn't save it. He lurched forward
and threw out a bracing arm, only to have it plow a furrow,
the heel of his gloved hand sliding away as if it wanted to
steal third base. Jason, for all his trying, landed hard, pin-
ning the body, missionary style, in its bed of filth, his face
inches from Harris's bagged head. Jason's tongue surged at
the back of his throat and he scrambled to the edge of the
grave, flinging himself belly down in the grass to wash his
lungs in fresh air. He sagged on his hands and knees and
rode the bucking nausea until the sweat cooled on his face.

Spurred on by a sudden solo from Mrs. Truesdell's dog
in the near distance, Jason scuttled back into the hole, limbs
quaking. He planted his knees wide, sipped a deep breath
over his shoulder, and wrapped his arms back around the
body. And pulled. His face flushed hot against his reluctance
to breathe up the filthy air.

The body shifted when it wasn't sticking, a puppet of
physics, but feeling for all the world as if it were resisting
eviction. Jason pleaded with Harris, with God, with himself,
in a desperate whine against the direly inconvenient while
vowing in his heart never, *never* to do anything wrong ever
again if only he could get this body out of its hole and onto
the waiting tarp. Fireflies of strain flitted at the edge of his
vision as he struggled for inches in the yielding ground
and fought, against all probability, his dead nemesis one
more time.

Jason's lungs clamored to fill. He tottered at the threshold of choice—black out or let go—but the hindrance suddenly gave way, flinging the body into his arms. A long rope of glistening, viscous, bit-of-Harris slingshotted from the breached wrappings and curled around Jason's exposed neck to slap against his cheek and slide thickly onto the useless protection of his third shirt. His guts recoiled into a low, greasy knot, and the blood pulled heavy in his ears as it rushed from his head. Shivers twitched and chased circles, looping down his spine, away from the scene of the insult—the putrid, wet streak on his face that burned like a brand.

To Jason, the sound signaling the end of his tether was a sharp crack, like thick glass giving way. To Harris, had he been able to hear it, and the creatures in the woods that didn't care, it was only a feeble bleat trickling from Jason's throat. His arms lost the imperative of their nerves and he let Harris slide back into the mud.

The breaking-glass sound had put an out-of-place period on his internal dialogue. The constant narrator in his head was banished to silence at the resounding clink. But there was no peace in the quiet. Jason was just as blind and nearly as slack as Harris was, but one sense had usurped the potency of the other four, drawing every scrap of aware-ness to the cooling, gelid trail that Harris had drawn down the slack curve of Jason's jaw. His mind was a void, save for one achingly keen sensation—the itching outline of slime already drying at its edges in the night breeze.

The spark of self-preservation is the last to go. It needs no cheerleading from the body's other systems. It doesn't celebrate the company of civility, and it certainly never asks sanity's permission. It allowed Jason his moment of disconnect, while it kept its own radar sweeping away in the silent background. Back there, in the recesses of Jason's mind, it registered the stealthy thunk of a car door being closed by someone trying to be quiet. The engine had cut out just opposite Jason's driveway.

So, the force that fights until the last, that elemental wish to continue, pulled Jason to his feet and moved those feet furtively into the deep shade of the trees. And it remembered to bring the shovel.

The snuffling at the window plugged her back into reality. A bellowsy exhale against the glass snapped her eyes wide open. For Leah, sleep, especially the inadvertent nap, was sometimes less like rest than it was a model of total annihilation. In these upright comas, she simply didn't exist. No dreams, no twitches. When she came to, there was no groggy transition. The world was precise, freshly drawn in colors that had just been invented, like watching Genesis unfold for her approval. The clarity would fade with a pang after a few heartbeats spent in awe of awakening at the alien edge of creation.

A tawny dog snout sniffed along the gap where Leah had lowered the window to let in some fresh air.

"Tessa! *Mercy!*" A woman tugged at the dog's collar. "I'm sorry. She's very friendly." The woman dragged the dog's head away from the window. Her hair was braided into an impressive rope that hung to her waist, and it swung with her battle to corral the straining Tessa. "And very nosy."

"It's fine," said Leah.

"Are you okay, honey? It's awfully late." The woman smoothed the wispy strays back into line against that remarkable plait of graying hair. It was as thick around as Leah's wrist. The dog had abruptly lost interest in Leah and strained to the limits of the leash, and to the teetering of its mistress's strength, to jam its nose into an abandoned fast-food bag. That the bag was on the ground four feet from an overflowing trash bin at the park's entrance spoke to the general upkeep of the place.

"I just meant to close my eyes for a minute." Leah bookmarked the receipt into the paperback that had been steepled on her lap and laid it on the passenger seat.

The woman pulled her sweater closed and looked at her watch. "Well, it's a quarter to one in the morning, honey. Tessa and I are insomniacs, but I wouldn't be out here at this time of night without her. It's a sad thing, but times as they are, I think I'd have to warn you off snoozing alone in the park."

"Right." Leah smiled and squirmed a stretch against the seat to circulate some heat into her limbs and numb backside. She wished she had thought to bring a sweater. "Thank you. I was just killing a little time."

The dog gave the woman a yank and an imploring look. The deserted park was beckoning, and if you had a wrap or a pelt, the night was beautiful.

"You sure you're all right?" Both the woman and her dog watched for Leah's blessing to move on.

Leah nodded. "Thanks for the wake-up call. And for looking out for me."

The woman smiled back as the dog trotted away with her in tow. "It should always be so easy," she called over her shoulder.

Leah watched them on the path until they were swallowed up by the gloom that hunkered low under the trees. The glow of the moon was generous, even feeding the shadows a second helping of contrast. On a night like this, you either knew where you stood or you were invisible. Leah started her car and double-checked the directions for the route back to Old Green Valley Road.

In the starlit night, the drive back to the Getty house took on the air of ritual. She had pinned her peace of mind to this ceremony of her own devising. She'd kneel and cry. She'd absolve and, in turn, be granted absolution. At the last bend before the house, Leah held her breath and thumbed the switch, extinguishing the headlights. She eased off the accelerator as her eyes adjusted, finding that the moonlight was enough of a guide at that tame pace. She coasted to the curb opposite Getty's driveway and twisted the key slowly, as if the jangle of her key ring would make the difference between success and discovery. She reined in the closing door to a muted thump.

The house was dark, as she had hoped it would be. Leah closed her eyes and, not believing it for a second, reached out for a sense of Reid—for which sad, police-taped plot to approach first. Drawn to the right by intuition or perhaps by just the pull of her dominant hand, Leah skirted a wide path around to the west side of the house, eyes glued to the windows for light or movement. And with barely a pause and only a cursory scan of what she'd come for, she kept to the tree line and continued around to the backyard, a magpie, distracted by the glint of light from the far edge of the lawn.

The human animal is the only creature that willfully suppresses instinct. Admittedly, there isn't much left of it in the mostly hairless, thin-skinned monkey, softened by air-conditioning, bottled water, and mall melodies piped in so that we don't feel lonely while we shop. But such as it is, excuses to meddle in shiny other business trumps innate knowledge all the time.

Leah's scalp crimped in tingly patches, and chills stippled the backs of her arms. Some unlabeled sentience swimming in the pit of her stomach waved a flag of warning, and the ominous banner rippled in hot and cold surges, but she kept to her course. The moon was high and white, but the golden glow of two camp lanterns rose from the ground near the trees at the apex of the curved border of woods. Curiosity drowned out the mewling certainty that something was terribly wrong with this scene—it was the middle of the night and a gaping hole in the ground was bookended by battery lamps. Ribbons of stench were layered in with the perfect night breeze, wrinkling her nose midbreath. A rumpled tarpaulin had been laid out on the near side of the hole.

Keeping just inside the shadow of the trees, she laid each footfall gently, and as silently as she could, on the pad of leaves and old pine needles. She stopped her breath to feel the crush of quiet around her. It was heavier than the sum of just the wind whispering and the boughs clicking. Paranoia put the weight of watchful eyes on her, but she shook off the notion. She'd twice looked into the trees and both times found only trunks, branches, and moon shadows. Her concentration flicked back and forth between the back facade of the darkened house and the lanterns at the pit's edge.

She drew even with the hole in the ground. The light skimmed the edges and showed that the crumbly rim was still moist, but the slope was steep enough to shade the bottom from view. Leah swept another wide-eyed look over the lawn and inched from the safety of the shadows to peer into the pit. She quick-smothered a scream against the back of her hand. Her heart, which had been hammering since she'd diverted from Reid's erstwhile grave, thrashed out of rhythm, flinging terror into every limb. The lamps showed her the shape she'd almost expected to find lying there; the only outline that would sensibly complete the macabre tableau.

But the bright glare had also pinpointed her pupils, so that when she whirled to the snapping rustle rushing up from behind her, she saw only blackness. She heard the flat clank of metal on bone, but crumpled senseless to the ground before she felt it.

14

THE DARKNESS wasn't as much of a hindrance as was the undergrowth. The wind through the leaves fluttered the moonlight, strobing everything to the beat of a murky, old newsreel, but it was enough light for him to get by. The cords of ground cover twisting underfoot, though, were relentless. They yanked him off stride every time he'd stray into any sort of confident pace. Forging ahead at anything more than a crawl was becoming a surefire bid to eat dirt. But he didn't have all night to get done what needed doing, and he came as close to cursing the booby-trapped trail as he ever got to cursing at all.

He had no quarrel with the distinction between right and wrong. He appreciated it better than most, that was for sure. Heck, he'd beat the snot out of Greg Plumb in the sixth grade for swearing and talking filth about Miss Avery's chest. He watched the preachers on television most Sunday mornings to keep the Sabbath. He even always held the door for old people and pregnant ladies, and he'd never been cruel to an animal that wasn't asking for a good, strong swat to guaran-dang-tee its attention. But what *did* scorch him a freshly chapped backside was the sheer stupidity of people who couldn't admit that there were, from time to time, circumstances beyond a man's control.

Show Boyd Montgomery a man who claimed he would stand idle after watching his wife wiggle her hips underneath another man's zipper and he'd show you a liar. At first he'd thought it was a girl on top of Katielynn, kissing her and tickling up under her T-shirt to set her giggling. The soft-looking, brown curls had dipped low enough to cover both their faces and mingle with Kate's straw-straight, straw-colored hair on the bedspread. Boyd had wrestled a moment of muddled conviction, because while he'd brook no infidelity from his wife, he'd sometimes read the letters at the front of skin magazines, tall tales about men walking in on this very type of thing. As unnatural as it was, he couldn't deny that those stories had always left him shuffling away from the rack, titty mag left tucked into the hot-rod weekly he'd covered it with, hunched over a bit to hide the urgent bulge below his belt buckle. The letters, with their detailed descriptions of surprised and delighted sin, had sorely tempted Boyd to buy a few of those rag sheets, but bankrolling pornography was immoral, and he'd always resisted.

As soon as that tickling hand had scuttled from Kate's bare ribs, Boyd had seen his mistake. The man's watch was a giveaway, but Boyd's shame was spurred into full-fledged disgrace by the rising pressure in his Jockey shorts. He'd not recognized, at first, the firm shoulders for what they were, or how they tapered down to hips narrow enough to fit snugly between his wife's. That he had swelled to the sight of it made him sick.

He'd ducked back behind the doorframe to catch his

breath while his hard-on shriveled to disgust. Then the revulsion partnered with the fury that was biting and clawing its way up his spine. A loaded .357 waited in the nightstand, but Boyd wouldn't risk getting beaten to it by that poufy-haired faggot.

He had crept down the hall, his full attention aimed at rolling heel to toe to mute his steps, so the shock nearly knocked him over when he saw his brother. Bart stood in the living room, sad-faced and lost-looking as always. The instant the ghostly image didn't fill in more completely, Boyd recognized his own reflection in the glass of the gun cabinet. This happened to him occasionally. He'd see an image in a mirror or a window, and before placing himself in the picture, he would stand in all-out wonder for a fraction of a second at the coincidence of running across his twin in such an unlikely place.

The scare had spiked his blood with acid, and now he had the shakes to deal with, though he'd been calm, even if absolutely furious, just the second before. Boyd's feelings always tagged along like a third twin, or a second shadow, sort of one step behind and off to one side. He was resolutely a head man, knowing what he knew, but never quite feeling what he felt. Not even enough to be concerned that this constant double-exposed state was less than normal. Shock and surprise, and gooey suffering over sad stories about animals, seemed to be about the only things that could build a temporary bridge from his heart to his mind, and he found that he wished his brother were really there, forcing a reason for him not to do this thing. Bart's slower wit and easy smile softened every edge that had ever come down on the boys. Trouble had rarely found anyone in Bart's mild company.

Imagining Bart's influence was nearly as good as having it, and Boyd considered his other cheek. He was a good man after all, only ever drinking on Fridays and Saturdays and the Fourth of *Ju*-ly, whatever day it fell on. He had, hand to God, slapped Katielynn exactly once, and even she would have admitted that she'd deserved it. He knew what he *should* do. He imagined how sorry Kate would be, how pretty she looked after a good cry. . . .

Katielynn's bright laugh cut loose the pull of his conscience, and his rage sprang back twice as hot. The rifle lay ready in his hands before the laughter's sparkly echoes cleared his ears. Any reconsideration he'd wrangled died at the sight of the other man's naked butt shining full at him from alongside the bed, *Boyd's own bed*, pants pushed down around his ankles. His shirt had been tossed, teasingly, all the way to where Boyd now stood. Katielynn saw the movement in the doorway and jerked up from her sashay down the son of a whore's body, and Boyd pulled the trigger before he knew he meant to.

The one bullet took them both, the young man from back to front, a neat hole pouring red through his middle as he staggered over his denim-bound feet. Katielynn had risen high enough to take her shot under the collarbone. Her eyes went wide as she clutched and swatted at the blooming, hot stain on her chest.

"Boyd!" she screamed. "Boyd! What the fuck did you do?"

The profanity stung. She would never speak to him like that. She knew better. That boy must be some no-account, pothead bastard, making her talk like that. She knew what he thought of foulmouthed sluts.

"Reid! Oh my God! Reid!" She was reaching for the kid—he looked so young—and his name rang off the walls, *Boyd's own walls,* as she wailed for him, so Boyd shot him again. The slug, more by accident than by aim, almost overlaid the first shot, but the boy, Reid, jerked rigid this time and crumpled, arms flung out pleading toward Katielynn.

"Boyd, no! Oh, fuck! What have you done! Reid! Oh, God! Boyd, help me, you son of a bitch!" She crab-crawled away while at the same time begging Boyd for help, her lame left side dragging her in a small circle, until he found himself standing over her.

"You're crazy. You're crazy," she panted. She'd gone pale and they'd stared each other down while at the corner of their vision her bare-butted Casanova pulled at the carpet and gasped like a landed bass.

Whatever life passes before your eyes as you die, Boyd could only attest to the shared life that plays out at light speed before someone you knew dies at your hand. All that Katielynn had promised to and simpered for flared up as pictures in his mind. And it was all a great burning lie. She'd made a joke of their vows in their own bed. No matter what anyone could or would have to say about it, he had loved her truly, albeit jealously. But jealousy is hardly a crime. She'd known his mind on that score, too, and had flown right in the face of it, which could hardly be his fault. She was suffering something terrible down there on the carpet, fire in her eyes and blood drenched clear down to the waistband of her white panties.

"Fuck you, Boyd" were her last words. He put the skinny barrel of the rifle against her chest and pulled back on the trigger one more time. The dogs barked insanely in their pen until Boyd ran out and shushed them, rubbing their ears while straining his own for any neighborly commotion.

There was none. Sunday services in town would have swallowed everyone who was near enough to be bothered by
close gunfire, and anyway, weekend target practice rang
through these woods often enough so that no one minded
as long as you didn't start too early or finish too late.

He wasn't proud of the whole business, but he wasn't
exactly sorry either. No one could expect a man to be spit
on and not wipe it off. Laws and commandments were fine
things, and criminals who disregarded them were worse
than rabid animals. But when it wasn't planned and you
mostly did good, and you still got shameless insult shoved
up your nose while your wife sat there in her Skivvies cursing you for shooting a trespasser, well, that wasn't quite
the same thing, now was it? He'd be damned, yes *damned*,
if he'd let faithless wives and soulless pretty boys steal the
heat from his blood.

Boyd waltzed with his righteous indignation while he
sorted out the particulars of cleaning up the mess and hiding
the filthy punk's car. His blameless logic watered him up
like church hymns and "The Star-Spangled Banner." He
hadn't meant to do it. Would have sworn that he wasn't the
sort, until it happened. And he wasn't about to be kenneled
with thugs and thieves for the rest of his days over it.

It had been so dry that the weedy flower beds by the
house were the only ground soft enough to dig up. Boyd
had always had uncanny night vision, so half a moon was
more light than he'd needed, and more than he had liked
for privacy's sake, but the dogs patrolled the perimeter for
him and he'd have known well in advance should anyone
come close. The neighbors never did, though. It seemed as
if the entire stretch of road was mostly dotted with people
he never saw, just their colorful outlines caught every now

and again, quick and rare in a distant glimpse, as they were closing their doors behind them or maybe mowing their grass as he drove by.

He buried her first, sobbing and cradling her head onto a little, crocheted pillow he'd snatched from the sofa. Her baby pillow, made by her granny, the one she'd always wrung during scary or sad movies or after a quarrel. The guy went in on the other side of the house as a necessary afterthought, hastily dumped in with the packages he'd had with him. Boyd had strewn fresh mulch and said a little prayer for Katielynn, but he had spit on the fellow's, that *Reid's*, dirt blanket. Then, he had abandoned his temperance and stayed blind drunk for four days. In his soppiest moments, he took to stashing those possessions of Katielynn's that he couldn't bear to part with in hidey-holes throughout the house with a mind to take them out from time to time in her memory. The rest of her things he'd stuffed into a suitcase, then into the trunk of the rotten little runt's car and, once he'd sobered up enough, drove it to a seldom-used gravel track at the edge of the big woods and burned it in enough kerosene to melt the ice caps.

Boyd hadn't handled the emptiness of his house as well as he could have. Strangely, he slept fine in the bedroom where it had all happened. The drab carpet cleaned well enough with some weak soap and the wet vac, and some-how not even a drop of blood had made it onto the bed. The foreplay-defiled comforter had gone into the car to burn with everything else that reminded him of the scene, but he had plenty of other blankets so he hardly missed it.

It was the living room that felt haunted. The front room kept a chill that wasn't seasonal, and after that day, the gun case next to the mantel never seemed to want to stay closed. But it wasn't fear that seethed in that room. It got so that he only had to pass the doorway and his hands buckled into fists all on their own and the breath whistled through him as if he were sucking it through a straw. It made sense, sort of. In that room, he could still hear her laughing, as clear in his head as it had been on the day he stood there trying to talk himself out of violence.

Boyd never quite got beyond the notion that the front room had soaked up something from him that day and held it like a pitcher, ready to pour it back over him if he ever lingered in there too long.

Depression had driven him to sell the house in a haze of booze, spearmint chewing gum, and little beige OxyContins scored from Phil next door. Phil the pharmacist led a mostly benign double life, the obvious joke being that he'd "phil" any prescription and ignore that it was written on photocopied doctor's stationery, as long as it skimmed across the counter on a little pad of extra green. He was mostly harmless and minded his patients, as he liked to think of them, by doling out Valium or Xanax or painkillers in friendly little quantities, keeping people, as he saw it, off the streets and away from the hard stuff.

Phil believed very much in people's taking the edge off hard times or bad days without the grand hassle of copayments, but he didn't partake himself, and because he cared, he kept a sharp eye trained for people dipping dangerously often into his charitable sensibilities. And he made all of his customers swear an oath on whatever was precious to them not to let his wife find out. He loved her, and their gaggle of plump children, in a sappy way that had made Boyd want mostly just to punch him in the face.

Phil's sentimentality had, though, been Boyd's inspiration

for the sob story of Katielynn's leaving him for another man. The lie's (and alibi's) father was a pill to help him sleep; its mother, a shameless Tuesday six-pack of beer. And the bull-crap story grew to maturity on Phil's front porch before being abandoned by Boyd when he left town altogether a few months later with his dogs, their pen, and all the hidden memorabilia of his marriage that he could call to mind.

Stillwater drew him back eventually. It was easy there. When he'd hightailed it across country from what he'd done, he'd found El Paso too hot and too full of spics. And though Boyd didn't see himself as a man to shy away from a hard day's work, he didn't see any harm in getting by with a little less effort than all that, especially if that's what it took to let him keep himself to himself. All things considered, he knew on some deep level that it was probably best for everyone that way.

If he could steer clear of a rent payment, a decade-old workman's disability claim kept him in checks big enough to feed himself and his dogs, with enough left over to dampen his sorrows, now that he'd found his way around a whiskey buzz and had grown attached to the comfort he found there. His brother, Bart, had seen to it that his boyhood bedroom lay ready for him at the old family homestead. His brother took him in, and the dogs as well. Then Boyd faded into a ghost of himself and lost track of Fridays and Saturdays, so that he sometimes drank and blurred the calendar until every day felt the same.

The loss of Bart was the unkindest blessing yet. Boyd had never quite considered that his brother had a life full of hopes and worries and disappointments of his own. He knew that Bart had been sad-sacking over something or another for a long while. He'd been grim over the drudgery of his day-in, day-out routine. Bart had always been unlucky in love, too, and he sighed about it a lot. It had seemed all the usual stuff to Boyd, not worth crying over, and he'd told Bart so dozens of times. When Boyd sped through the house at the sound of the rifle blast, his first thought had been for how cussed inconvenient this was going to be.

But after a good long think, Boyd had decided that sometimes the smartest thing was actually the simplest, and that if he kept things just as they were, except turn himself into Bart and quit Bart's job for him, he'd be at least twice buffered from his deeds. It had been gnawing at him, in his more sober moments, that the bodies weren't much more than rosebush deep and that the house had been sold to God only knew who. Bart could hardly mind. So Boyd burned the letter that Bart had left his good-byes in and wrote a new note over Bart's blood on the phone bill and tucked it away for safekeeping, just in case. He was sad for the quietness of the house, but quite pleased with his own cleverness.

Boyd and Bart had mapped the woods together as boys, literally. The project started in the seventh grade after a geography assignment had ignited the idea. By graduation, the forests around Stillwater were drawn all to scale in a series of four three-ring binders, one for each compass point, and the Montgomery brothers could get into town over thicket and bramble faster than their mother could in her Honda, if she caught the light at Ledbetter and Route 10.

Traipsing through the woods for a day and a half, now under another fat moon, Boyd smoked at the ears over how stupid it was that a man who had never taken a dime of welfare would get anything more than a slap on the wrist for spending money the government had been more than willing to pay out. He had always expected to be told, if found out as "Bart," to stop with the checks, if it ever came to that. But a felony? An arrest? What a mess.

The forfeit of the dogs was a pity. With nothing but time on his hands, and Bart no longer flinching every five seconds at their unruly play, Boyd had trained them into better companions than anything on two legs had ever been for him. They'd held a path for him to the back door, and he'd been more than a half mile away before one of the cops had risked a reach for his gun. Boyd had heard the shot, but was too far away to be sure he hadn't heard a yelp.

For all he had lost, Boyd Montgomery was no closer to giving up than he had ever been. He hadn't eaten in more than twenty-four hours and his piss had already gone dark and scanty by the afternoon, but so far, his weakest moment was still years ago, flinching scared at his own reflection wavering in the glass of his living-room gun cabinet. If he'd given in to his conscience back then, yelled or even punched instead of shooting, things might be different, but that was far away and as done as done gets.

His hands hadn't even shook when he'd spoon-fed that load of bunk to the first two policemen who had shown up. It would buy him some time before they'd turn from looking for Bart to guessing where Boyd might be. He would leave Stillwater and find his way elsewhere, first over thicket and bramble as he had already managed plenty of times, and tonight with more than enough light to show him the way. He'd hit the road after a visit to his old next-door neighbor Phil the pharmacist.

Phil collected cars. He sought out decrepit, old ones and restored them to functionality, if not to glory, and he could surely spare one in repayment of Boyd's long silence. Boyd could find a way to ask nicely, but if that didn't work, he knew where Phil kept the box of keys. He was owed a favor anyway because it wasn't right, what Phil was up to at the pharmacy. And Boyd had only ever taken just a handful of those pills, after all.

15

JASON came back to himself by degrees. The sad fact was that a sliver of sense rekindled at the crest of the backswing. On primal autopilot, he'd seen only "intruder," and the push of the shovel's arc had dragged harder than the pull of maybe-I-shouldn't. It was a blind impulse, the violence of it uncalibrated, but the split-second debate on what he was about to do weakened his commitment to the follow-through. He didn't strike as hard as he might have, but still plenty hard enough.

His soul slammed back into its borders once the girl completed her graceless crash to the turf, but reason had gone AWOL in the shuffle. His place in time flickered in and out of focus, and the swerving of his mind felt just the tiniest bit on purpose. Something was wrong enough with the "now" that it wouldn't seem to settle over his thoughts.

Jason smiled down at her fondly. He knew she'd been tired. He'd been asking her all the time lately if everything was all right, and she kept saying nothing was wrong. She said she was just tired, but he couldn't understand why his wife was sleeping in the grass. And why she was wearing a skirt—she'd worn a dress at their wedding and, reluctantly, at her sister's. Otherwise it was strictly slacks, jeans, or shorts. And her hair—his eyes slid away because something was definitely wrong with her hair.

"Patty, get up, silly." The shrillness played in his ears a little too much like begging. He cleared his throat. "Come on, honey. It's late." (*Why in the hell is she sleeping in the grass?*) His eyes rolled like loose ball bearings on a lazy Susan—most reluctant to light on any one thing because, each time they did, his stomach vaulted a little hillock of terror in his midsection. His gaze could skitter and dance at will, but his hands, weighed down as they were, could not. The shovel kept announcing itself, a clumsy anchor looking to tilt out of his grasp. He didn't want it to slip and hit Patty by mistake, so he gripped the handle until his knuckles went pale.

A voice, his own—but whether inside him or out loud he didn't know—proclaimed, "It was an accident. It doesn't count." Try as he might to avoid it, his glance kept roving back to her hair. It kept nagging for an explanation. Patty had faithfully dyed her short, dark hair a deep auburn, but the red here was a bright delta, vivid enough to make even the grass lush with ruby highlights. Tendrils lay heavy and glistening on her cheek. *Not unlike the mark Harris just left on*—Jason shook his head and the horror spread through him on pace with the widening funnel of blood through the long, honey-brown hair of the girl at his feet—the girl who looked not one thing like his late wife.

"Oh, God." He planted the shovel blade in the ground and bent double, hands on knees, trying to breathe through the panic stacking up like wet bricks in his throat. He raked his hands, twice-gloved in filth and sunny yellow latex, down his face. "No, no, no, no. I didn't do that on purpose. It was an accident."

He straightened and craned his head back to take in the sky, all sapphire and cobalt and white stars fading into the fringe of a blazing moon. His arms fell limp at his sides. All the way to his bones, he ached in maudlin appreciation of what he stood to lose. And it was not much, but it was absolutely everything. A tremor racked him, and also the notion that the ripples from some events never stopped curling over your life. It wasn't fair. That sulking sense of injustice was just enough to prompt a rejection of the facts at hand and wrap logic, once again, in a gauzy cocoon.

Since he'd mostly forgotten to breathe, or feared that maybe he wasn't allowed to anymore, light-headedness pulled another swoon over his rationalizations. Jason cocked his dizzy head, face blank, at the heap at his feet. He saw white and red and golden brown, a vague oval, a patterned cloth, some leather, a glint of metal. But the equation wouldn't complete. His head felt full of cotton wool, and his ears strained to hear against a pressure as if there were cups clapped over them. His vision swam. His lips trembled.

Salvation was a sudden, scolding reminder that shook him back to his purpose. An unpleasant chore still needed doing, and it was better than falling apart—again. He didn't know what was going on in general, but he knew a job was left unfinished. The other matter would have to be an improvisation. It wasn't fair. It didn't count.

Harris came up easily this time, loose and heavy, but as cooperative as could be expected from a guy in his condition.

Jason snatched the tarp closed over its now doubled load with only enough visual accounting to assure himself that no stray appendages were sticking out to snag on anything. He balled the edges of it in his fists, finding that although the kitchen gloves had failed to make the task any less disgusting, they at least guaranteed a decent grip against the plastic-coated nylon. Bent low, he locked his arms and threw his weight back through his hips, his feet staggering to stay beneath him. He hadn't banked on it being so heavy, but nothing was as it ought to have been and Jason was exhausted, body and soul. Momentum was bought at some expense to his shoulders, each hitching stutter-step pulling his arms hard in their sockets and sending shocks into his elbows. Scooching became gliding as he gained several steps without a stumble. The long grass bent, glazing the way toward the bricked-in carport and the car. He'd lined the trunk with another waterproof tarp and an excessive layering, even by these dire standards, of old towels. If he could manage the heap even that far, there was going to be barely enough room left for Harris, much less anything else.

He'd stowed the rake and shovel out of the way and put out the lanterns, and with the moon drifting out of its optimal angle, Jason found himself much more alone in the dark than he'd been all evening. Even the most famil-iar terrain can sprout treacherous shifts in the gloom. So, considering that Jason had mostly avoided looking at his backyard in the last year, much less keeping acquainted with the rise and fall of it, it was no surprise that a small swell took out his feet two-thirds of the way to the carport. His speed dropped him hard onto his tailbone and his teeth clicked together through the meat of his tongue. Jason howled behind clamped lips, and tears leaked from the corners of his eyes as he lurched back to his feet. He grabbed at the edge of the tarp, and his overtaxed left hand delivered the final insult to his composure in a cramp that burned deeply, curling his fingers into his palm. He unfolded them gingerly with his right hand, only to have the misery spike through to his knuckles.

Jason sobbed into the crook of his elbow. His tongue ached all the way down his throat, and a sickening clarity bloomed in the wake of the pain. If he could taste the iron in his own blood, if he could feel the hot muscles in his palm unfurling, if he had to plant his feet to keep his quaking legs from dumping him over onto the ground again, then it was all real. The tarp didn't cover a pile of abstractions and the smell wasn't an authentic touch to a particularly vivid nightmare. Since meeting Harris, Jason had become some sort of an anti-Midas; everything he touched turned to shit. He needed to scream. It was rising up like lava through his lungs and pressing against his voice box, and unless he was to surrender any hope at all of making it through this ordeal a free man, he couldn't very well do it in his backyard in the dead of night.

Then there was the other problem. Bile and despair boiled in adrenaline had left his guts cramping in sodden, heavy waves all night, but in the pause, his intestines looked to make their complaint a bit more urgent. Jason gritted his teeth against a bout of churning. His face burned in solitary humiliation. The spasm passed, but with a lingering ache that promised a showdown that he was pretty sure he'd lose. He wasn't going to make it all the way to the car, never mind past the clenching it would take to get the trunk loaded. Jason yanked off the gloves and hurled them onto the tarp and stomped off into the house for a ridiculously reality-affirming trip to the toilet, then to bury his face in a pillow and bay like Mrs. Truesdell's dog in a bear trap.

"Ford Watts!"

Ford gasped and inhaled an eye-watering throatful of bootleg chip dip. He coughed and spluttered. "Good God, Margaret! You scared me half to death."

Tessa nosed along the floor under the counter to recover the crumbs launched by his startle.

"Better I do it for you than the doctor catching you eating gobs of"—Maggie's eyes took inventory under arched brows—"sour cream and onion salt? Honestly, Ford."

"I was hungry!"

"Then eat the hummus with the carrot sticks. Or an apple. Or the whole-grain—where did you get these?" She rattled the foil of a potato chip bag. Her shoulders sagged. "They've upped your pills twice in the last year. . . ."

"I know. I know. I'm sorry." He put a hand to her shoulder and drew her long braid over the other. "I don't cheat much, I swear."

She leaned her cheek against his hand and pouted prettily, the years falling away with the practiced flirt. "No, you just wait until I leave the house."

"How was the ladies' moonlight stroll anyway?"

Maggie shrugged out of his hold with a smirk and rolled her eyes. "Nice deflection." She swept chip crumbs into her hand and brushed them into the sink. "You should have come along. It's a beautiful night. But Tessa nearly panicked a girl sleeping in the park, though."

"In the park? It wasn't that Siffert girl hanging around again, was it?"

"No, no. This girl was in her car. I didn't recognize her." Maggie cleared the countertops and tidied automatically. Ford watched her hair, swinging like a metronome, keeping time with her industry. The spell of order, as worked by his wife, soothed a soft-focus peace over Ford. It always had, and better than any heart medicine ever could. Maggie didn't seem to realize she was puttering, or indeed that she was being watched. "She was a tiny little thing. I thought she was a kid until she woke up."

This snapped Ford out of his reverie. "What was she driving?"

"A little, blue econobox. I don't know. It had a smiley face doohickey on the antenna. Why?"

"Did she say anything? Was she all right?"

Maggie shrugged. "I just told her it didn't seem safe. She looked okay. She was friendly. Said she was just killing time."

"Really? And this was just a little while ago?"

"Yes. Why?"

"I talked to a little, tiny girl who drove a blue car earlier today. Smiley on the aerial and all. It was way earlier this afternoon. I would've expected her to be long gone by now." He slid the tip of his tongue over the edge of his teeth. "You staying up or going to bed?"

"I'm meeting Cyndi early to help her set up at the garden show, so I'm to bed."

Ford nibbled his thumbnail. "I'm gonna take a real quick drive."

"Ford, it's so late."

"I know, but I have tomorrow off. I'll sleep in. I just want to do a drive-by."

"The neighbors will think we can't stand to be in the same house together. I come in, you go out."

He pulled her to him. "The neighbors are all asleep. Your reputation is safe, Miss Margaret." He leaned down to kiss her.

She granted him a tight-lipped peck. "Don't kiss me. You smell like onions." She pushed him toward the door. "Get it over quickly and come home."

Leah woke up dead. The silence was wet in her ears, and her eyes scratched barbed swirls in their sockets. The left side of her head was surely missing and felt red and black, and the pain dripped all the way down into her jaw, while the right side sang an echo of the damage. Her chest wanted more than the stingy nips of air she'd been sucking in, and that was her first clue that she may not have passed on after all.

She rolled from her side onto her back and was assaulted by a spike of intensity through the pulpy spot on her head. A roll of nausea welled up her throat and a strobe of panic pounded in her chest as a crinkly blanket settled over her face, blocking her nose and mouth. Then the smell hit her and with it, another dense fog of confusion. The family cat had slunk off to the garage to die one summer. The clinging stench had ruined just about everything in there made of cloth or plastic. Rot and worms and jellied hell could only mean death, but if she could think it, could she actually be it?

She pushed the smothering cloth away and held it off her face and tried to see. She was blind. The blackness vibrated with purple and acid-yellow branches of lightning that faded as she tried to catch them in focus. She put a fearful hand to her eyes, suddenly terrified they wouldn't be there, that she'd find only squishy pits in their absence. But the lids were smooth and rounded over, just as they should be. And closed. She slid them open and still wasn't sure she hadn't gone blind.

Vertigo yanked at her bearings and Leah threw out a hand to stop the spinning. A random survival tip came back to her from an article she'd once read on spelunking—if you fell and became disoriented, you could spit to figure out which way was up. So she tried it and was rewarded with a sprinkling of saliva over her cheeks. Then she knew she wasn't dead because she could feel stupid. She was pretty certain she wasn't in a cave, if not of much else.

She held the blanket off her face with one hand and, with the other, explored her confines as she took inventory of hurting, of not being dead, and what the hell was that smell? A remote call of *No, don't!* came from some exiled store of know-better, but a second too late to make any sense of it.

Leah's hand closed around an irregular cylinder wrapped in soggy stuff that shifted and squelched between her fingers. She remembered being twelve years old and hauling her cousin out of the swimming pool by her cool, wet forearm, only to have the little snot clamp down and yank her off the edge. She'd almost drowned that day, and suddenly she was back there, thrashing, flailing, clutching for her cousin's arm (*It's not Allison, Leah, stop!*).

Leah kicked the tarp free and a blast of clean night air shocked her back to the untethered present. She sucked in gulps of it, wild-eyed. The starlight pricked her aching eyes like flecks of foil confetti, and the chill drove a peg deep into her temple. She shut her eyes and rolled away from the pain, onto her right side and up against—a snapshot flashed into her mind, of standing at the edge of a hole in the ground, a body slumped in the mud, mostly covered in a filthy cloth and slimy plastic.

Her hand still held the *stick, it's a stick, a bat, the neck of Reid's guitar, ohGodLeahwhatisit?* . . . She kept her eyes closed tightly, wishing the dead dream back. The psychedelic lightning played again against the pitch depths, and she squeezed her fluttering eyelids tight against the urge to open them, denying the frenzied need to know what she held in her hand. The night breeze wafted between her face and the shape in front of her, eclipsing the current, bouncing back a fetid vapor. Leah opened her eyes, and then her mouth to scream.

16

"WILLS AND WAYS, Boydie. Wills and ways. You got one, you got t'other. Like bull's-eyes and buttercups." Boyd's mother had always said it with such an inspired gleam in her eye that he'd never thought too long on how the axiom didn't actually make any sense. That it came by way of his crusty and perpetually ironic grandfather should have been a clue. PapPap had never seemed overly impressed by his middle daughter and her pair of matching rug rats, especially the stubborn, ornery one. But just as the word *cute* had meant "cross-eyed" and "bowlegged" in its origins, Shelley, Bart, and Boyd Montgomery had taken one thing and declared it another. And by continued misuse, it had become this other thing. In this case, a bit of nonsense had bloomed into their own personal mission statement, a rallying call for getting through life's rough patches. And Boyd certainly owned enough of the bull's-eye will to win him a way through most everything he had pushed up against in his time.

He had kept track of Old Green Valley Road, a silvery river of moonlit asphalt winding alongside him just a whistle-distance away. He'd eyed it for landmarks through the gaps in the trees, he was sure of it, but he came out of the woods into confusion and only just barely ahead of a galloping defeat. He rechecked the lay of the lawn and recognized the back of Phil's house, but the big backyard, which had never been home to fewer than four cars, was empty. Boyd scanned the house and tried to pin down the deserted mood echoing back at him. The grass was trimmed, the shutters gleamed of fresh paint in the moonlight, the—Boyd's eyes slipped back to the windows. Behind the reflection that glanced off each pane lay a square of darkness that yawned deep into the house. Boyd saw straight through to the gray silhouette of the front-porch posts. Neither shade nor curtain protected the home inside. It was empty.

Boyd confirmed this in a frantic scurry from window to window, dashing from one to the next, while his mind chased its tail. He'd known for sure after the first bare room gaped back at him, but his grand plan still whined for its life. All he wanted, needed, *deserved*, was a car, and maybe a little cash, and definitely a few hours' head start. Phil had cars to spare and likely a little pill money besides. Boyd had been counting on it. He prayed for a break, batting away the unrighteous pangs that nudged him to really consider what he was asking for, and why he might not be exactly worthy of it.

No new options presented at the front of the house either, but the FOR SALE sign sunk into a grassy patch near the street erased the need for any further window-peeping. At a single stroke, Boyd had no idea what he was going to do. Knowing the woods as well as he did wasn't going to get him far enough out of town in the hurry that he needed, and he'd already wasted too many precious hours on this great idea to start all over from scratch.

A whole herd of curse words reared up in his throat and trampled on his courage. Little fireflies of terror flitted behind his eyes, and he was huffing like a train gathering speed, the breath loud in his own ears and floating in his head as if he were taking on helium instead of oxygen.

I want to go home. The sudden, dizzying lament that welled up in him seemed only remotely connected to a sound he'd just heard in the near distance, a small sound that his distraction wouldn't allow him to replay for naming.

He hadn't thought far beyond the need for a set of wheels and the convenient fact that Phil owed him *big-time* for keeping his hush promise. Boyd hadn't been looking forward to the exchange, but drug pushers didn't always get to choose their hassles, and that was just Phil's own darned fault. But now, marooned in a sea of failure, Boyd's attention had been yanked yonder past the trees dividing the properties, over toward the house that had once been his own. There might yet be a car there for the taking, or at least something there that would spark an idea. *I want to go home.* The word *home* usually never rang in his head without meaning his family's roost in Branson Heights. For good or for ill, it was where he'd formed his ways and grown his spine. Only just now, that wasn't the place he wanted.

Boyd hadn't felt the loss of the house on Old Green Valley Road as much more than a tactical regret. Katielynn had been so house-proud, always painting and curtaining and fussing, but Boyd's thoughts had always been on other things when he'd cut the grass or banged at the plumbing. A roof from the rain and a place to go after he'd been somewhere else was mostly all he'd ever required of the word *home*.

But now, the image of Mamaw's quilt tucked up nice and cozy over their brand-new sofa flared up in his memory, and Katielynn's sugared corn bread—he could smell it. A rain squall of remembering soaked him: him rolling on the rug with his pups, making love, digging graves. He savored the recollection of his courage and even of his sweet regret at what she'd brought down on him, brought down on them all. He itched to be there, to stand in those same places and draw the strength of his old life (and their deaths) back up through the ground that held the record—the whole truth, not the law truth—of these things. It sparked first and then fizzed like a lit fuse, twisting through the dark toward his house, drawing him along. Just a peek. Just to see the spot one more time.

He slipped back into the ranks of the trees and rode the shadows sideways into the tangly back hem of his old backyard.

Boyd had only once before approached the house from this direction, through the back boundary of woolly bracken and tall, ancient trees. It had been on the night he'd trekked home from burning (and burning, and burning, oh my Lord, how that thing had cooked) the dirtball faggot's car full of Katielynn's stuff.

He'd run out of the house, sprung from a nightmare in a deep, afternoon sleep. His vigor was plain old panic, but he wasn't entirely sure that he wasn't going to die of the hangover he'd woken with. His heart quivered every time he tried to take a deep breath, and his swollen tongue tasted of mold. His liver, or something down that way in his guts, throbbed hideously out of rhythm with his brain, which leaped up against the walls of his skull with each heartbeat. He would probably still have blown a mite picklish on a Breathalyzer, but his rebounding sense of self-preservation spurred him into action nonetheless.

So, he had forced down three aspirins and a bottle of Gatorade, taken in small sips after throwing up the water he'd chugged in a Legionnaire's desert thirst.

Boyd had come to his more or less sober senses absolutely furious with Katielynn. He'd thundered through the house, punching pictures, shoving her T-shirts and panties and her stupid Snoopy toothbrush down the throat of her flowery overnight bag, and pummeling the rest of her things into a couple of pillowcases. Then he packed kerosene into the car. A great deal of kerosene. Every drop he had stocked away, in fact. The stores always had more to sell and it wouldn't be cold for months, so hell—yes, *hell*—with it.

On the way home from the bonfire, he'd been winded and sick at the stomach from all the alcohol and no food, and the thought of his empty house had both pulled and repelled him in waves like a deranged magnet.

Now, better than three years later, he fought and fell again through that same tidal drag, simultaneously wanting and not wanting to be *home*. The lay of the land worked for Boyd in the same way a long-remembered fragrance sparks memory in other people. Hunger and thirst and the sooty after-buzz of adrenaline were the same again, and each step forward felt like a tick backward in time. The light drag of his feet ruffled up the layers of seasons that had settled on the forest floor since he'd last been there. It turned them over fresh, and he imagined bringing up the very leaves and twigs from that day, all of it back up under his boots—*My God, they're the same boots*—so that as he drew nigh on the thinning edge of the tree line, he would have been hard-pressed to say for certain how long it had been since he'd shot Katielynn.

The ghost of a smell slid past him on the breeze, punting his heart up into his throat. Only a privileged few live to full grown without being able to recognize the smell of rotting meat. When it's coming from the fridge to remind you of a neglected electric bill, it's merely disgusting. But out in the open, all he knew was that something had died close at hand.

For Boyd, on this night and in this place, the smell of death was just about enough to send him bolting back the way he'd come, all the risk of it be hanged. But the sound that had nipped at his ear in Phil's yard came again, this time clearer and unmistakable—a plaint, a whimper, an undeniably feminine mewl floating up to him from a dark heap a short ways ahead in the clearing, halfway to the house, and right smack between him and the mulch bed where he'd put Katielynn.

All the clarity he'd ever owned tilted away, and a terror-senseless thrill blazed up every nerve. It pulled him forward while desperate reasoning spawned a litter of explanations for why injured-girl sounds mingled with grave stink hung in the air only a little more than spitting distance from the spot he'd buried his murdered wife. His beautiful wife. His young, sweet, laughing, faithless wife.

Boyd flung himself sideways into a tight gap between two bushes at the far wall of the shed. A hailstorm of possibilities clattered against the full-on surety that Katielynn was dead, dead as dead had ever been. Moaning or no moaning up ahead, there was no coming back from what she'd made him do, no matter how much he'd wished it at the bottom of his whiskey glasses. That the cops had been poking around was proof enough. She was stone-cold and just as silent, as was her rat bastard lover. Moreover, she'd been gone for years. He gripped this fact between his temples to clamp down on the wavering doubt that was trying to throw a load of what-ifs over the certainty that Katielynn couldn't possibly be making that noise.

He crouched in the weed-skirted shrubs, the smaller twigs snapping against him, while the sturdier branches of the bush dragged at his skin and hair, ripping payback from his hide for busting up the tender spring fronds. Boyd, not breathing, not moving at all beyond the thrumming pulse that forced his temple against a broken stem, ran through his choices as he listened for the sound again. He could stay put, or he could crash through. The hedge curled around him, clotting up the darkness and blocking the breeze.

Only two things could steal the will from Boyd Montgomery's bones. One was a tall drop, and the other was a tight space. He pulled against the urge to thrash his way into open air. His body hummed with the sudden, stupid desire to stand tall, to fling off the greenery and turn giddy somersaults into freedom. The rational part of his brain, without hesitation, argued very much for the opposite—to wait out any chance of ever seeing what was out there in the grass from just exactly where he was, thank you very much, not making a sound, no matter that it took till sunup. He was going light-headed in the debate. A leaf, or something crawling on one, tickled Boyd's ear, teasing him to swat at it and yell. Self-control tightened down like a straitjacket.

Someone was messing with him. Maybe they'd guessed he'd come, set him a trap. Boyd shimmied out from between the bushes through the eye-watering pull of branch-combed hair, and he pressed himself against the shed wall. He ducked a look around the corner and saw the mound on the grass snap to a peak, another muted cry calling out to the raving soft spot that was blooming over his common sense. He flattened back against the wall, his eyes squeezed tight to keep the sight of the roiling nightmare from going any deeper. It had to be the cops. Please, God, that was the only explanation. Either that or something hell-sprung wasn't the least bit impressed with the reasons why he'd done what he did on that long-ago day. The thing had come to intercept him, waiting for him here on the very ground where it had happened, just to have a go at his soul.

He swung around for another peek, but a foot too far this time to keep him from stumbling out from behind his cover. He threw out a hand, catching only the loose hasp of the shed's open latch, but the metal plate and the wobbling, loose padlock were hardly enough to reel in his misstep. A racket of wood on metal brought a shovel handle toppling over his toes and the noise of it ruined his stealth, but it also rattled loose the cage door of his recklessness. He swept up the handle, swinging the head of the shovel into position high over his shoulder, and made for the murmuring bundle.

It rolled and bucked as he approached. Ten paces out, Boyd could see whatever it was wriggling under a plain, old camping tarp. Something that unremarkable, so very of this world, gave him pause to think more clearly, though his feet didn't bother to take advantage of it and propelled him onward anyway.

Eight of the ten paces spent, Boyd's calculations abruptly snuffed out on the last breath his lungs looked to replace. The tarp crackled and flew open at the far edge.

As much as he immediately decided that he would prefer to take his chances with the police, Boyd was convinced that the other scenario had opened up a portal and he was indeed staring down a hell horror that would play on everything he loathed. Two figures slithered into view on a waft of decay—one dark and still, a man made faceless and anonymous by his tattered wrappings, and the other a pale woman, turned from Boyd, and nuzzling up against her gruesome lover. A contorted chortle climbed the woman's throat and raced up to merge with the replay in his head of Katielynn's last naughty giggle.

17

M OST NIGHTMARES are caged in their realm by implausibilities. The sleeper slogs through quick-sand in a fun house of frightening nonsense and disjointed mumbo jumbo. But everything's all better once the bedside lamp is back on, because reality, even when it's bad, is easily distinguished from night terror. Except for the trying-to-scream dream. That one's pretty much spot-on.

Leah's throat strained to cry out, but the weight of the fear bogged down the sound and pressed it thin. She managed a hiss, high in her throat, then a guttural, warped whine. And just like in the dream, that deformed sound was even scarier than what caused her to make it in the first place. The thing beside her was simply a biology lesson.

The sheet had shifted open, the plastic ripped away from the shoulder and torso. Pale ribs peeking through a mushy gap and a glimpse of collarbone oriented the shape of her tarpmate, but the head remained mercifully hidden in its bindings. Leah still clasped the forearm fleshed in dark sludge, now gone warm under her grip. She snatched her hand away, fingers splayed to keep the jam from mingling.

She scrambled to her hands and knees, but the aspect change wreaked havoc on her head wound, which throbbed a booming tempo. A look ahead only brought on the spins—house-woods-thinginthetarp; a swirl of moon-stars-treetops. She swiped her slimy right hand through the grass and kept it flat on the ground for counterbalance as she drew into a crouch. She held her head together with her left hand and winced at the pulse clumping along in the goose egg that bulged there. Her heart whirred and her vision grayed as she wobbled to her feet, but an unsteady three-count was all it lasted. One trembling half step and her clay legs showed their true colors, dropping her back onto the grass. Leah slapped at the ground and whined through gritted teeth. She rocked onto all fours, and without waiting for the merry-go-round to slow, she launched an attempt that not only didn't work, but toppled her over backward. Her shoulders scudded up against a squelchy something; her head was cradled in an almost comfy nook. The crackling rustle of plastic sheeting was loud in her ears. Her aching eyes rolled to see what she already knew: the rest of the covering had been nudged aside and she was cheek to jowl with the livid, grinning horror.

Jason yanked the towel away from his face and scowled to sharpen his hearing. He thought he would have grown used to the taste of his heart at the back of his throat by now, but there it was—metallic, warm, and sickening again. Fresh beads of sweat sprung up in the stubble on his upper lip. And once again from outside the window, the low, halting moan, louder and grimly for certain this time. It was the lethargic pause between bleats that renewed the watery warmth in his innards. All his mind's eye would show him was a groaning Harris: trailing his shroud, bagged blind, and staggering through the back door.

He considered closing himself up in the closet and counting to ten thousand, but the only thing more terrifying than the thought of seeing what was yowling out in the backyard was the stealthy silence that played in the spaces when whatever-it-was went quiet.

Jason crept back to the narrow window over the commode. He'd nearly sprained his neck trying to keep his porcelain seat and a simultaneous watch over the covered heap on the lawn. He'd abandoned the view only long enough to rinse his hands and face. Now he drew the curtain back, one finger sneaking it open one eye's width. His heart, which had been crashing red thunder through his temples for most of the night, stopped cold.

Guilt wears track shoes. Sprint, marathon, or cross-country, it doesn't matter. It runs tireless to catch you, and it carries a sledgehammer. From the backyard to his bathroom was a short dash for the dread reflex, and that he hadn't even considered that the dead girl might not be dead made the blow all the heavier. The light of relief at having not killed a perfect stranger was well smothered under the bushel of new anguish—how was he ever going to account for any of this to a live person?

But the new addition to the scene in the backyard pushed that problem to a distant second place on the podium for prize-winning disasters. It left him blinking, but not breathing. It was simply impossible.

His car had been stolen from outside the library once when he was a teenager. He'd walked to the spot at the curb where he'd parked it and stared, dumbstruck, at the bare blacktop. His brain had, over and over, laid down the card showing him the little red hatchback, trying to match it to the picture of empty space in front of him, but a phantom game-show buzzer insistently voided the transaction. This was very much the same. His senses were overflowing with unpleasant trivia, but his brain offered up nothing but plain white banners where the explanations should have been. Urgency, though, whispered a cold clarity into his head; this time, he couldn't just stand there and fret.

She was fighting to her feet, chest heaving, limbs flailing, and terror flowing out from her in waves that he could feel right through the window glass. But far, far worse than all that was the improbable new addition to the cast. A man was standing behind her. It wasn't Harris. Thank God. That was the only thing that could have been more horrible, but this man was blessedly too tall, too blond, and too dry. And from somewhere, somehow, more recently familiar. The man had cocked Jason's own shovel back over his shoulder and he stood two giant mother-may-I steps braining distance from the girl.

In only seconds he would finish her off or she'd whirl and discover him. In either case, chances were better than average that she'd scream, waking the neighbors or, God forbid, the dead. Her fear and vulnerability bored through the wall, straight through Jason's hesitancy, and he was out the door before he'd formed a strategy that could possibly yield any good result.

Boyd didn't seem capable of moving beyond the trembling that rattled the shovel in his upraised arms. The girl had flung herself back and forth over the canvas with not so much as a glance spared in his direction. Her performance clearly wasn't for his benefit or, thankfully, for his damnation either, but before he had the chance to hazard a guess at what was going on, her eyes found his. She'd spun and swiveled as if the ground under her were layered in greased marbles, and her final fall had left her tucked under the chin of a glistening skull that, in the scuffle, had mostly popped free of its plastic hood.

When she did see him, he was instantly reminded of his threatening pose by the naked terror in her expression, but a rough call of "Hey! No!" reached him from near off his right side. Before he could decide which way to play it, a speed-launched weight slammed him sideways onto the ground. The unseated shovel rapped at least three spots on his head on the way down, the sharp edge of it slicing a notch into the sweet spot at the tail end of his eyebrow. The hard spindle of the handle bit into his hip as it dug in under him.

The man landed half atop Boyd, driving the shovel's haft against his hip for a second sting, and the pain made up Boyd's mind for him—he'd had about enough. The first people he'd dealt with since the cops in his kitchen were turning out to be near as much of a hassle as the police themselves had been, if not more so. No ghosts. No demons taking sport from his blame. Just two roadblocks. Noisy, blundering idiots who ought to be in bed. A thread of blood turned the corner at his lashes and slipped into his eye, so that the other one watered up in sympathy. He raised a hand to scrub the blood and tears away, but the man on top of him swatted his arm down, struggling to pin him into place.

"Go! Go!" the man called to the girl, who stood stunned, transfixed by the body on its tattered wrappings.

Her pale skin shone through swatches of dirt and blood. "Oh, God. Is that Reid?"

The name set Boyd's head fizzing and he lost track of the fight against the man holding him down. "What did you say?"

"Is it?" She put the back of her hand against her mouth and shook the other loose on its wrist. A shuddery exhale threatened to escalate into a full-fledged breakdown. "Is it Reid? Why is he still here? I thought they'd taken him. They just left him outside? On the ground, for Christ's sake?"

Boyd felt the old, smoldering school-shame flood into him. He'd almost always had the right answer somewhere in his head, but could never get to it and get his hand up before some other kid earned the gold star, the place on the team, the smile from the smart girl in class.

"What is this mess?" he muttered through clenched teeth. "Is Katielynn out here, too? What have they done? Where is she?"

Jason held his breath as he watched the girl behind him and the wiry man underneath him take in the vision that had plagued him into paranoid seclusion. Whatever these two thought it meant, Harris, as an image, had lived alone in Jason's mind since the last time the bastard had shouldered past him over the threshold on his way in and flopped lifeless in his burial bindings on the way out. But the world didn't end. No rumble ripped open the ground and swallowed Jason whole. The fact of it sizzled through him—he was still here. And, for a change, he wasn't the most clueless person in the group.

"You people are sick." The blond man upended Jason,

pulling himself free with the strength of indignation. "Y'all can leave that *Reid*, that no-good piece of trash, just wherever you'd like, but you oughtn't drop Katielynn that way, out in the open for God knows what to get at her. Where is she?"

The woman's gasp drew them all to a shared stop. "Oh my God. I've seen your picture! It's him. They told me he was dead, but it's him."

"Who?" asked Jason.

"Run!" she said. "He killed them. He killed them both!"

Kill and run and hi-fi hysterics fed into Jason as if they hadn't always been the order of the evening, and indeed an integral part of his entire week. He scrambled away toward her call just as the bits came together for him. Jason worked the important words from the stream of everyone's overtaxed consciousness. *Girl* and *blond guy* took up their rightful name tags in Jason's mind—the fiancée, Leah Tamblin, and Boyd *flipping* Montgomery. That's where he'd seen him. Bayard had shown Jason a picture in the case file.

"Now wait!" Montgomery hooked his arm over Jason's lurch. "I ain't got traffic with you. I'll have your car keys, but that's all I want."

Jason had never been particularly attached to his car, but the thought of being left with no way to cart Harris off the lawn or drive himself out of town, if it came to that, which was looking more and more likely by the second, had him swearing a silent vow that the very last thing he'd see before he died was his key ring dangling from Boyd Montgomery's fingertips. He lunged upward quite respectably, but not as far outward as he needed to, so Montgomery was up and on him before he'd cleared two strides.

They struggled over a small patch, trampling divots out of the grass and bruising each other's feet until they staggered over the slick edge of the tarp. Jason enjoyed a split second's triumph when the other man lost his legs first. The gloat faded once he realized what had caused the slide, half a heartbeat before their tangle landed. There wasn't enough firm substance left in the pile to technically fall *on* Harris, so the finale was more of a splashy dive into him.

For the first time all night, it seemed, Jason held the advantage. He was already familiar with the sound and the stench and the slip of it all, so even though the bile ran north in him, the horror of it had largely been spent. Boyd, however, squirmed and retched and hissed little hacking yelps during his wet skid through the center of the wreckage. Harris's acid-eaten bones broke beneath them, and what had been pulp was ground to paste in their wrangle.

Jason clambered over the other man and was nearly free of him, but a lucky bit of flailing married one of Jason's belt loops to a one-fingered death grip by Boyd. He pulled Jason back down, but Jason, one horror for the night stronger than Boyd Montgomery, drove an elbow sideways into Boyd's windpipe and thrashed free. He bolted for the house, as best he could on rubber legs, catching Leah, who stood suspended in petrified fascination, and dragged her with him.

Boyd had heard it said, and even from his own lips on occasion, that something or another had made his skin crawl, but he realized now that he'd never meant it. He had scraped specks of his twin brother's brain off the radiator with a table knife and not wanted to leap from his own hide as badly as he did right here in his old backyard. A cool, wet reek matted his hair, while his fouled collar buttered the back of his neck in shivery strokes.

The blow to his throat had made the dry heaves agonizingly interesting, with the waves of nausea roiling upward against his lungs sucking downward, struggling for air. The fight under his breastbone seemed fit to crack it, but he had to put aside the wonder and the pain and manage a flat-out run even without breath. No time for hurt or sick. He had to run so he could flee.

He hadn't thought of this whole tromp through the woods as a retreat. In his mind, even as he'd flashed his fingers at his pups to have them hold the cops to their places, he'd only thought of it as "moving on." In seconds, those two ijits who'd just tottered up the back steps and into the house were going to shred his lead on being able to get himself out of there before the cops found him out.

Boyd wasn't a man who devised harm to others, though harm he had certainly done. No matter what had happened here, or anywhere else for that matter, no one could say that he'd ever crossed anyone's intentions that had steered clear of his own. As such, he didn't stand for being crossed. Whatever had brought these two danged fools out in the middle of the night, this one and only night he'd needed something here, it was not his doing. He would not be held to fault for what he didn't plan.

There had to be a working car between them, and he meant to be in the driver's seat before the only thing he had between himself and a standoff with Johnny Law was his list of reasons. Fine and true as those reasons were, he couldn't very well see them as the only thing for him to live or die on.

He swept up the shovel with hardly a falter to his stride and cracked the junction box at the side of the house with a mighty swing. A brief shower of sparks and a clanging swell of shock waves through the bones of his hands, and the power and phone lines were cut straight through. The silent night fell apt to stay that way.

18

THE URGE to run crawled deeper into Jason's bones and set them humming. The soles of his feet had an itch that only the slap of asphalt could scratch, or better yet, the resistant nudge of the gas pedal. If he kept straight though, he could make the front door and beyond before anyone could stop him. He ached for a blurring wall of trees just off the side-view mirror. All he wanted now was the sigh of a speed-forced gale over the windshield and the surety that all this disaster was falling behind him with each turn of the tires. But it wasn't. Not yet.

Leah hung on his arm and dragged them to a full stop before they'd even cleared the kitchen.

"Where's your phone?" she pleaded. "We have to get help. He tried to kill me out there."

The insight that had flared for notice during the scrabble over the shovel sparked in his mind again. The woman he'd walloped wasn't afraid of him, and Harris, in all his venting glory, was still unrevealed as any sort of new problem. Nobody knew anything yet. Jason's opportunity was indeed tunneling down, but it wasn't yet an utter cave-in. Dialing 911 was out of the question.

"It's okay. Just hang on." Since it had primarily been for self-soothing, he wasn't aware he'd said it out loud until she responded.

"What? What do you mean? You already called the police?"

Jason flinched. His moment of revelation, of course, hadn't helped the girl one bit. Her fingers dug, demanding, into his arm. He plucked a string of true words free of their meaning and plugged the silence with them. "It's Leah, right? I'm Jason. It's okay. The police have been here. They're coming back."

A muted bang at the side of the house clapped off the kitchen lights. A sudden unplugged silence shoved out the civilized electronic background buzz. The computer's fan purred to dead, the refrigerator fell silent, the central-air blower held its breath, and the blackness pressed a primeval quiet down over the two of them.

Jason's mental replay of locking the dead bolt, and a gulped "Oh, God!" from Leah took up all the time there was to be had from the blackout to the first blow against the kitchen door. The brass latch proved sturdier than the doorframe, tearing through the wood at the second kick. The door sailed back from its slam against the rubber-tipped stop and clobbered Boyd Montgomery into the shredded doorway as he lunged inside.

Jason had named himself a coward many times and sometimes even fairly. He'd lost count of his regrets, but kept a running tally of all that his yellow streak had cost him over the years. In this case, though, he was blameless. He wouldn't deliberately have left her there as a gift to his own head start, a speed bump in the middle of the kitchen floor for Boyd Montgomery to slow down on. Jason had taken for granted that she, in the face of a huffing, bloodied intruder—someone who had killed her fiancé and, as far as she knew, whacked her in the head with a shovel—would have run with him.

Mutual surprise froze Leah and Boyd to their respective places. She'd felt the space beside her fall empty, the air around her rippling just slightly cooler in the breeze of Jason's abandonment. He'd left her. Like a locked turnstile, Leah's mind lurched forward only to rock back into it—he'd left her, alone and dead center in the path of a man who had already shown more than willingness to cave her head in. She stared him down, her short-circuiting thoughts standing in for defiance. The spell broke for both of them simultaneously, and they danced the grocery-aisle two-step: both to the same side; stop; lurch to the other side; stop. They mirrored their movements into each other's path, left and right over the linoleum.

"Now just hang on," he said, instead of taking his next slide-to-the-right turn. It gave way for Leah's extra cut to finally break their synchronized sway. She dodged left to put the kitchen table between them.

"I only want a car," he said. "That's all. I swear."

The room wavered gray at the edges and Leah sucked in her cheeks and locked her lips against a sob. The cannonade of her heartbeat swelled into the bump under her hair, and her legs trembled as if God himself thought it a good idea that she sit down, but she gripped the back of the chair in disobedience.

To save her life, which felt very much at stake, she couldn't think back to the point she'd last been in her car or what the hell had happened to this crazy day to leave her running desperate circles around a stranger's kitchen table. Her knees wobbled and everything reeked distractingly of rot, while her mind zipped through the checklist of what was hers: her name, her house, her job, what she'd done that day. She flashed over her visit with the big detective and the first trip out to the house on Old Green Valley Road. She'd come back again to pay her respects to Reid. Reid. The world, and the whole sorry state of her plight, was wrenched once again into focus. The back of her free hand flew to her mouth. Her knuckles rapped her lips painfully against her teeth.

Whatever telegraphed over her face, Boyd Montgomery read trouble. He reached out for her. "Now, wait! I ain't gonna hurt you."

She bolted from her place, tapping some lightning-spiked reserve of strength, but after only two blundered steps backward, Leah's legs met with a tangle of too much chair and not enough space. Her arms windmilled in vain as her feet slid from underneath her and she crashed down against one of the chair's upended spindle-legs, snapping it off.

He scrambled around the table, but Leah grabbed for the broken chair leg and swung it, catching him lightly across the cheek with the jagged end. "Stay away!"

He scurried backward, then regained his feet out of Leah's reach.

She pulled herself up, bracing against the window frame and brandishing the bristling chair leg. "I mean it. Stay back!"

"Just give me your car keys and I'm gone. I'm not lookin' to hurt you. I promise."

She patted her empty pocket for keys and searched her foggy past for a clue as to where they might have fallen. "You already hurt me, you goddamned son of a bitch," she said, but her jousting arm trembled.

"Don't you cuss me, you little . . ." He dove off to the right to herd her from behind the table, but she was around it and through the dining-room doorway before he could reach her.

Leah couldn't keep up the dashing pace for more than a few steps. The pain grinding into the side of her head pulled her off-balance, and only the ambient moonglow through the front windows made the black a barely navigable gray. She held the chair leg close and tight.

She glanced through the dining-room window and her pulse redoubled. Her car. It was directly in front of the house, intact and, as she now remembered, at the ready with the keys still in the ignition. She considered and discarded the notion of a scramble out the window as horribly likely to leave her half in, half out, and defenseless by the time he reached her. Instead, she edged to the doorway, heartbeat jackhammering in every cell.

She looked to the left, back down the hall. Jason was nowhere. The back door beckoned, closer than she would have thought, but farther than she dared without knowing exactly where Boyd Montgomery was. Across from her, another room glowered deep in shadows. And to her right, no more than four steps away, was the front door, with a thumb-latch bolt and a brass safety chain spanning the doorframe. If there was time to undo it . . .

"I just want to get on out of here." Montgomery seeped from the gloom in the passway between the kitchen and dining room. "Now be a good girl, put down the spike, and help me do that." His tone was gritting frustration, but the words were pure mild reason. His posture, on the other hand, was all linebacker: arms poised to catch, legs cocked to run. Leah didn't believe for a second that he wasn't plenty angry enough to finish what he'd started with the shovel. She finally found her voice and screamed a full-throated wail. She darted across the hallway. Three strides in and her shins slammed into a low table, spilling her onto the carpet and launching the chair leg truncheon out of her hold.

A bit of shadow at the corner of her eye broke free of its murk and rushed up at her faster than another scream could rise through her throat. A hand clamped warmly over her mouth.

"Shh. Shh," Jason whispered. "Where is he?"

Boyd felt insult raking up the hairs over the back of his neck. The affront at being thwarted and cussed on his own turf—but even worse, the familiarity of it—was too much.

"If you'd just listen!" Each of his words grew in volume as he took the rest of the hallway at a run, but he left off his pace as he neared the front of the house. The living room held its cold breath, just as it had since the day he'd taken up his gun in anger.

"God-dang it!" he bellowed. "You people will *not* like it if I have to run you down and take the ever-lovin' keys myself." Boyd gave them to the silent count of three. He sucked in his last of the hall air, balled his fists, and stomped into the living room.

Jason hunkered down in the dark corner beside the sofa and raked the carpet for the lost weapon. Leah huddled beside him and clutched his other arm as if it were all that was keeping her off a steep fall.

"And it ain't like I can't see you, stupid."

Jason jackrabbited from his crouch. Beyond all likelihood, he felt the glow of embarrassment stirred into the mix after thrusting the spiny, and now obviously inadequate, broken chair leg out in front of him. He hauled up on Leah's sleeve and pushed her toward the den behind him. "Go! Through there!"

Clutching his free hand, she hustled to her feet. Her eyes had grown more accustomed to the gloom, and she drew away through an open French door into a small room, trying to pull Jason along with her.

Boyd's hesitation evaporated over the threshold and he pounded off the paces to the far corner of the room, his long arms slapping at the broken lance. He caught up the stabbing hand and crushed Jason's fingers against the wood, before snatching it away from him. Boyd took a handful of Jason's shirtfront in the other fist, ramming the whole works up under Jason's chin.

"Give me your keys!"

"Jason, just give him the keys," Leah pleaded.

"Give him *your* keys!" Jason countered through the choke hold.

"Mine are still in the car!" she wailed.

Boyd shoved off and broke for the door. He'd only just cleared into the hall, with a passing wonder if the living room had only ever been haunted by his own moods and not an ill will of its own, when all the remaining hell that had surely been biding its time crashed loose.

Boyd had rounded the corner squarely into his path. *Too fast. How could he have gotten 'round that fast?* The man loomed up in front of him, taking his same corner simultaneously from the opposite direction, arms outstretched to catch him. Boyd locked his knees and tried to reverse, but his momentum was more than the maneuver could manage. He slowed, but didn't stop. Hand to God, he meant no harm, but he would not be stopped. Boyd drove his arms, and their splintered wooden extension, forward.

There was only a brief resistance, then the spiked end sank into soft belly. After a halting friction in the other direction, the spindle pulled free, and the two men staggered back from each other. His hands landed heavily on Boyd's shoulders, and grappling, they fell together out of the darkened entryway. He was so much bigger than Boyd had thought and so heavy as the man tugged at Boyd's arms for balance. The man's legs folded and he dragged them both to their knees. He still towered over Boyd, and Boyd raised his head to look into the man's face as they tumbled through a patch of refracted moonlight on their way to the floor. The chair leg slipped from Boyd's numb fingers.

"Oh my God. What did you do?" Jason asked, running out from the doorway of the den behind them.

In the last reaches of the weak light from the windows, Ford Watts lay on his back in the main hallway of Jason Getty's house—what had been Boyd Montgomery's house—and his blood mingled with the ghosts of the three who had bled here before him.

19

THE SAME goes for distinctions as holds for slivers: oftentimes the smallest are the sharpest. Jason had committed murder, but being blinded in the moment with Harris, he had never actually seen a killing in real time. Now though, front row and center, in the most candid 3-D that life can offer, he watched the big detective fall.

Boyd Montgomery, still on his knees, spun away from Detective Watts. The frayed end of the chair leg glistened an indeterminate dark color that Jason's mind screamed red for him anyway. Jason remembered the fever-sick prayer he'd said in those first few seconds after he'd pulled away from Harris's body, begging to undo it. He searched Boyd's face for what that might look like from the front view. But what he read there could have been horror, regret, or just unfulfilled rampage. It was hard to tell, and that couldn't be good news, so he decided in all but his feet to remove himself from the equation.

Then Jason felt a brief statistical curiosity over how many people died annually because they couldn't move when they should. He couldn't think as far away as his feet, and they weren't going anywhere on their own. It seemed that the internal conflict should have screamed in his head like a sold-out theater on fire, but in practice it felt stupidly bovine, like shoveling in more dull food when you were already full.

An electronic purr overlaid with the tinny-but-still-ominous first bars of Beethoven's Fifth Symphony blared from the foyer. Jason yelped. Montgomery startled, tipping his crouch into a half sprawl, while Leah full-on screamed and clamped a towing hand down over Jason's arm. She had pulled them away from Montgomery and the fallen cop, and they were nearly clear of the hall and into the kitchen when Jason finally placed the sound as a campy cell-phone ringtone.

The ringing phone made a word-association game in Jason's mind: ring-phone, phone-call, call-help, help-this poor lady (probably to the hospital), help—Detective Bayard solve his case, help—Jason Getty into an orange jumpsuit and then a prison cell for the rest of his life.

The back door beckoned. His car stood ready in the carport. It was time to run.

Boyd staggered up and roared after them. Low-blood-sugar fireworks dazzled his eyes, and the floor canted and rolled beneath him with each step. His mind howled for time to think, and his fists buzzed with fury, but a glittering black-ness feathered the edges of his eyesight.

"Don't you quit," he murmured to himself as he reached the kitchen. He remembered the open padlock dangling from the catch on the shed and saw the chance to herd those two pains in the ass—*oh, yes, Lord help them, they've surely driven me to cursing, now*—inside it, locking them clear out of the path of his getaway. His will reasonably restoked at the doorjamb, Boyd launched himself through.

Jason's rush was faster and more sure-footed than Leah's concussion. He'd had to clutch her elbow twice to steady her on the way out. She'd been at his side, then no more than a pace behind him—he would have sworn—but Jason realized he'd lost the sense of her again, once he heard Montgomery's boots pounding down the deck boards.

Jason checked behind him to find her closer to Montgomery than she was to him. How had that happened? He ran back for her, recalibrating the distance with each stride in hopes the math would work out better for them. It didn't.

Boyd clamped a hand over her mouth and lifted her clean off the ground. "You!" he called to Jason, his voice lowered. "Don't you make a sound. I *will* hurt her. I don't want to, but hand to God"—Leah was small enough that he could hold up one hand, palm out, to God presumably, and still keep her pinned and half-smothered with the other arm—"I will hurt her and more if you don't just walk straight to that shed right there and set yourself inside." Boyd boosted a choked squeal from Leah, her feet dangling even higher off the ground, just to show Jason how easy it was. "And I do mean now," Boyd snarled.

Jason stopped on the far side of the splatter-heap of Harris and turned to them, his own palms out. He couldn't just leave her in Boyd Montgomery's arms and lead the way into the shed like a bad dog skulking into its pen. He'd eventually be freed, probably by the cops. Then he'd trade his garden shed for a jail cell.

"Okay, just hang on a second," Jason said.

"Don't you stop," Montgomery warned.

It startled Jason to find that, once he got going, he could lie with an agile talent, especially when the stakes tugged at the gambler hiding somewhere deep inside him. He stared strong into Leah's bulging eyes and ticked an almost imperceptible nod of encouragement to her. Then he dropped his voice as invitation for Boyd to do the same.

"Is this really your wife out here? They told me it was," he all but whispered, eyes steady to catch clues to Boyd's reaction. "Did you do it like they said you did?"

"No. It ain't her."

"Is it? I mean, who does that? Shoots his own wife? In their home?"

"Shut up. I said it ain't her. You don't know me. Anyway, lookit, there's a hole over that way. I don't even know what that is. It don't matter, I'm just gonna close you two up in that shed, and I swear on the Bible, I will not hurt you. I just need to be getting outta here."

"I dunno," Jason said, shaking his head, but looking Boyd dead in the eye. "Did you offer Katielynn any kind of deal, too? Did she get a chance? Did she let her guard down and do as you said? Or did you just get off on it? Is that why you came back here?"

Boyd roared and lunged, angrier than he was careful.

Leah felt Boyd's bellowing as a tickling hum in her back. She hammered his shins with her heels and shimmied out of his grasp.

"Oh, no, you don't," Boyd said. And it was meant for both of them. He stepped forward, his long legs spread wide enough to trip her escape and he stopped Jason's charge with his fist. The blow landed dead center and Jason staggered back, gaping soundlessly, trying to take in air over a paralyzed solar plexus.

Boyd's fingers scrabbled over Leah's ribs to get a good grip, and he hauled her back to him, but this time she fought it, snarling and twisting instead of shocked and compliant as she had been.

"You asshole! You son of a bitch!" Leah raked at his face with her nails, but he held her back easily. They fell short and only tagged a short stripe into his neck, then caught mostly filthy collar, then shirt, then buttons, then air. "Reid!" she sobbed.

Boyd caught up a fistful of Leah's hair close to her nape. "What are you yowlin' about? He was with my *wife*!" Boyd yanked her closer and growled into her face through gritted teeth, "He wasn't worth the bullets it took to drop him."

A flash in Leah's eye sparked a flare of cruel amusement in Boyd Montgomery's. He sent a teeth-rattling shake down his arm that snapped her head back. "Ha! And what's more—you know it. Yes, you most certainly do, don't you, little girl?" He jerked her head again.

Leah looked into the eyes of Reid's murderer. They met in an instant of recognition, and hers flickered one part hatred, three parts loss, and a dram of disgrace as the small, mean truth burned acid into her tears.

"You go to hell." She was trapped in a less than ideal fighting posture, but swung her foot anyway.

Montgomery, who seemed unable to keep score against all the little girls he'd underestimated in his time, took the blow in the groin, a glancing shot from the side of her heel that laid him hard to his knees and, in his fall, set her free.

Jason, with his first lungful of air settling back over the pain in his middle, stumbled after her. "No, wait! Hang on," he wheezed.

She disappeared back into the house. Jason fell inside, just seconds behind her. He pulled the door into the wrecked jamb and slotted home the top slide bar, which by every suspense-film standard should have juddered out of his quaking fingers at least three times, but didn't. He caught up with Leah in the hallway.

"You have to make a run for your car," he said.

"No, Jason, please. Please don't leave me. He's out there. He killed Reid. He killed Detective Watts. I can't make it. He'll get me."

"You can do this. There's only one of him and two of us, if he's even still out there. If it's clear, run for your car and lock yourself in. I'll stay between you and the house. Drive slow. You can make it."

"Oh, God."

"Let's go."

Leah would have been the first to admit that she had some abandonment issues, but the cosmopolitan fear of losing a boyfriend or parental approval, or a job or social status, barely compared to the fundamental terror of drifting out of reach of the last human being standing between her and a murderer. But she didn't argue. She simply nodded and fell in line without the slightest intention of letting Jason get any farther than grabbing distance away.

She could make it. Of course, she could make it. Bit by bit, Jason had lost all of the relief that had come with Leah's assuming it was Boyd Montgomery, not him, who had cracked her skull. Every time he looked at her, he felt worse. Blood had slipped down through her hair and pasted a curl to her temple. A fan of red crept across the white corner of her left eye, and tears cut shining tracks through the film of dirt and blood on her cheeks. Despite all hideous evidence to the contrary, Jason was harmless. He was nonviolent to the next to the last degree.

And now he meant to leave her. A worm of shame curled into the back of his throat. But her car had the keys in it. She could make it. She'd expect him to go for help because good people wouldn't imagine it any other way. He'd have to cash in on that, too, her decency, so that he could buy a margin.

"I'm sorry," he said.

"For what?" she whispered.

"For everything."

"We're going to be all right, right?"

"You're going to be fine." He believed it. More than that, it didn't require belief. It soothed to a certainty, as if somewhere on a parallel thread of time and circumstance, it had already happened. To keep her safe, to allow himself to do this, he cast her in his future memory, her face destined to come to mind from time to time. *I wonder how she's doing; if she has nightmares; if she wonders about me . . .* She would drive off to an ice pack and a harrowing story to thrill everyone who loved her. It required no more faith than knowing where he'd parked his car.

Hand in hand, they crept down the main corridor. Jason leaned his ear to the front door and heard solid wood, nothing more. He freed the bolt and led Leah onto the stoop. Jason's die-hard habit pulled the door closed behind them, and as it shut, the cell-phone symphony orchestra pealed Beethoven's score of doom from the hallway again.

He turned on the top step and saw that where he'd parked his car, where he *always* parked his car, was the very thing that would capsize his new plan right into the crapper.

The big detective had parked smack in front of Jason's car. Stout brick pillars framed the entrance of the carport, without enough depth to the structure to even entertain the idea of running a stunt-double crash through the posts. He was utterly blocked in. Hope was a wisp of exhaust from the running truck, but before it could waft any inspiration over Jason's next move, Boyd Montgomery limped out from alongside the carport. The truck was his for the taking.

Jason was snared in the desperately stupid alternative of leaving with Leah or running down the road like a lunatic all on his own. What was he going to do, steal her car right under her nose? Ask her to drop him at the train station in his stinking clothes? The sheer size of the problem blocked his airway, and the panic backed up in his throat. It was so wrong to do any of this in the first place, and so exponentially more wrong to involve Leah any more than she'd already fallen into it.

"Come on!" she said, and ran for the road. And not being able to think of anything else to do in its place, he followed.

Jason and Boyd looked at each other over the lawn that already needed mowing again. No way would Jason ever get to the truck before Boyd. He was standing right in the path to the carport, and bruised balls or no, he was standing strong. Insects scritched in the woods; a shred of cloud streaked across the moon; tires whooshed and faded out down the distant highway. Most of the drama had played indoors, muffled by brick and drywall. Outside, with only a few short squeals from Leah and one growl from Boyd, they'd brawled over the yard in quiet hisses and undertones. No more fuss than a cat fight or a fox taking a bit of rabbit home for supper. Old Green Valley Road slept unaware.

But something seemed more wrong to Jason than even the night's troubles allowed for. The maddening subliminal squeak of a loose end. Harris had been pummeled to paste. There was nothing to be done about it. Except for the mush pressed into everyone's clothes and hair, he would remain there, ground into the grass and smeared across the tarp for the detective to find. The plan, however ridiculous it had ever been, was lost. Jason briefly wondered if he'd been inside his own house for the very last time. He left the idea to haunt the place in his absence and sprinted to Leah's side. She dove for the passenger door.

"I'm a wreck," she said. "You drive. The keys are in it. Run! Go!" She slammed the door behind her.

As he climbed in behind the wheel of her car, he heard the truck drop into gear and flare to life. Boyd Montgomery flailed at the dashboard controls in the cab, screeched locked tires over the parking brake, sorted out that little problem with a lurch, then rumbled down the long driveway. The driver's-side wheels churned up grass and half a shrub as the truck arced into the street.

Seeing that Boyd wanted the road to the right, Jason immediately fitted the reverse gear and started backward to buy as much distance in the shortest amount of time, but Leah's scream drove his foot reflexively into the brake.

"The phone!" she cried. "The detective had a phone! Jason, stop! It was on the floor by the door!"

He'd just begun teasing with the notion of letting Boyd drive away from them and then convincing Leah to part company right where they sat. He'd tell her it would be good for them to have their own cars. He'd tell her that he'd be right behind her. It was a good idea. Just let him go and then let her go. That's what he was missing, yes? No? It tickled *maybe*. But Leah's hand was already on the door handle. She would, if he didn't stop her, call down the authorities right in Jason's own foyer—from a cop's phone, no less.

"No, we should follow him," he said. The words came faster than any sense they didn't quite make. Jason knocked the transmission into drive, hit the gas, and whisked her away from her eureka moment and any opportunity to call in the cavalry. The truck ahead bounced over the curb.

"What? We have to call for help! Jason, no, wait!"

"He'll get away. We have to know where to tell them to go, right?" The crazy lie rolled out smoothly on a common sense tone.

"I don't—"

Leah's nimble little car ran right up on the bumper of the truck, but the bellowing eight cylinders easily pulled a widening gap. Then the switch clicked in Jason's mind; the squeaky uncertainty snuffed out. A cop's phone.

"Leah. We ran right through the house. Where was he?"

"Where was who?"

"Detective Watts. His phone was on the floor, but where was he?"

Slack wonder turned their heads first toward each other and then to the tailgate lights receding ahead.

20

MAGGIE WATTS opened her eyes in the dark. She'd known before she'd woken up that she was still alone in the bed. A breeze played over her shoulder where there should have been warm bulk shielding her from the open window. Year-round, Ford insisted on having it open, if only a crack, while they slept. His mother had drummed it into him that fresh air while sleeping was second only to a daily dose of fish oil and apple-cider vinegar for warding off colds, flu, the blues, bad humors, and hay fever. He'd almost never sneezed in the thirty-seven years she'd known him, so arguing the point was little more than an exercise.

The whisper of air on her bare skin had tickled her subconscious into sending up an alarm. She wondered how long she'd been asleep, then wondered at her wonder. All she needed to do was turn over and look at the clock to know how long she'd been there. She was stalling.

Maggie had always been plagued by a muddled radar. Often, and usually for no reason at all, the face of a friend or a loved one would spring to mind, hemmed in by neon exclamation points, blinking distraction. Thoughts of someone would ride shotgun to every task, fuzzing her concentration until she gave in and phoned the person to check if everything was okay. These feelings, heavy and textured as they were, rarely produced news of any kind, much less any advance warning of doom or even garden-variety emergency. A few times, though, the caller and callee had felt uncannily connected to each other by the coincidence of mutual thoughts. Probably not enough for a supernatural label, but still. And the numbers she'd regularly dreamed had only twice won her prizes—fifteen hundred bucks in a lottery once, and a year's supply of dog kibble in a jelly-bean count at the Pet Depot at Easter.

But awake and bothered, the track record of her unreliable clairvoyance was of no help at all.

Ford throbbed in her mind. She rolled over and saw that she'd been in bed not half an hour. "Oh, good Lord, Margaret. Go to sleep." Maggie talked out loud to herself with ease and always had, without apology.

She managed to doze off again, but was snatched from a dream, breathless, already half sitting up by the time her eyes fully opened. "Ford!" She reached out in the darkness and found his side of the bed still empty. Her dream left no images for her to replay, but the tone of it held her dangling over the void of sleep, wrapped in an echo of black panic. She slid searching hands across the cold sheet as if Ford, of all people, could somehow have made himself small enough to miss.

Fully awake and jangled at the nerves, Maggie, as was her habit, pulled on her bathrobe before dialing the bedside phone. She refused to speak on the telephone in the altogether, even to her own husband, although she couldn't

sleep comfortably any other way than bare naked. At bedtime, Ford always switched from his long list of pet names
to calling her Lady Godiva. She only wanted to hear him
say that and to tell her to go back to sleep.

The ghoulish green of the backlit handset struck a mood
in keeping with how a phone call in the middle of the night,
incoming or outgoing, is not often a good thing. One ring:
Fine. Two rings: *Well, he has to get to it, Margaret.* Three rings:
Come on, Ford. Four rings. Five rings. Click. "This is Ford
Watts with the Carter County Sheriff's Department. If you
feel you have an emergency, please hang up and dial 911.
If you just want to talk to me, wait for the beep and leave
a message. I'll get back to you."

Maggie cleared her throat. "Yes, Mr. Watts. This is Mrs.
Watts, alone under the Wattses' blankets. It's not an emergency. Not yet, anyway." She giggled in the pause. "Anyway,
just checking on you. Get yourself home or call me and tell
me not to wait up."

She disconnected and her smile faded with the seconds
that ticked away from having heard his voice on the message.
She sat in the dark, staring at the phone-shaped black hole
in the nightstand shadows. She started to shrug the robe
from her shoulders, but caught it as it slipped down her
back. It wasn't cold enough in the house for goose bumps,
but Maggie had them anyway.

She pulled the chain on the old bedside lamp, and the
details of their bedroom, hers and keenly now Ford's with
his robe over the footboard and his change jar on the dresser,
leapt at her, overbright and too colorful for the middle of the
night. She jammed her pillows behind her back, but two
paragraphs of her nightstand novel frustrated her. She'd
had to read each line four times to get the words to stick.

She tapped her front teeth with her thumbnail. Twice she reached out for the phone and twice she recoiled before an exasperated sigh put a halt to the dance. She grabbed it up and redialed.

"It's me again," she told his voice mail after bouncing her knee through the endless ringing. "I'm being silly. Will you call me anyway? I just want to know you're okay." There'd be no more sleep until they spoke.

Maggie rebraided her hair, but kept to only the silk kimono over her birthday suit. No sense in dressing as Ford would be calling soon or, better yet, be home in the flesh, and she'd be back in their bed shortly.

She lasted halfway through a cup of chamomile tea and up to the first ad break of an infomercial extolling the wonders of a rubber rug rake.

The number pad took the brunt of her restlessness as she dialed Ford's cell phone a third time. The call rang to his voice mail, and she hung up before the message tone demanded comment. He'd either gone out of range or turned the ringer off.

If he'd drifted into a pocket of dodgy reception on the outskirts of town, Maggie was only a little annoyed. He should have called her if he was going much farther than the park. It was the middle of the night for heaven's sake, and his night off what's more.

And if he'd turned it off, there was going to be a quarrel. Maggie mostly stifled her instincts because, more often than not, they left her with nothing but a red face to show for it. She was a practical woman in the interest of peace, and at some cost to her nerves. But Ford knew, if she'd called—and twice at that—she really needed him, if only to tell her that he'd be home soon.

Her patience didn't make it another ten minutes. "Tessa?"

The dog had followed Maggie from room to room, matched at both ends by droopy eyelids and a sagging tail, bobbing in time atop shuffling paws.

"What do you think?" Maggie drew resolve from the automatic consent to be found in Tessa's steady brown eyes. Tessa always agreed first no matter what, out of loyalty, then again once the question was actually asked out loud. "Want to go for a ride?"

The dog's ears perked to cinnamon-fringed peaks at the string of her favorite words. *Is it time to eat?* ran a close second, but riding always took precedence over food and sleep.

Maggie tried Ford's phone one more time as she dressed. "Dammit" was the only message she left.

The park was deserted, just as it should have been at that hour. Maggie pulled into the space where the little blue car had served as a makeshift cot for the tiny, time-killing girl she'd spoken to earlier. She stared out through the windshield at all the nothing going on in the park. The engine ticked and the dog shuffled her anticipation in the passenger seat. And it was all the news to be had.

Maggie clipped the leash to Tessa's collar and stood aside to let her out of the car and into the park. Tessa ran the length of her lead, snuffling and darting between invisible troves of interest, leaving Maggie too aware of the weight of her unease and fidgeting for a reason not to feel foolish. She didn't know why Ford had wanted to check on the girl in the park, and she didn't know where that curiosity would have led him beyond this spot. She didn't know anything more than that it was well past their bedtime. Her intuition fretted away in the back of her mind like an itch that squirmed just past the longest contortion of her reach. The buzzing of the lamppost only highlighted the quiet, and it irritated her. "You could have just asked, you know. It would have been a simple enough question as he walked out the door. But, no. And so here you are, in the park, in the middle of the night with your dog, but not a clue. You're really slipping, Margaret."

Tessa paused, alerted by the tone, and checked Maggie's face to be sure the scolding was not intended for her. Satisfied, the dog bowed back to her sleuthing, as Maggie muttered on in her tirade against her own lack of foresight. In the near distance, brakes squealed and the gritty pattering of tire-stirred gravel echoed down the bricked facades of downtown.

Maggie's monologue faltered at the sound and she listened for more. There wasn't any more. She sighed and reeled in the slack of Tessa's leash. "This is silly. Let's go home." But Tessa stared ahead, lock-legged and rooted in place, pulling against the shortened tether.

"Come on, Tessa."

The dog looked to her mistress and back across the open lawn.

Maggie gave the leash a grumpy tug. "Not now, Tess. No strays or trash-digging for you tonight. I'm not in the mood."

Tessa dropped her head, the equivalent of a dog shrug, and fell agreeably in step, back to the car.

*

Experienced bird-watchers can identify a hidden warbler just on the pitch and variations in its call. Sometimes they'll pinpoint the seasonal plumage and the mood of the creature, too, just by the sound it makes. Savant music students may be able to name the arrangement and performer of a well-loved piece by listening to merely a few bars. They can hear a Stradivarius or a Steinway, where most would hear only a violin or a piano. And the simple secret of mothers-with-eyes-in-the-backs-of-their-heads is the ability to discern that only one combination of items in the house could make a sound like that: the new stainless-steel toilet brush clattering along the spindles of the open staircase railing.

But what even the most canny and attentive human being discerns by straining at the eardrums would disappoint the average mutt.

Tessa was always game for a late walk. Night smells and night sounds were so different and, without the sun toasting her dark fur to distraction, much more pleasant for her. Her ears twitched constantly and her nose cataloged trace scents by the hundreds. Rabbits had been in the park earlier, and sometime recently, a kid sick from too many sweets. She could already feel the leading edge of a storm that wouldn't roll overhead until tomorrow afternoon, and she could hear squirrels turning against dry bark in their fretful sleep deep in the hollowed knothole of a dead branch. The second hand on the clock tower in the square whirred in its loop to underscore the night music for her. All of these tidbits flowed over Tessa with as little notice taken as Maggie had paid to the tiny shifts in the wind against her face. Tessa didn't react because it wasn't important.

Obviously, Maggie was agitated. Late-night drives and strolls on their own in the deserted park would have clued Tessa to that. But anxiety has a taste that doesn't tingle on the human tongue. It sours the edges of a person's aura. The tang was only vague around Maggie just now and was nothing Tessa could remedy anyway.

Apparently, it was nothing for Ford to attend to either. Otherwise, Tessa couldn't account for why Maggie hadn't perked up at the sound of his truck. The slight arrhythmia of the engine's firing made easy work of picking out Ford's ride from other sounds. Gun the throttles on a dozen identical pickup trucks and Tessa would find her own (because, of course, everything that was Ford's was hers as well) in seconds flat.

He had headed out of town, out onto the forest road, and not in the smooth way they usually rode together—the truck lurched into the distance, erratic on the go, jerky on the stops. But now Tessa and Maggie were humming along due opposite, back toward home. Tessa chuffed a sigh and twisted her head with the passing guardrail posts. She could hear the interruptions they made in the airflow past the car. It was all so interesting.

21

B OYD DROVE in silence, flicking his eyes rhythmically from the street to the rearview to the speedometer to a quick check at both sides, all the while holding a precise line through the bends of the road. He'd spurned the speed limit, sometimes by nearly double, to put plenty of asphalt between himself and those two loonies from the house.

But Boyd hadn't driven all that much in recent years. The bank, the liquor store, and the market were all in the same strip mall. Fifteen minutes to get there and another fifteen to get back, twice a month, was about the size of it, and although his twenty-year-old Nissan rattled a bit in the trim, its mild engine ticked like a clock. This mammoth rumbled like a logroll in a thunderstorm, and it flat-out unnerved him. He had never wrangled a vehicle as modern, complicated, and howlingly loud as the pickup. And he'd never been worried about being chased before, either.

It had never occurred to him how much concentration it would all demand, but it was surely enough to bring on a headache bad enough to compete with the soreness in his balls. He hunched over the wheel and squinted a hard focus on driving inconspicuously while trying, with limited success, to shake off the teasing prize of all puzzles—how to ride a fast rail out of Stillwater in a dead cop's stolen truck. Then all he had to worry about was what to do with the rest of his life.

There were boondocks and backwoods in the near distance, some of them even peopled with Montgomery kin, but Boyd's standoffish ways had hardly endeared him to most of them. Any of them, if he was honest. A cold flutter dropped right through him. What if he made one of those cop shows for killing that detective? There'd be no sure safe haven in all the world, even under a Montgomery roof. Everyone knows that juicy gossip runs thicker than the sap in a family tree.

It wasn't fair.

Boyd had always thought of time, his time, in the same way he regarded a vast forest full of sunlit hollows and shadowed thickets. He'd conceded to the natural way of things, but he wouldn't apologize for clearing some space of his own. Every man had a right to that. Now that he was alone, he only wanted to stay that way—bothering no one and earning a little peace and quiet in return. He had tried it the regular way. He'd bought up a pile of debt and called it a home and married up and let her set out her plan for their lives while he took out the garbage. Katielynn ought not to have done him like that. And that long-haired, little peckerhead? Boyd wished he were still alive so that he could shoot him again. He was still that pissed off.

The strobing pools of yellow light from the streetlamps worried him. His route out of the county was a winding series of dark side roads with only one short run across a corner of town. This was the span that concerned him most. Crossing the well-lit, open stretch left him feeling as bare as an egg.

The storefronts were unlit, their shadowy window displays hidden in the gloom, then opaqued in the sliding glare of his headlights. Boyd's eyes darted back and again over the scene to mark the difference between mannequin and security guard, his paranoia inventing stealthy movement where there was none. Preoccupied as he was with his imagination, he was sluggish in responding to the very real tomcat that darted into his path from the alley between a closed tavern and a still-bustling all-night diner. The cat flinched to a petrified arch, its yellow eyes wide and fixed on the truck's grille.

Boyd swerved and braked hard, freeing the cat from the spell of the headlights, but kicking up a racket in the strewn gravel at the far edge of the lane. The truck skated over the grit, then hurled him against his seat belt as it jerked to a standstill. The cat loped to the opposite sidewalk and glared back in contempt. He watched it slink away in the rearview mirror, scanning the street and the diner window for clues that he'd drawn any unwanted notice. He curled his lip over the newly familiar urge to curse. With shaking hands, he steered the truck back to center, a heavy dose of asphalt pebbles clattering in the wheel wells.

The fright had jolted all of his senses high. He sniffed the air and immediately wished he hadn't. He'd been sucking in the reek of his clothes, off and on, since he'd shut himself up in the cab, and it brought back to mind his wrestling around in the dead glop that could not have been, would not have been, absolutely was not, Katielynn. A deep, nagging tingle marked an alarm that had suddenly switched on in his guts.

And then a sound. Boyd had felt the wheels pick up some rocks off the shoulder. They clacked off the rims as the tires spit them out of the way. His brows came together in concentration to look, listen, smell, and think over the painful thumping of his heart.

Boyd hated to admit it, especially coming as it was just on the heels of having conjured Katielynn to mind, but as the rattle of dispersing gravel grew fainter, the other noise gained ground—a muted drag, scraping against metal and a soft thump, coming from behind him, but nowhere near the tires.

His foot forgot its job on the accelerator and the truck slowed to a crawl. He looked again into the rearview mirror, at a red and grimy smudge raked across the back window. He knew full well that it hadn't been there a few moments ago. He also knew a more complete analysis was due, and right soon at that, but somehow his mind was still stuck on the notion that Katielynn shouldn't have any red left in her.

Boyd let the truck drift to a stop on the shoulder, eyes glued to the mirrored view behind him. The last of the streetlights were a block in the distance, but still close enough to throw wet glints off the smear on the glass. Boyd had never fainted in his life, but as a blackness rose up to blot out the view of the street behind him, his heart squeezed down small and hot in his chest. He found that, somehow, unmanly or not, a forced nap might not be the worst thing he could think of at the moment.

The trail of muck on the window disappeared into the rising shadow. The harder he stared, the more he wasn't at all sure he was still awake. The black void moved and, in doing so, betrayed its edges. Boyd's attention shifted closer to home. He found his own eyes in the mirror, strange and double exposed, his own face eclipsed by a human-shaped shadow that didn't quite match up in size or contour to his own. Two men materialized, overlaid in the same dim reflection.

As hard as he'd started to wish for it, unconsciousness didn't rescue him, and only because he had to, Boyd sucked in a dose of sour air. To his horror, he was left stranded in his seat, very much awake with his heart banging to drown out every other sound, staring through bloody glass into the furious glare, reflected back into his own eyes from someone behind him in the truckbed.

Spirit totems are usually grand things: eagles, bears, rushing rivers; any number of elemental or noble symbols. Jason's soul, though, was probably best represented by a bit of rope: a bundle twisted in on itself, a stringy thing, terribly easily knotted. And as such, he now understood the tension at the center of an evenly matched tug-of-war.

The undead Ford Watts hadn't been successful in his crafty break for the truck, not all the way to behind the wheel, anyway. By her gasp alone, Jason knew he wasn't the only one seeing the camel work boot as it dropped stealthily under the sight line of the side wall. And he found that he was dragged exactly neither way by the pull of doing the right thing, striving as it was against the hundred ways he could still slither away from his problems. So, in lieu of a decision, he choked the life out of the steering wheel and let Leah's concern for the policeman drag them forward.

"Oh, no! Go! Go! Help him!" she cried.

The truck was almost out of sight faster than seemed the least bit safe, and when counting up horse legs, you wouldn't bet on Leah's car in a race. But the gate had opened and race they did. Their route rode a plain stretch of thoroughfare, straight through to an eventual corner of town, then out into a series of mild hills, each rise blocking the long view. Jason's dread ran ahead, cresting each intersection and knoll before them. The thought of what it would mean to catch up to the truck kept nudging Jason's foot off the accelerator, and Leah countered every lag with a howled prompt to go faster.

"Oh, God. This is all my fault," she wailed.

"*Your* fault? How could this be your fault?"

"Detective Watts wouldn't have even come except for me."

"Huh? Who knows? Maybe someone saw Boyd Montgomery and called the police, or saw me—" He stopped just before the *maybe someone saw me digging* slipped out. Regardless, why *had* Ford Watts come? Why had any of them come?

In getting the body out of the ground, the night was always going to have been traumatically unpleasant. Jason had signed on for that and had already made the down payment in nightmares for the privilege of even trying to move Harris out of the way. But the intersection of everyone's purposes had gone all the way to end-of-the-line disastrous, and he couldn't help but wonder beyond his normal agnosticism. What the hell was happening here? Was there a higher power drawing a line under his life as he'd lived it? Was there ever any intervention? Or better (or worse) yet, was it all preordained?

"Saw you . . . what?" Leah asked.

Panic brushed against the top of Jason's throat again, closing it up like a tickled flytrap.

"Nothing."

His little slipup spiked down through his middle, and he felt her staring, her eyes heating up the side of his face. He hunkered deeper into the seat. He wasn't cut out for this in any extended play, no matter that he'd proved quite good at faking it for short bursts.

"I don't know," he said. "Maybe someone saw me run out after you. I mean you *did* drive up and park an unfamiliar car on the street in the middle of the night, right? Maybe it worried the neighbors." He tried on a Detective Bayard-style pause and felt the power of it, but none of the rightness. *Low blow, Mr. Getty.* He belatedly tried to soften it. "But still, that doesn't make it your fault."

"We're losing him," she said.

Way up ahead, a curve and a hill swallowed the truck again. The options rolled over Jason's perfect tightrope, a unicycle high-wire act—with no net and a storm gale blowing through the big top. He was sorely worried about anything that pulled them closer to the moment of having to do something, anything. And he was well aware that his worry was some sort of metaphysical catalyst for fiasco.

He'd said so himself, everything he did was the wrong thing. So how long could he get away with doing nothing? He didn't know. How much gas was there left in the tank? How bad would the next wrong words out of his mouth make him look? And there was always the odd telephone pole to plow into. He cut his eyes to check that Leah had her seat belt on.

"Jason, look!"

The final hilltop gave way to a mile of road, plumb-straight, the yellow dividing line spearing through the night under the headlights. Far ahead, a set of taillights flared under braking, tilted around a right turn, and vanished.

22

THE EVOLUTION of a species takes millennia, but dread can leap from a single-celled organism to an agile, nagging parasite in minutes. By the time Maggie had hung her sweater back on its hook in the closet, she was already launching into an argument with the strong urge to raise the alarm.

"Maggie Watts, if you stir up the night shift for nothing, Ford'll have your head."

Tessa lifted her nose from the kitchen floor at the outburst.

If he's still in the head-having business. The voice ringing in her mind's ear feigned cool detachment; hinting at the bleakest possible outcome with the light, maddening touch of spider's feet.

"That's ridiculous. He hasn't been gone that long."

Tessa looked from Maggie to the door, clearly perplexed by the one-sided conversation.

But it's the middle of the night. Wouldn't he have called?

"Yes, it *is* the middle of the night, which might be exactly *why* he hasn't called. He no doubt thinks I'm sleeping like any sensible person would be at this hour."

You're probably right. Maggie held her breath to see if she'd scored the point and made peace with herself. *But he knows you; knows you'd worry.*

She didn't respond right away. Maggie was not fond of arguing, especially with the part of herself that sounded more than a bit like Sister Patricia Ignatius, the only haughty, habited hater of children who had taught at St. Joseph's Primary Academy. And Maggie was polite, always. She didn't speak out of turn, even when debating her own dark side, nor did she forge ahead before she'd thought her comebacks through.

Instead, she made tea and tried to ignore the ticking mantel clock. She retrieved the telephone from its cradle and fetched a stash of chocolate/cashew snack mix from a covered saucepan at the back of the pots-and-pans shelf. Glancing again and again at the receiver didn't make it ring. She stirred milk into her tea and wiggled her finger through the nuts to root out the chocolate pieces. No message icon appeared from the voice mail, but Maggie dialed into the system all the same, just to be sure. She stared deep into the pattern of the stone countertop and tapped scattered salt from the shiny surface to her tongue.

"He would have called by now, wouldn't he?"

Sister Patricia said nothing.

"If I call the station looking for him at this hour and it turns out he's over there having a laugh with the guys, or if he's on the road helping some stranded motorist out of a ditch, they'll say he's got a mother hen, not a wife."

Wouldn't want that.

"I'll just give him a half an hour more."

Of course.

The voice had its pacing down to a science, and Maggie

knew the full stop was hardly an indication that the debate was over. She relented and ate a nut while she waited, as there appeared to be no more chocolate.

Honestly, what could happen in thirty minutes anyway?

The cashew paste in Maggie's mouth was suddenly cloying and difficult to swallow. She was surprised to see that her mug was empty.

It's gotten quite cold out tonight. Unseasonable even.

The clock's patient clicking grated away. Maggie scrolled through the phone-book entries on the speed-dial. "I can at least just give Tim a call. He'll forgive me. Christine would do the same if he'd gone AWOL in the middle of the night. They'll understand."

Tim Bayard would have woken up at half-past dead sounding as if he'd just knotted the crispest double Windsor the world had ever seen and was still running smartly ahead of schedule. As it was, he was simply sleeping, so he was good to go when Maggie called. His wife never even heard the phone ring.

"This is Bayard."

"Tim, I'm so sorry to call this late. This is Maggie Watts."

"No problem, Maggie. What do you need? Everything all right?"

He closed himself into the walk-in closet, his voice low, but never wavering, as he jostled into his jeans and T-shirt. He wanted his wife and daughter to stay sleeping and for Maggie to hear only soothing reassurance while she gave him the details, his own mind racing ahead.

"So he didn't say where he'd spoken to this woman you

met in the park? The office, maybe? Was it a new complaint
he'd taken?"

Maggie's sigh was heavy with self-disgust. "I didn't
even ask."

"It's okay. I'll try to get him on the radio. I'll make like
I needed something and I'll call you right back once I've
found him. All right?"

The pause bothered Bayard.

"Okay, Tim. Thank you so much. I know I'm being
ridiculous."

"Maggie, how worried are you?"

"I'm okay."

But it rang down the line as a mannequin *okay,* the kind
to hang your happy coat on, seeing as you're not wearing
it at the moment.

"No, you're not," Bayard said. "You know, Ford always
wears his lucky socks whenever he buys a lottery ticket and
laughs at himself for it. But, he's not kidding when he goes
miles out of his way to check out things that have weighed
on your mind."

"He does that?" Tears crowded tightly at the top of
Maggie's throat, driving her voice up an octave.

Tim pulled the loops of his shoelaces tight and tiptoed
from the closet and out the bedroom door. "Yeah, he does.
And I have yet to write the man off as a fool."

"I'm silly. I get jumpy all the time. Ford knows that. It's
never anything."

"Yeah, but it's also never Ford who you worry about." Tim
began the hunt for his police radio under and in between
the stacks of papers on the desk in the den. "Stay by the
phone. I'll call you in the next fifteen minutes."

*

Tim Bayard, for the first time in a few days, held both his switched-on phone, in its shiny new belt clip, and his radio. As he'd suspected, the combo wasn't the cure-all everyone seemed to think it was. Neither of the gadgets raised a response from Ford. The little screens and display lights stared back at him blankly. Nothing chirped or vibrated or squawked with any news. Tim called the dispatch desk.

"Can you put the word out that if anyone sees Ford, or hears from him, to have him give me a ring?"

"Try him at home. He's not working tonight," said the dispatcher.

"I realize that, but he's not there."

"Is there a problem?"

"Not that I know of. I just need to talk to him," said Bayard.

"Will do, Detective. I'll give the heads-up."

With that, Ford became missing in Bayard's mind. He had never been one to deliver solemn news over wires if he could help it, even when he had them at his disposal, so he left a note for his wife, donned a jacket, and drove over to the Wattses' house.

Practice fretting had made Maggie somewhat of an expert, and oddly, it was worth something. With Tim having paired his concern with hers, there was no satisfaction in the I-told-you-so from Sister Patricia in her head, but it also didn't take the knees out of her. Maggie knew how to bear up in the face of distress. She'd done it hundreds of times in rehearsal.

Bayard broke the brooding quiet between them. "He could call at any minute."

"I know."

"And even if he doesn't, there are a lot of reasons why he could be out of contact. Not all of them are dire."

"I know."

"If it was a breakdown or even an accident, we'll hear something soon," Tim said, as if she'd argued his reasonings.

"I know."

"You okay?"

Maggie managed a small smile. "I am. I just don't want to move. Somehow, sitting in this chair, right now, with this cup of tea, well, as far as I know, nothing terrible has happened." Her cup had gone tepid at half full, because even though she felt thirsty, she was reluctant to see it empty, hesitant to advance the scene forward to the need to put it down on the cocktail table or to get up again and refill it. She extended no invitation to what came next.

Bayard's needs, however, played out differently. He'd taken up pacing. "Maggie, I think I'm going to go drive around a little bit. Ford wouldn't have gone far without telling you. That's not like him."

"Take Tessa." The words had leapfrogged her logic filter and left her stunned and a little pink in the cheeks, but attached to the idea, nonetheless.

"What?"

"I don't know. It's just—" There was no explanation waiting its turn at the back of her throat, but the notion still begged attention. "Will you just take her with you?"

"Maggie, you don't want to be here alone."

"She's Ford's dog."

"I'm just going to be in the car."

With the heavy blush of looking foolish already well under way, Maggie's dedication to this impulse held its ground without cringing. "Ask her. Ask her if she wants to go."

Tim wasn't a dog person. His wife and daughter kept cats, replacing one snobby furball with another, sometimes even in twos or threes, as they died or ran off. He moved them aside when he wanted to sit down and sometimes scratched their ears if they deigned to come near, but he never spoke to them. In twenty years, he couldn't remember having even discussed the pros and cons of adding man's best friend to the Bayard household. It wasn't that he disliked them, he'd just never felt the need.

He looked from Maggie to Tessa, feeling ridiculous, yet obligated to their anxiety, both as a friend and as a cop run fresh out of good ideas. There was no kind way to get out of it. He could feel the dog's eyes on him and dragged his gaze to sink into the golden-brown patience there.

He swallowed past the lump of absurdity in his throat. "What do you say, Tess? You want to go with me?" Bayard kept an eye out for some signal from Maggie, some small gesture that would betray a trained maneuver.

But Maggie, hands in her lap, only spoke to Tessa. "Do you want to go look for Daddy?"

In answer, Tessa left Maggie's side to stand at Bayard's knee, her tail sweeping a slow arc of alliance around his legs.

Bayard laughed in spite of himself. "It's like she knows what we're saying." He ran his hand along the smooth curve of her head.

Maggie drank down a mouthful of cold tea. "I never stop being amazed by what she understands."

The dregs in her cup stared back at her, throwing light up the sides of the china and into the tears stacking up at the edges of her lashes. She drank the rest to buy a moment of privacy behind the cup's rim. Left with an empty cup and no way to make time wait any longer, she set it down and walked Tim and Tessa to the door.

They had circled the park and cruised the town grid without success or inspiration. Back in the park, Bayard gnawed his knuckles in concentration. Tessa sighed from the passenger seat.

"What? You're tired of me already?" he said.

Tessa panted back and looked sympathetic.

"Well, it's your move, smarty-pants."

Tessa's brows peaked and her dog-smile widened.

"I'm serious. Where should we look? Talk to me."

Her eyes darted to the window and back shyly, embarrassed for him.

"I know you don't talk. So let's do this telepathically." Bayard closed his eyes. "Send me a thought. Some doggy wisdom." He opened one eye at her. "Come on, Tess. You're not even trying." He settled back into his headrest, eyes squinched tight. "Send me a message."

Then his eyes flew open. "A message," he said again, and reached for his phone.

Tim dialed into his voice mail and advanced through several recordings, listening only for the time stamp and Ford's voice. He didn't find any, so he went back to the beginning, through the most recent messages. Leah Tamblin had called three times that afternoon, announcing her intentions and advising him of her progress en route to Stillwater, specifically, to his office. And she fit the description of the woman that Maggie Watts had spoken to, the woman that Ford had gone checking on.

"Tessa, you're a genius."

23

B OYD'S BOOT seemed to have a mind of its own because his brain most definitely hadn't moved past the horror-movie scene rising up in the rearview reflection. A memory or some sense of recognition tapped for attention above the fray, but Boyd's foot wasn't paying any attention at all, and it knocked the pedal to the floor. The apparition in the mirror winked out with a swiftly following thud, and in an instant Boyd was tensed over the steering wheel as if he could beat the front bumper to the next mile marker with his chin.

The truck heaved to the edge of his control with every swell of the road and bounced to the bottom of its springs in the troughs. By the final hill, Boyd's mind was all but blank, and he'd ground his foot into the floor mat as far as it would go. The big truck caught air and gave up whatever grace it had on the landing.

Boyd snapped to attention as the impact shuddered up through the seat. He sawed the wheel and begged for mercy. What he got instead was a gift of physics—the resultant spin somehow didn't bring on a somersault. The truck lurched back to right, and Boyd hit the gas again, but this time with a little restraint poised in his ankle.

He fought himself against straining to listen toward the back of the truck, and he slapped the rearview mirror out of his sight line without looking into it. But as fine as the denial felt, there was still the little problem of inevitability. Try as he might, there was no way to outrun his own tail. He could fly until the gas tank ran dust and air, but at some point he was going to be at a standstill with whatever was in the back of the truck.

He hadn't worked himself up to a solution by the time he'd run out of road. State Route 10 loomed up across his path, with a backbreaking rise of median beyond, cut through with a narrow chute for left-hand turns. But Boyd couldn't bring himself to slide his foot to the brake. He imagined the monster in the back, held to its place only by the speed he was keeping. If he stopped now or slowed down too much, he was sure a ragged arm would punch through the glass and drag him through, and before he could say Jack Robinson he'd be flat on his back at the mercy of something right out of a midnight creepshow.

But something in the gloomy reflection had been familiar, something that made, if not sense, at least a point of reference somewhere deep inside his head. Boyd's fear shifted a little toward the sidecar where his emotions usually rode, and this freed his feet and hands to crank the truck around the right turn at State Route 10 without flipping the whole works. He felt the far side of the truck lighten on its tires, the tilt of the cab teasing his guts into sliding along with its lunatic pitch, but it decided all on its own not to go over or dance a reel.

As he untangled himself from the fear of gravity, and

of the bogeyman besides, Boyd began to appreciate the bind he was in.

"Wills and ways, Boydie," he whispered into the darkness. A fast ache gnawed down through his jaw from clenching it. "First things first."

There was a person in the bed of the pickup truck. Not Katielynn, nor the ghost of Katielynn. *Just a person, Boydie, as there ain't nothing else in this world but men and animals.* And why ever somebody was back there behind him, that person needed to go.

Boyd didn't allow time to second-guess himself. He jerked the wheel to the right edge of the road and slammed the brake and the gear selector together. The truck ground to a spine-rattling stop. A loud bang shuddered through the frame as the monster behind crashed into the bulkhead. Boyd didn't look into the crooked mirror. He didn't even close the door after he sprang from the cab. The keys bristling from between his fingers were the only weapons he'd had time to consider. He brandished a spike-knuckled handful of them as he grabbed over the side wall at the hunched figure, fetal-curled and scrabbling at its own feet.

As majestic as Boyd Montgomery's resolve had always been, the convictions of other people caught him off guard every time. His savage handling of the ride had spurred the person in the back of the truck into a frenzy. Stunned to a white standstill, Boyd noticed two things about the figure lunging over the side wall at him: the man was enormous, and he definitely recognized him.

The cop crashed onto Boyd's chest, crushing the breath out of him. The keys jangled over the pebbles and disappeared into the moonlight shadow of the wheel well. But the cop seemed spent in one charge. He lay slab-heavy over Boyd, lamely trying to push off with trembling arms.

"Bart Montgomery?" he said, his voice hoarse and his breath coming in tight rasps. He pinned Boyd's shoulder to the ground, levering himself up from his sprawl. "What have you done? Have you lost your fool mind? Did you hurt them? What in the name a God were you doing back there?" Ford Watts stretched down his own side, wincing and reaching.

Boyd wiggled his right side free and swung his fist at the policeman's temple, no awe at all spared for the good news that he hadn't killed the cop back at the house. Two knuckles sank into meat, but two bit bone. Boyd whooped in a breath from the pain, only to have it mashed out again by the other man's weight falling back down onto him.

Boyd couldn't pull in sufficient air from under the press of the fallen detective. His ribs ached and sparks burst behind his eyelids. He reached into the darkness, fingers following the replay of the clanging tin notes in his memory until he touched the keys splayed at the far end of his stretch. Quick and nimble in the burn of suffocation, he snatched them up and laid the business end of a longish key under the shelf of the cop's jaw.

"Get offa me, old man. And I do mean now. Git up!" he seethed.

The pair struggled up as one, and Boyd held his advantage with the key. He could feel the other man's pulse rippling along the side of his hand where it pressed against his neck. Darkness bloomed at the edge of Boyd's vision while he recovered his breath. Watts heaved in strained gasps.

The cop's voice had steadied, the key fast-prodding him to somber attention, but he held a protective hand to his belly. "Son, don't take this any further," he wheezed. "I know you're scared. Those government checks ain't that big a deal. Don't make this mistake."

Now that it had come to it, Boyd found, both to his relief and annoyance, that murder wasn't on his mind. He'd suspected it earlier when he hadn't pounded the daylights out of that mealymouthed sissy back at the house. He'd worried at times, mostly alone in bed in the dark, that maybe killing came a little too easily to him. Katielynn flashed in his mind like a single poppy in a green field, not to mention the bold, trespassing hard-dick who'd helped himself to Boyd's happy home, and that one stupid dog that had snarled with more of an edge than Boyd was willing to tolerate. He saw Bart, the twin this man mistook him for, begging with his soft eyes and gentle ways for understanding, for just an ear to take in his troubled thoughts and a brother to share his pain. But this time Boyd's hand didn't ache to twitch deeper. Just now he wasn't angry, or affronted, or even indifferent. He was busy. That was all.

The cop, Watts, was hurting. Boyd heard the injured hitch in his inhale. His own breath he'd been keeping shallow, trying to take in as little of the smell from his clothes as possible. The roll through the dead man and his wrappings would not fade from the foreground of his mind. Given any sliver of attention, every time the reek hit the back of his throat, the thought of it crawled down, soggy and green, into Boyd's empty belly. Waves of sick threatened to buckle his knees.

He shoved Watts with his free hand. "Go on. Git."

Watts fell back a half step, but held the rest of his ground. He warned, "Montgomery."

"Don't make me fight you. Look at you." Boyd shook his head. "You'll lose."

The big man tensed, but for balance or attack, Boyd wasn't quite sure. He clenched the keys and reconsidered the wisdom of letting Watts go. It wouldn't take much to send this cop right through the Pearly Gates. And Boyd could surely make good use of the head start. In the instant he contemplated the deed, he gave up a strike.

Ford Watts launched a wild swing and connected a double blow. Weak as it was, the man was still halfway past six feet tall and sported enough muscle to tote his weight, so Boyd's head rocked back on a jolt that moved him off his spot more than it hurt him. The punch's follow-through caught his arm just below the elbow, and a wicked sting raced up his forearm and numbed his hand. The keys took flight again in a high, glittering arc, clinking out of sight into the blackness under the truck.

The detective staggered away, taking full advantage of the surprise he'd delivered. He loped off, as best he could while clutching his midsection, up the hill and toward the trees.

Bayard didn't try to talk himself out of it. Jason Getty was an iffy link from Leah's arrival in town to Ford's absence, but the nagging idea was bolstered by the messages she had left, which had been demanding in tone, if still reasonably polite in content. She had driven all the way to Stillwater just for more information. She was hell-bent to own all the details, needed to know everything in its precise order to be able to move on. He knew the sort and even admired the moxie. The only things left for her in Stillwater were the case file and the crime scene, and since she wasn't looking at the case file in her car, in the park, in the dead of night . . .

Sitting in Ford's living room hadn't helped. There'd been no word from the station. Driving the town hadn't turned up any cast bread crumbs. The lateness of the hour was a nuisance, but also a fairly reliable shield. Either it would help the situation to look around for Ford and Leah at the crime scene, or Getty would be asleep and left to dream on, none the wiser.

The street in front of Getty's place was deserted—no Ford, no Leah Tamblin. Bayard tested the balance of his reaction, relief against disappointment. He leaned his head back on the headrest and looked out over the last of his ideas.

Bayard had always thought that things watched too long or too intently seemed somehow to watch back. The pressure of staring down a blank-faced house in the dark for more than a few minutes tickled at his common sense. Tendrils of nothing tracked through his hair, raising it at its roots, and stationary objects swore up and down to his peripheral vision that they could move—just a little bit.

People rarely rattled him, though. He could entertain his overactive intuition for hours by reading the fine print of another man's face. But inert things had only the subtext he gave them, which was never a problem unless he had nothing to do except note that the hedges beside him were hunkering down in a suspicious manner. The impromptu stakeout nibbled at his nerves.

He watched a sudden wind in the trees make the night shadows lower and raise over the windows, looking, for his discomfort, like a set of blinking eyes and a mouth flexing fearful or angry in a door-shaped snarl. Enough of that had been already too much to begin with, so he let off the parking brake and slipped the transmission into neutral and steered the car off the curb as it drifted back out of the sight line of the house. Nothing indicated that Jason had heard him. No lights had come on, he'd heard no noises. But Bayard felt better sitting out of the house's challenging stare just the same.

Tessa fidgeted in the passenger seat, unable to get comfortable in the narrow bucket.

"It's okay." He stroked her, fumbling to find ears to scratch without looking away from the street. His gaze bounced between the corner of the house that he could still see and his rearview mirror, and every few seconds he'd snatch a peek at his cell-phone display. No calls. Ford hadn't made it home. Tim's eyes stung for want of blinking. He wouldn't call Maggie until he had something to tell; wouldn't rattle her with news of no news. He shoved back at the prodding feeling that he should be somewhere else.

The air went stale in double time between Tessa's panting and Tim's mulling. He turned the key to spark the battery and ran the windows down. Tessa's immediate whine surprised him. She leaned out the window, rigid, chuffing at the ends of her whimpers.

"What?"

She glanced back to him, then twisted around again to strain at the window, keening high in the back of her throat and punctuating the song with low, whispery barks.

The hairs on Bayard's arm danced in waves. He grabbed a flashlight and looked at Tessa.

"You stay here. I'll be right back. This won't take long." One dog ear cocked doubt in his general direction. "Well, it shouldn't take long, anyway. I hope."

She peaked her brows at him and chewed the air, licking her chops.

"It'll be fine. Don't get all wound up." He squeezed his temples between both hands. "Why am I talking to a dog?" He patted her head. "Gotta go, Tess."

But Tessa had other ideas. Tim opened his door and she bounded out, scrambling right over him, oblivious to the sensitivities of the human male lap. Bayard's breath caught in his throat in a harrowing moment of anticipation between the dog's planting her paw in a safe-ish spot and the inevitability of its sliding into the danger zone at the relaunch. Physics and anatomy collided and Tessa cleared the door in a nimble spring. Bayard groaned and slumped over the steering wheel, sucking in air over gritted teeth, then growling it out again, not much better for the oxygen. Tessa waited for him, tap-dancing and smiling, in the middle of the street. Bayard gripped his knees as the swirling, green pain crawled into his belly and died a slower death than he had time for.

He eased his legs around and stood up, fighting a spine that was still intent on curving a belated protection over his nethers. "Tessa, get back in the car." He scowled at her and flung a guiding finger to the interior. "Go on, now. Back in."

Tessa crouched and chuffed a low, imperative bark.

"Get. Back. In. There."

She bolted off and ran back to the spot of her disobedience and repeated the relay twice, each time taking an additional stride toward Jason's house. Bayard didn't know how to argue with a dog. At this point, he wasn't even sure of the wisdom in it.

"Okay, fine," he said to no one in particular. And to Tessa: "You. Keep quiet."

He clipped the lead onto her collar. "You'd better not just have to pee."

24

LEAH FOUND HERSELF well out of practice of hoping for the best from this night, but she tried to commit to the upside in the scene playing out at the end of the headlights' reach.

Impossibly, Ford Watts was back from the dead. She'd seen a boot in the truck, but still couldn't get all the way to believing that somehow he was okay. Yet there he was, clearly and unmistakably alive, as he stumbled up the hill at the side of the road, clutching his middle. A starburst of butterflies blazed through her, making the blood fizz in her ears. She thought perhaps she was fainting, but instead of black gauze falling around her eyes, she felt wide-awake and poked all over with exclamation points.

Her voice was even more reluctant to leap to hope and she could only whisper, "Jason, look! Up on the ridge! It's Detective Watts!" And on the heels of that: "Oh, God."

Boyd Montgomery, with a rose printed across the front of his shirt, stood up alongside the truck and stared at them, pinned to his place by the headlights. He'd popped into sight from a crouch down near the front tire of Detective Watts's truck.

Leah knew that the rose was out of place, but couldn't slot it into its proper priority. Her head throbbed and her thoughts fuzzed at the edges. Who cared what was on his shirt? What did it matter? But Leah's newborn optimism couldn't build a wall faster than her common sense could tear it down. It wasn't a rose. The man's shirt was covered in blood. Montgomery scanned the ground again as they neared, then bolted up the hill after Ford Watts.

"Jason, look!" she said again.

But Jason didn't look. And he didn't answer her cry either. Instead, Jason sped up.

As they careened past the truck, Leah fell back against her seat and then the passenger window. She twisted around in time to see Montgomery reach the tree line. Her clarity came back online in a hot rush. There was pain left, to be sure. A direct sort of pain, though—burning straight down the offended nerves without distracting every passing thought along the way. If she squinted her eyes, she could think clearly, and beyond that, everything else worked fine. Especially her conscience.

"What are you doing? Stop!"

Jason didn't. He dropped the pedal, which, in turn, dropped Leah's sore head against the glass for that one last crack, this one of the sobering variety.

"Jason, stop!"

And still no response. The car bucked over the rough shoulder of the road and lost its hold on the fine gravel under the tires, the back end flicking like a mermaid's tail to get back onto the asphalt. Then she realized Jason couldn't see. She watched his face in fascination, almost detached from the moment. So strange—cataracts of pure fear fogging clear eyes. They may as well have been bricked over. He stared straight ahead, but whatever he was seeing, it was all much farther away than the band of blacktop spooling out under the headlights.

"Jason," she said, quietly this time, and touched his arm. "What's wrong? You have to stop."

Apparently he didn't.

"Where are you going?"

Jason only shook his head.

"We can't just leave him alone back there! For God's sake, he's hurt!" With the simple statement came a tidal wave of guilt, not unlike, if she had known it, the crippling blame Jason had felt watching her struggle to her feet in his backyard. And like a rogue wave, it slammed into her, dragging salty dread down through the pit of her stomach, drenching her in regret. "Oh, God. We have to help him. We have to go back."

Jason plowed ahead, trying to outrun a nervous breakdown by driving fast and talking faster. "I can't. It's too late."

"Too late for what?" Leah watched the needle of the speedometer nod over to her side of the car.

A crazy giggle bubbled up in Jason's throat. He laughed harder, snorting a little as he came up for air. Then his snickering congealed to a sob.

"You don't even know what you're asking. If I help him, do you think he'll help me?" He darted a look that expected the obvious answer, whatever that could possibly be. Jason shook his head. "I have to keep going. I can drop you somewhere. I'm so sorry," he babbled, squeezing the fight out of the steering wheel as if it meant to jump free.

Leah checked for turns ahead, but they zipped through a featureless black, overdriving the halo of visibility in front of them. By the time they would see a problem, it would already be two seconds too late.

"Calm down," she said. "And, for God's sake, *slow* down. What are you talking about?" He looked terrible. Leah knew the phrase *not a friend left in the world*. She'd said it herself, meaning no harm, to describe sad nobodies. But she'd never believed it, never thought that those people were completely friendless. Not really; not literally.

Jason was utterly alone with something that had taken up a hot and reckless presence in the car, leaving her stranded, also alone, locked out of his reality, but strapped on to its blind ride. "Jason, please. You're scaring me."

The hook of this plea was a brand-new barb. Jason had disappointed Patty, and he'd driven Harris to utter contempt. But as far as he could recall, he'd never scared anyone. It crawled like wasps over his skin. He had accepted, even in bewilderment, the changes that his time with Harris had burned into his character. But not this.

The line, although he couldn't have known it until he'd treaded all over it, was in that Harris had delighted in other people's fear of him, where Jason never could. He looked at Leah again, in hard focus for the first time since he'd tried to set her free in his foyer. It wasn't in him to put her in this kind of danger, to scare her so terribly. Whatever play he'd make, it wasn't this.

He drove on, his foot lightening on the pedal, his shoulders drooping. "Okay." He slowed and made a U-turn in the median and sped back the other way.

Relief wilted Leah and the road rattled up through the suspension, making a trembly, dark blur of the view outside the window. She dug a flashlight from the glove box and prayed they weren't too late.

The last bend in the road straightened out under their tires, and Leah tapped Jason's arm, excited and fast, with her full, flat hand. "Here it is."

Jason bounced over the grass and cut across the opposing lanes. He stopped the car in front of Ford Watts's truck.

Leah squeezed his arm. Jason knew he could just let her go. Take the car and leave her to hunt for Detective Watts alone. But Montgomery was out there. He had been adamant that he meant them no harm, but he'd also said that all he wanted was a car. A good bit of spilled blood since then had painted that little white lie a bright shade of pink.

Would Jason wear that on his conscience, too? Stranding her to watch her own yellow-smiley-face aerial fob fly off into the distance with no explanation and a double murderer closer at hand to her than the help she needed? He wouldn't and he knew it. He'd keep the keys. He'd wait to see what happened. It could still go a few ways.

Leah looked through the car's windows to both horizons, shortened in this stretch of road by the hills ahead and behind, searching for someone to flag down. She twisted in her seat to catch the white glow of headlights spilling over the rise. There weren't any. But they would come. There was always someone.

Just then, moments into hope's triumphant return, a muffled buzz purred against the seat and a song lilted up beside her: a catchy little jingle, a factory-bland, preset ringtone. Jason cried out and wriggled in surprise. His hands swatted at his pocket as if it had caught fire.

Leah couldn't precisely name the reaction that raced up her backbone and exploded into her head like stadium lights. The mutable wave twisted, changed color and temperature as it rose: confusion, shock, some dishwater-dull horror, and all tinged in a sour-sad disappointment.

"You've had a *cell phone* the whole time?"

25

THE HOUSE was completely dark and still, and Jason Getty's car sat locked and empty under the carport. Bayard flicked open the cover snap on his gun holster and somehow couldn't quite muster up feeling silly about it. Something was off. He kept his footfalls careful to preserve the quiet, but he wouldn't stoop to tiptoeing. If his hand had been in his pocket instead atop a .40-caliber pistol, he would have looked every bit the casual neighbor ruled by his dog's bladder. That is until he sidled up to the living-room windows, SWAT-style, for a peek inside. Luckily for Bayard, at that distance from the road, he was all but invisible. Shadows layered the front rooms of Getty's house, but nothing hinted at overtly sinister in the black outlines of the furniture and walls.

Tessa trotted at the length of her leash, changing directions, testing the wind, ears tugged every which way by sounds that Tim couldn't hear. At the side of the house, the breeze delivered the ghost of a reek. Trash? Compost? Tessa was off like a racehorse, dragging Bayard at the end of her strap. He fumbled with the switch on the flashlight and stumbled along behind the dog.

The smell had only to become a fraction stronger before it was unmistakable to Bayard, but by then Tessa had towed the both of them most of the way to the open pit at the back of the yard.

"What the hell?" Bayard flicked the beam over the edge of the hole while Tessa nosed in the dew-damp grass just behind him. Her snuffling went frantic as she dug at the ground, pressing her snout into the soil.

Bayard knelt at her side. "What is it?" He shone the light onto the patch of ground that Tessa raked with her paw and nose. He couldn't see past her. "Hang on, Tessa. Let me see."

She pushed his hand away from her discovery, but Bayard cupped her scuttling muzzle and guided it aside. "Just let me take a look."

The fur of her beard was clumped into sticky strands. His hand cooled where she had painted soggy swirls there, tossing her head to be rid of his hold. He let her go, and the night air lit up the damp in his palm. It was wetter than a dog's nose would have left it, and he didn't have to be an animal expert to know that. He drew the light over his hand and found it smeared with red blood and dirt.

Bayard's instincts hummed in every limb, but the confusion of the puzzle before him left him rooted in place. He traced the flashlight into the trees, then again to the blood on his hand, and over the rear of the house. Midway to the back deck, a shallow mound in a patch of flattened grass caught the beam and locked his wrist. Tessa took the light like a zip line and ran out the slack of her lead.

"What the hell?" In the back of his mind, Bayard began keeping track of how often he'd say that this night.

For Tessa, the ground from the front of the house to the back was tangled with trails. The rush of sorting the scents from all the many fresh, crisscrossing paths buzzed through her brain so that she had to work to concentrate, a rare thing for a mind so used to sifting intangibles.

The pit had scared Tim. The smell of dead things almost always spiked ammonia-fear from people, even if they didn't run. Smells didn't frighten Tessa. People had to be sized up, and animals had to be chased, befriended, or sometimes intimidated, but smells, for Tessa, were the best source of the daily news. Some smells felt like a smack to the nose, and some made her drool and beg, and then some needed to be marked over with a squat. Tessa understood all these things and minded accordingly.

For all that needed minding here, it had been a busy news day indeed. She didn't know why Tim passed right by, but they always did, the people. The yard was jumbled and too busy with trampling and bleeding when people were usually asleep. But she was not afraid, because the top story of the night was recorded right here in the grass. Whatever else might be wrong, her master had walked this very ground, and she would drag Tim to understanding if she had to.

It took some convincing to pull Tessa back to the car, but back they had to go. Tim's phone and radio were still inside, and it was time to send up the alarm.

"I'm going on in," Tim said to the officer en route. "Get here fast, but no lights or noise. The last thing I need is the whole neighborhood out in their jammies gawking at this mess. Hurry."

Moments later, Tim Bayard stood at Jason Getty's front door, finger poised above the doorbell. He had never underestimated the value of the simplest, most obvious etiquette. With all that he'd found in the backyard, he could have crashed through with a battle cry and been excused the dramatics, but over and over in his career, he'd followed the civilest path to often surprising results. A startled bad guy was an off-balance bad guy, and nothing is more startling to a red-handed outlaw than a polite knock at the door or a courteous *please* and *thank you*. They never saw it coming.

His phone had been connected to a patrolman named Mike whom Bayard only knew as an overstuffed uniform that he'd passed in the hall on occasion. Now Mike kept Tim company on an open channel.

Tim, in just above a whisper, brought the details into order for Mike. "This guy, Getty, he's a real regular. It shouldn't be a big deal." Saying it out loud, however quietly, to another person, snapped the circle closed in Tim's mind.

He'd talked to Jason Getty for a handful of hours and never once left feeling as if he'd asked the right questions. The Montgomery/Reynolds case seemed simple enough. Getty had given them all the right access and accommodations. Yet, here they were. When "all right" was completely wrong, everything was off—every smile a beat too late, every cadence just the slightest bit wobbly. A pretender's back was always so straight that his shirt sat funny on his shoulders. When they'd spoken, Jason's eyes had strained to drift, but he'd forced them to stay, irises trembling like a weakling pinned under a two-hundred-pound bench press. Jason Getty was afraid of cops and in the way that didn't seem entirely general. For the benefit of his new partner, Bayard kept the conclusion simpler.

"He's been really meek. Pretty helpful, to be fair. But somehow . . . I dunno. It's never really fit. I knew this was going to get upended. Something's been wrong the whole time. Just stay with me, Mike."

"I'm right here till I'm right there, Detective."

"Thanks."

Bayard rang the bell and immediately followed it with a mild volley from the side of his fist to the door. He craned back to look through the dining-room window for a better view of the main hall, scanning the shadows for movement. He repeated the sequence. Nothing.

Tessa's ears were flat against her head and tension swept back through her in waves that pulled her rigid as a stringed arrow.

"Let's try around back," Bayard suggested.

Tessa led the way.

At the back door of Jason Getty's house, Tim got more of the same from the door—a whole lot of nothing. But Tessa had gone frantic on the landing, prancing and woofing, shoving her nose into Tim's hand.

He ran his other hand across his mouth, then readied his pistol. He sniffed, wished he hadn't, and huffed out the offending breath hard. "Ready?" he said to the dog.

Tessa obligingly skittered left and right and gargled a hushed bark.

"Still with me, Mike?"

"Yep. Sure you don't want to wait? I mean, you know Ford's not there, right? And you said yourself it's dead quiet."

"His truck isn't here, but you should see the dog."

"So?"

"She's Ford's dog."

"Okay, well, do what you gotta."

Bayard clipped the phone to his belt, speaker on, and hammered once again on the wood, then on the glass of the back-door window. He looked to Tessa and she panted her enthusiasm. She tossed her head and rocked back on her spring-loaded legs, a dog nod if ever he'd seen one. Which he hadn't. Bayard shrugged, then drove his foot into the door, just below the handle, with the full force of his leg behind it.

The whole works took surprisingly little effort; the door bowed under only a flimsy safety catch at the top. It gave way with the sharp snap, banging open and sending Detective Bayard spilling over the threshold. He pedaled his legs to stay ahead of a face-plant and barely won out over his momentum, keeping everything upright.

But Tessa nearly toppled him anyway in her dash for the main hallway. She didn't wander. She didn't snuffle along the linoleum or linger to twitch her ears. The weak light from the front windows lit everything to a scale of gray shadows, showing a clear and empty path from the kitchen through to the front entryway. To Bayard, the house smelled faintly of the decay in the yard. He couldn't know what Tessa sensed, but the chills that bent every hair on his body to full attention were knowledge aplenty.

Tessa had fallen to her haunches against the wall in the corridor, her forelegs out stiff to allow her to crane as tall as her neck would go. Her throat rippled the sound forward, up to the ceiling, ricocheting off the walls, raking raw all who heard her: a howl of pure misery.

The ringing cry scrubbed every thought from Bayard's head. Never mind that it was terrifying on some primal level to be blind and deaf to whatever horror Tessa sensed; just the sheer sound of it made white static spike and hiss in the place where his logic should have been. Her warning wail set fire to his fight-or-flight instinct, but it burned at cross-purposes with his own weak senses. Nothing was there. Even sand through his fist at least let him know what he couldn't grasp. What only she could know sparked a tremble that sped through him.

"What the hell?" Bayard dropped to a crouch. "Tessa, what?" Her eyes were squinched tight, the sound rising from deep within her to blast the air with her anguish. The noise careened off the walls and through his head.

"Tessa, stop." Bayard wrapped his arms around the dog. He felt the shudders climbing through her, so he hugged her to him, his face buried in her fur. "Tessa, please." Her baying rang on until Tim's eyelashes were wet with tears that he hadn't felt crest.

Then she stopped suddenly enough to leave a hole in the hallway, so stark it tipped Bayard right off-balance. He caught himself with his hand against the floor and raised his face to Tessa's.

Bayard had easily believed that man's best friend could be taught to understand basic commands. He'd seen for himself how clever dogs could be at communicating their wants and needs, and at anticipating what their masters might require of them. But whenever it had been suggested that a dog could read a man's mind, or even bypass the internal chatter and scan a soul, he'd always indulged the idea with the same nod he reserved for UFO sightings and ghosts on the stairs.

But he forgot to remember that he didn't believe in that sort of thing once Tessa's gaze crawled through his own eyes and into the solitary confinement of his mind. For the briefest of moments she was there, their two wills separated only by a thin glass of silence. In the warm amber quiet of her eyes, understanding glowed between the crashing surges of his heartbeat. His scalp tingled as it crawled in awe at the realization that to the very edge of actual dialog he was, for a moment, not alone with his thoughts.

She opened her mouth and took Bayard's wrist in her teeth and curled around on herself, drawing Tim's arm over her. He hugged her and wiped at his eyes, but she butted him off. She repeated the process, wrist in mouth, curling herself into a comma.

"What the hell's going on?" asked the other officer from the phone on Tim's belt. Tim could finally hear him again.

"I don't know, Mike." Bayard stood, and immediately Tessa pulled him back through the motions again, curled nose to tail with Bayard's wrist gently, but firmly, in her teeth. He watched her insistence and precision, but kept talking. "Getty's not here, or he's really good at playing possum. I'm going to have a look around, but I'm not touching anything."

"Got it. I'm nearly there."

Tim took a step to leave the foyer, but Tessa wouldn't allow it. She blocked his way, pressing her side against his shins. She had his wrist again wound around herself.

Bayard tried to step away, but Tessa bounded in front of him, mouthed his wrist, harder this time, and ducked to the side. Then she bounced away from him and barked. She pounced on him to repeat it once more, complete with the punctuating woof.

"What are you doing, girl?" He tried on an authoritative tone. "Tessa, come."

She barked back, unimpressed.

Clearly she wasn't going stop her interference, so Bayard disconnected from Mike and called Maggie.

"Did you find him?" She hadn't even said hello.

"Not yet. I don't even know if Ford was here or not. But Tessa's acting really weird and I can't get her moving or get past her."

"What is she doing?"

Bayard explained, and fifteen miles away, Maggie sank to the floor. "Oh, God. He's not there? Are you sure?"

"Maggie, what? What is she trying to tell me?"

"She does that when something's wrong with Ford, like when he suffers one of his angina attacks. Whenever he has one, or is about to have one, this is what she does. She knows it's coming. She does it to him or she does it to me to make me follow her to him. She did it—oh Tim—she did it when Ford fell off the stepladder last year. Remember when he chipped his elbow?"

"Hang on, Maggie. Don't go all the way to the finish. He's not here. No one is. His truck's not here either, so that could be good. Call the hospital to check if he's come in. We're going to find him."

"Don't wait so long between calls, Tim."

"I'm not going to call you and send your heart into your throat if I haven't got anything to say. No news is just no news, okay? I promise. I'm out here. Know that. I'm not going home until I find him. Just check the hospital and let me know once you have."

Bayard knelt in front of Tessa. They stared at each other. "Tess, I don't know how to talk to you." He offered his wrist. "Take me to Ford. If you can."

She rocked back against locked forelegs and barked again, then sprinted for the front door, then pulled toward the left until she zagged right and whined, pawing a small, dark box before doubling back to puff over a spot in the rug.

Tim tried the hall switch, but it clicked dead in the wall. Stuck with only the garish pointer of his halogen flashlight, he traced Tessa's pacing. His beam showed blood on the floor to the left, and then to the right, he knelt to look more closely at a cell phone, battery side up in the carpet. This evidence needed to be left where it was.

Tim flicked open his phone and first selected Jason Getty's number from his call list, then watched the phone on the floor. The tone in his ear rang through to the default electronic mailbox, no recorded greeting. Grim to the back teeth, Tim dialed Ford from his speed-dial roster. He held his breath for a hopeful interval, but the phone on the floor lit up, twisted half a turn, and Beethoven's Fifth sang out into the too quiet house.

Tessa bayed to break the walls just ahead of her heart.

26

"I FORGOT!" Jason blurted.

It was cold-water bracing and strangely anchoring for Leah that anything in this hellish night could feel familiar. She'd been primed a dozen times for this brand of flimsy con in every one of Reid's absurd reaches for distance from his sins.

"You *forgot* that you had a cell phone." While she fit the puzzle edges of the last few hours together, a reasonable fear fought for ground against the distinct and disorienting impression that she had nothing at all to fear from Jason. So instead, Leah was furious. "Police and ambulances, ours for the asking, in your pocket the whole time and you forgot?"

She ground her teeth over his silence and set loose the simple test through them. "So call 911, then."

He made no move toward his pocket.

"You won't," she said.

"I can't. Please."

Leah scrambled out of the car and Jason mirrored her to face off over the hood. No set of headlights was anywhere in sight, nothing to offer the hope of any help, but for the first time all evening, since the moment her trip to Reid's temporary grave had gone haywire, Leah felt like herself. She wanted answers even more than she wanted a white knight or an aspirin.

"Oh my God," she said, her realizations now steadily thudding into place in time with the pulse in the side of her head. "I am so stupid."

Leah's eyes ran back and forth, snatching to the foreground bits of the scene that had brought the two of them out into the night together. "You were filthy before you fought with him, and then he said he didn't do it—oh, yeah, I know! I heard everything." She lobbed Jason's startled look back at him. "You were quiet and I was falling all over myself, but sound carries real well when the whole goddamned world is holding its breath. I didn't know what the hell he was playing at, but *he* wasn't playing, was he?"

Jason gaped like a fish horrified at drinking air.

"Did you hit me?"

"I—Leah, if you'll just let me—"

"It's a pretty simple question: Did you hit me?"

"It was an accident."

The thrill of wringing him with questions registered on a scale from unkind to unwise, but she couldn't seem to help herself. The Q&A burned away the pain and the terror, and it kept the rest of the night at bay. She was fairly certain that whatever came next for the foreseeable future was going to be chock-full of things she didn't want to see and didn't want to do, so she kept tossing questions onto the bonfire instead.

"Were you going to kill me?"

"I would never hurt anyone!"

And there it was. The rarest specimen of falsehood—the elusive, nocturnal, true lie. Leah considered herself the reluctant curator of a world-class collection of honest untruths; most of them she'd stockpiled were just different variations on Reid's I-love-yous.

"Well, there's a fucking relief."

"It was self-defense!"

"Hitting me was self-defense?"

"No, no, the other—the—" His hands fell to his sides. "Harris. In the tarp."

"I don't want to know."

"I'm not a bad person. I didn't tell the police because I was afraid, but I'm not like that."

Not like that. Leah wondered what *like that* would look like and thought of Boyd Montgomery. He would likely also have a good story justifying why he'd shot Reid and his own wife. But would he ever wear a look like Jason's? Would it fit his face? Would she believe it if he even tried? It was difficult to imagine. Jason could have left her to Boyd half a dozen times already and he hadn't. She wanted to make less of that fact, but she couldn't.

In spite of herself, a faint pity welled up, vying with anger as the source of the weight in her chest. She sighed, disgusted, and with herself for starters. Out of practice, she didn't have her usual stamina for confrontation. A breeze rolled through her empty fingers where Reid's hand hadn't been for so long.

"You know what? Prove it. Show us how much you're 'not like that.'" She scanned the tree line and pointed. "He went in about there. He can't have gotten that far." She thrust the flashlight into his hands. "Jason, hurry. You just go find him, and I'll do the rest."

"The rest?"

"I'll get Detective Watts to the hospital. You can take the truck and go wherever you need to go. Just get in there after him, bring him out, and you can run or whatever you were going to do."

"Why? Why would you do that?"

"Because if you help me and this doesn't work out for you, it was never going to. You had a plan tonight and it was my stupid luck to fall into it. But whatever. You have to get in there now or it'll be too late. Jason, just hurry. Run. I'll stay with the car."

Jason recoiled as if she'd slapped him. "Go after him by myself? You won't. You'll leave. As soon as you get a few minutes to yourself, you're going to freak out, Leah. You're going to drive away and leave me."

"No, I won't. Right now I want to help the detective more than I want to burn you. You can take the keys, if you want."

"Yes, you will. You'll run. You'll flag someone down." He looked away, red to the ears. "I would." She heard him swallow. His nose went red and his eyes watered. "And anyway, what if Montgomery comes back? You'd be here all alone. You can't be out here by yourself. It's not safe."

"Not safe? Not safe here? You can't be serious."

His eyebrows leaned plaintively up his forehead. Again, Leah sifted her thoughts for fear of him and came up empty. Something, or a domino row of somethings, must have tipped the world on its head for him. She couldn't disbelieve him or pry what she did know of him away from a nagging inclination to sympathy.

"Look, I don't know what I'll believe tomorrow, Jason, but I swear to God, I won't be stopping anywhere until I get to the hospital. It'll give you time. This has nothing to do with what you've told me, anyway. I promise. I was never going to be able to go into the woods. I just can't—I can't go in there."

"You have to. You have to come with me."

"You're not hearing me. I cannot go into the woods, Jason. I can't go into the woods because I will freak out if I do."

"What are you talking about?"

When Leah was ten years old, she had been on a camping trip, a rare family outing. While her mother and stepfather made a booze run, her oldest stepbrother, lazy and stoned, had bribed Leah from her splashing at the lake's edge to go back to the campsite for his radio. He'd offered $4, and then sweetened the deal, since she wasn't a baby anymore, with the grown-up dare of the swill-half of the last beer from his secret stash.

It had been wickedly hot, the flies buzzing overloud in her ears and the forest floor tilting and wobbling under her feet. Leah had kept to the shade, just off the path, as the alcohol zipped through her virgin veins. Within half an hour, she was hopelessly lost. They didn't find her until the next morning, and then only with the help of a handful of park rangers.

Since that day Leah had never been able to stomach beer and had not gone deeper than three strides into a stand of trees.

A quick version of the tale told, and her palms were already slick with sweat. Jason stared at her for more, eyes expectant for a bigger and better reason, but she didn't have one. In the face of Jason's titanic fear of whatever he'd done and how close he was to being collared for it, her phobia had been skimmed and shown shallow. At the brass base of it, even without Jason's demands, it wasn't a very good excuse to sit in the open, alone and concussed. Not with Boyd Montgomery on the loose.

"Goddammit." She pounded the hood of the car with both fists and yelled, "Just tell me one thing!"

Frozen in the expectation of a rhetorical hailstorm, Jason didn't even breathe.

"Just tell me I didn't take up with the wrong fucking murderer!" Leah snatched the flashlight out of his hand and hurled the door closed with a force well set to break the frame.

Jason's voice box felt folded into an origami swan and it couldn't be trusted to deliver more than a papery quack, so he followed her, silent and ungainly in the wake of her fury.

Leah gripped the light and started sweeping the spaces between trees. "Detective Watts! It's Leah Tamblin! We want to help you. Please tell us where you are. Detective? Mr. Watts? Please! Can you hear me?"

Jason and Leah crunched off into the woods, through the ankle-deep drifts of old leaves. He stayed close to the light and to Leah's back and he felt the last opportunity for his confession zipping up behind them. He'd never have another chance to explain. One way or another, it soon wouldn't matter anymore.

Jason cleared his throat and, in a low voice, started his tale.

Tessa's nose never left the ground between the house and the carport, her direction tugged this way and that by an invisible string of the past, over the traces where people had lumbered and shed the elemental ghosts of their intentions.

Her head snapped up and she bolted down the driveway. At the street she turned to the right, but slowed straightaway from a gallop to a trot.

Tessa swung her head back to Tim. Mike had joined him, arriving just in time to find that the initial search of the house had not turned up many clues as to what had happened. The dog loped back to Bayard, and she touched his wrist with her teeth and flew back down toward the street, taking the right turn with a paw-pedaling, graceful dog-skid.

The deliberateness wasn't lost on Mike either. "Why does she keep doing that?"

"I have no idea. Ford's wife thinks it has something to do with him. This is nuts. Mike, it's no good us standing around doing nothing." Tim looked back to the house with longing. Wood and shingles. Closets and rooms and evidence. Investigating thin air and dog sense was not his specialty. "All I've got is a dog going berserk." He puffed out an exasperated breath. "I'm going to walk with her a bit. See if I can figure out what she's doing."

But when Bayard tried to walk down the road at her side, Tessa reversed her direction and made for his car as if her tail were on fire.

"What now, Tessa?" Tim bellowed before catching himself. He grimaced a silent apology to the dark houses at hand and waited for the neighbors' lights, which never came. He'd got away with one, and his tension was better for the small release. Tessa stood by the car, wagging urgently, dancing in little hops.

Bayard met Mike halfway up the driveway with Tessa padding at his heels. "Mike, do me a favor, just wait for the team and keep the peace once they get here. Watch the place until I get back. You don't have to do anything. Just watch. Call me on the radio if anything happens."

"What's going to happen?"

"How should I know? I'm going to take the damned dog for a drive, but I need you here in case I'm making a mistake." Bayard bit his lip, immediately regretting saying it. He peeked to see if she had heard. He felt guilty for having even thought it. Following Tessa's lead wasn't wrong. Their progress was only banging up against that barrier of silence that made theirs an inexact partnership. She knew things he couldn't begin to guess, but he *did* believe now that she could help if only he could follow her the right way. He had no doubt they'd understood each other's purpose, but the gap in being able to convey the details could render the whole marvel completely useless. And Tim Bayard was far from used to throwing himself down rabbit holes.

As he buckled himself behind the wheel, he reached over to pat her head in apology. Tessa pulled away from her rigid windshield vigil long enough to lick his hand, but only just. She drilled through the darkness on the street ahead, seeing and knowing what Bayard could barely guess. They left Getty's house behind and crawled down Old Green Valley Road, two sets of eyes and ears, but more of one mind than Bayard could ever remember feeling before.

Boyd groped the front of his shirt, poking around for a sore spot or, heaven forbid, a hole in his middle. The oncoming headlights had lit up his shirt like Christmas, and kind of like Christmas, it had been mostly a field of white and red. The woods had got him out of sight faster than the road would have, and he just plain didn't know the lay of

the land on the far side of the median. Route 10 marked
the boundary of his expertise, so he'd run to where his feet
could think for him. At any cost, he was glad to be clear of
those two maniacs who would have mowed him down right
there on the shoulder of the road if he'd dallied. The relief
was short-lived. All the fighting and running had rekindled
his own heat and sweat. The reek from his clothes set him
gagging. His empty stomach tried to turn itself inside out
up his throat. At the edge of the woods, he tore the stinking
top shirt from his back.

Dashing through the trees in his undershirt, he could
barely see the branches flying up to slap his face, much
less any detail of his belly. His prodding fingers bounced all
around as he stumbled, most likely missing the problem at
each pass. He didn't feel injured, but that didn't lend itself
to the sort of serenity it might have. Boyd had once put the
square base of a key through the palm of his hand when
he'd slammed at it in a fury for being stuck in the lock. He
hadn't felt any pain for hours then either.

The more he thought about it (as much as he could
think about anything beyond getting far away and getting
there fast), he figured it was the cop's blood on him. What
he'd seen of the guy's face in the moonlight was enough to
know that the man was on the wrong side of fine, even if
Boyd hadn't full-on killed him back at the house. It wasn't
really his fault in light of the way things had worked out,
nor any of his concern.

However and why ever it had happened, the cops were
near onto him, so Boyd forced himself to a stealthy walk.
He was running on nothing. In a day and a half, he'd been
nervous, tired, confused, terrified, furious, and occasionally
full of swagger in great swinging blocks of time, and he

realized he was just about wore out from feeling things. Given a little time and a short stretch of quiet to think, he'd be able to right himself to the map in his head, even in the dark and even having plunged into the trees without strong heed to where he'd got in. His sense of direction was that good. But he was a lousy tracker. Sound didn't play to him like clues. Shifting winds only left him cooler on a different side of his face, and the passage of other creatures left their impressions too low for Boyd's eyes, which were always scanning ahead for landmarks. He did not want to find that detective. And he certainly didn't wish to be found by him either. So he made like a shadow and crept on, near as silently as was possible.

An obscene violin version of some pop song shredded Maggie's patience. The hospital operator had left her on hold forever, all alone with the fight to stay focused while part of her mind, Pavlovian-style, played Name That Tune. Her attention hiccupped in the middle of the endless chorus. Her rambling thoughts plucked the sound of gravel rasping under squealing brakes from her imagination or her memory, she couldn't tell, but it was faint and clear, and married to the disconnected idea of trees flying past her at a gallop. The vision flitted against the desperation that hopped up and down to know what news might be coming down the line from the nurse. The quick daydream distracted the idiot savant in the background, who had almost placed that stupid, cheerful melody.

She pulled the phone just far enough away to hear the wind in the eaves of the house, to make sure she hadn't heard Ford's truck pulling into the garage, and her skin prickled at how the gusts rattled the spring leaves, demanding that she think again of trees. Maggie clapped the speaker back over her ear to hear the last notes of the orchestra waver and fade. She had it. It was "I'm a Believer." And simultaneously, a spike of terror.

Maggie had been looking for, waiting for, praying for, Tim Bayard's number to light up the telephone display ever since she'd sent him out into the middle of the night with their dog. She'd narrowed her hopes to that single line she'd cast, had concentrated all her efforts there, to the exclusion of everything else. But the image of the trees was so strong and so—

Maggie nearly dropped the handset. She jabbed the button to get a clear dial tone. "Ford!"

27

AT THE T-STOP of Old Green Valley Road and State Route 10, the dog-and-cop show came to an impasse. Two lanes streaked off to the right, and a cut-through in the tall, grassy median made a twin set of highway lanes headed opposite, sending just as logical a choice streaming to the left.

"So, what now?"

Tessa said nothing beyond a clipped whine.

In the hour before dawn, the town center of Stillwater didn't own enough urban urgency to warrant a peep. Out in this far-flung border, they may as well have been on the moon. Bayard parked squarely in the middle of the deserted lane, flicked off the engine, and threw his back hard against the seat. But he tapped the hazard lights to life, just in case. A moment of knuckle-chewing yielded no inspiration, so he got out to listen for the whisper of more nothing to breeze past him. He released Tessa into the night and watched her scour the asphalt and grass verge with her snout.

"What do you know, Tess?"

She ignored him.

He gave her a minute to pick up the scent and leaned against the warm hood of his car, hypnotized by fatigue and the tick and buzz of the engine. By the second burr between the ticks, it was obvious that cars didn't vibrate like that. But cell phones humming in their fancy new holsters did. Tim nearly snapped off the clips in getting to it, and he scooped up the call before it could tumble to voice mail.

"This is Bayard."

Maggie yelled into his ear, "Tim! It's Ford!"

"Oh, thank God. What did he—"

"He's in the woods. I think he's in the woods past town!" Her voice was shaking, and what Tim had taken for exaltation was actually frantic tears. "I don't know why I think so, but I think we heard a tire squeal—park, and maybe—out there into the woods off 10—nearly out of my head"—her sentence was perforated by a gap in the reception—"this feeling."

"Hang on, Maggie. I didn't catch that last part." Bayard jogged to the other side of the car and shook the phone in hopes of rattling loose a few more bars of signal. "What?"

"They're checking the hospital, but I don't think he's there."

"Okay."

"What? I can't hear you. Tim!"

He banged the phone against his thigh. "Maggie, I'm at Route 10. Right now. Can you hear me now? This is where Tessa brought me."

"Tim, you have to find him! Something's happened. I just know it."

"I'm going to drive Route 10."

"I'm coming out there."

"Maggie, no! If he can call, he'll call you at home. You have to be there if he tries. Stay there. I'm going to go on with Tessa to see what I can find."

Lit up as he was, Bayard still had to choose—left or right. "Anything, Tessa?" he asked as he waved her back into the car and scrambled around to his own seat behind the wheel. He rode the window buttons, pumping them as if it would make them go faster, to let in the night for her, with all its invisible clues. But at the crossroads, she had found no markers. Her ears twitched and she lifted her nose to the wind, but the guiding pull was out of range. She panted sympathetically, but that was all.

Computers have no forethought. They can calculate at terrifying speeds without any ability at all to leapfrog a gap if the next step isn't weighted by logic and the proper syntax. Even Tessa, with all her awareness, didn't show the capability of making the odd guess, of plotting it out by drawing on past experience, unused trivia, and pure fiction to lead the way. That was exclusively human.

If Ford was hurt, he may have tried to make it to the hospital, which would mean a left turn. If he had headed for home instead, it would be a right. Left or right? Right or left? Tim's head swiveled with the options knocking back and forth. Tim took a deep breath and then a giant step over any sort of surety and turned right.

He drove slowly, letting Tessa hang her head from the window without any way of knowing if it was useful or merely pleasurable for her. He crept up over the steering wheel to see what was to be seen a foot and a half sooner. A few minutes felt like an hour. Finally, around a bend, his headlights threw back a refracted red glow from the corner of an extinguished taillight. Bayard held his breath as the tight cone of illuminated road swung into place and dragged the details from the dark shapes on the side of Route 10: red paint, tailgate, wide cab like a flexed bodybuilder. Ford's truck. And ahead of it, Leah Tamblin's car.

"I'll be damned."

In the dark, through the trees and underbrush, there wasn't so much a path as there was a path of least resistance. Thickets sprang up and closed off avenues with no warning, and all forward progress bent to the will of the woods. Trespassers went, with little option, to where it guided them. The two terrors, of nighttime forests and of having possibly been party to the murder of a policeman, balanced Leah in their tug-of-war and kept her upright. Her head was killing her. She swung the beam of her flashlight over a soothing pattern in time with her crunching footfalls: light to the left, right foot down, light to the right, left foot down, top left, right foot, top right, left foot, down to the left . . . She tried hard to be searching as diligently as she was counting the cadence, but it staved off the panic, at least.

"Leah!"

"What? Do you see him?" Fear and hope pressed in on her neurotic bubble.

"See who?" Jason asked. "I called you a bunch of times and you didn't answer."

With that, her dread recurdled to fury. "See who? Are you crazy? Are you even looking for Detective Watts?" She shoved the blade of light into Jason's face and he fell back, wincing.

Jason shielded his eyes and peeked through the slats of his fingers. "You didn't say anything about what happened."

"Why? What happened?" Confusion protected some mustard seed of faith that they were still speaking the same language.

"About what I just told you. About me and Harris."

"Jason, Jesus!" She came at him again, flashlight raised above her head like a club. She stopped just short of bashing him. "Are you out of your mind? There is a man probably bleeding to death out there because of us. I'm *trying* to save him." She glared a few thousand volts at him. "So, in a word—no!—I wasn't really listening to you." The unevenness of the terrain vibrated up through the stomping soles of her thin work flats. Her marching rhythm was ruined.

She heard him trotting behind to catch up. "But it's important that you believe me."

"Why?" she yelled without bothering to stop or to look back at him. "Why is it important, Jason? Just now, why in the hell should that story matter at all?"

This stopped him to silence so suddenly that she turned to see if he'd fallen into a hole. Her light found him tall, sad, and utterly lost. His hands hung limp at his sides. "Because it's the truth."

She shook her head at him. "The truth? Look, if I don't go to jail over this, the best thing that can probably come out of tonight is that I'll have to live with what's happened to Detective Watts for the rest of my life. The rest of my life! *That's* the truth. You, too, you know. But you don't do much of a job of looking out for yourself, do you? You're a mess." She sighed. "But I get it. You don't trust yourself with anything. Not even your own best interest. Pfffft. You're in here with me when you could be across the state line by now. But you let me drag you along. Not that I don't appreciate it, as it turns out. All things being equal, I'd rather be home in bed." Leah pressed her hand to the sore spot on her head and groaned. "But thank you, for what it's worth. You probably should have run, though. Really. You should have a vote in your own life. You just let me decide for you. And that Harris—even a guy like that. Yeah. As long as they're someone else, they're always more right than you are. That's sad. *There's* the truth."

The analysis hung there, awkwardly, between them.

"I thought you said you weren't listening."

"I wasn't listening, but I heard you. There's a difference."

Ford Watts would have got off the shot if they'd made it there a few moments earlier. His hand was still curled around the pistol he'd finally freed from its holster. He'd carried it strapped to his ankle all day, every day, since his return from Vietnam, but his ankle had seemed a reach too far each time he'd tried for it, gut-stabbed as he was and fighting with Montgomery.

He'd watched the bobbing light winding a track toward him, feeling his strength draining into the ground and leaving it warmer beneath him than his own limbs. He'd followed the beam's progress back and forth over the path he'd taken earlier, where he'd stumbled on roots and snagged invisible branches in the dark. The length of white light dragged his eyes left and right like the swing of a hyp-notist's watch until his lids slipped down and closed. He fought the wave of peace that settled through his shoulders and laid soft, warm hands around his aching heart. He thought of Maggie in her coral sundress on a hot day, years before. The sun was going down behind her and she handed him the screwdriver he needed to fix the gate latch. She was laughing and her eyes met his. Nothing special. Everything. His gun hand drooped to the ground, his finger slipped from the trigger, and the pain snuffed out like a doused candle.

Her flitting foot-and-flashlight drill wouldn't have left the illuminated circle in one place long enough for her to have picked out Ford's legs from the scatter of fallen branches. Instead, now with Jason beside her, her phobia of the dark woods had relented enough for her to concentrate. She stroked the beam in a slow, wide sweep of the forest floor ahead of them.

The flashlight kicked in her hand, a reflexive twitch, as her brain caught the inconsistency in the deadwood. At the end of the hunt, there's always what you were looking for and what needs to happen next, but Leah froze in the grip of discovery. Then she slid the quivering bright fan of light up the long, denimed legs and brought Ford into the center of the beam.

Jason gasped in confirmation, then saw that Leah had been struck motionless. He took the flashlight from her, and holding her wrist with his free hand, he eased her behind him. He broke into a run, pulling her along. They kicked away the covering branches and fell to their knees on either side of Ford.

"Is he still alive?" Leah asked.

"I don't know." Jason lifted the gun from Ford's loose grip with one hand and gently shook Ford's shoulder with the other.

"Is he?" squealed Leah. She scuttled closer, hand hovering, tentative at his chest. "Mr. Watts? Oh, please God. He can't be dead. If he came out here tonight just because of me, if he—"

"Leah, you wouldn't have come out here either except for Boyd Montgomery. You didn't hurt Detective Watts. You didn't hurt your fiancé. You didn't do any of this." Jason took Leah's hand in his free one and ducked his head down to draw her wild eyes up to his. In the farthest glow of the flashlight's halo, they could just see each other. "Don't do that," Jason said. "Put it where it belongs, on Boyd Montgomery. Let him take the blame for what he's done." Jason bent back to Ford and checked for a pulse, poking inexpertly at his neck. "Or even on me, I know. But none of it is your fault."

Leah was desperate to turn back and make one different move, just one, somewhere, anywhere, along the line of this day, this week, this life, to make this scene not true. The flood of random regrets poured out. "I shouldn't have been out there tonight. I shouldn't have had to see. It's like—gloating. I always have to know. To snoop. It's nothing! Nothing! And I wanted . . . It was easier with him gone. But Reid didn't deserve it. Oh, please, oh, please. God, I'm so sorry. I shouldn't have come. . . ." She rocked in her chant, lost in a begging panic.

Jason, being lately attuned for confessions, heard every word. Leah presented normal, good, innocent. He'd just said so himself. *It was easier with Reid gone.* All of a sudden, it wasn't a fantastically sick notion unique to him. If he could take that out of the woods with him if nothing else, it would be something.

Ford's eyelids fluttered.

Jason sagged onto his heels. "He's alive." He shielded the light from Ford's eyes and scanned down the front of his shirt. He touched the glistening, dark patch and his fingers came away only tacky. "He's not bleeding too much right now, but he looks terrible. We have got to get him out of here."

He bent to Ford's rolling eyes. "Mr. Watts? Don't worry. You're going to be okay." Jason took his hand and Ford gripped back. Jason smiled over tears. "That's it. Hang in there. I'm so, so sorry. Hold on. We're going to get you out of here."

"Hurts," Ford croaked.

The run was still ahead of Jason and he had no idea how to manage all he should do before he made a try for it, but, for him, a moment of absolution was like water and sleep.

Relief for Leah, however, was too much. "Oh, God. My head." She doubled over, then scrabbled at the tree bark to pull herself up, and staggered away, hands on knees.

Jason dropped Ford's arm and ran to her.

And to turn everything on its ear, his hand forgot to drop the gun.

He draped his gun arm over her shoulder and guided her up, holding the light across her face to get a look at her sweat-greased shock. She looked awful—too pale and blank. "Leah, hang in there. It's going to be all right."

There was a rustle in the undergrowth. And then a blast of light in his face, just in front of a pistol-slide's grating snick into place.

"Put the gun down," said Tim Bayard. "Let her go, Jason."

28

TIM HAD pulled up behind the truck and called for one of everything in Carter County's emergency services. There was no one, upright at any rate, inside the cab. Leah's car nosed crookedly off the edge of the ditch a few yards beyond. Bayard leaned over to get the flashlight from the glove box while Tessa crowded his efforts and scratched at the window, whining and prancing in her seat. He stretched over her, yanked the handle, and pushed the passenger door wide, more to be rid of her interference than to put her on point guard. But she was scouting at full alert and working hard before he'd closed his own door behind him. He watched her bustle back and forth, her nose pulling her every which way over the shoulder of the road.

He checked the back of the truck and found it empty. A dark smear trailed down the outside of the window, and a faint stink wafted out of the cab, which was, as he'd guessed, empty. "What the hell?" he sighed.

Bayard scanned the cars and the side of the road within the shallow arc of the flashlight. Other than the keys to the truck, which had been kicked up under the front axle, nothing looked as interesting to him as it did, apparently, to Tessa. He cupped his hands to his mouth and called, "Ford?"

Tessa cringed and cowered, then trotted to his side in a crouch, ears swept back flat against her head. She looked up at him from low between her shoulders and chuffed softly. She crept forward, glanced back, and coughed the breathy woof again. Bayard, almost tired of being stunned by her, shook his head in amazement. Given the height and flexibility, she would have clapped her paw over his mouth and shushed him. She kept her head thrust forward and scrambled down the trough beyond the brink of the road and up the hill in front of them. Bayard had to jog to keep up.

Only one thing was stronger than loyalty for Tessa, and that was the pull of interest. Obedience brought her close to her two-legged pack, but her forever struggle was to keep at their side. Their wants weren't exactly leashes, and she loved them. So, Tessa wrestled with disobedience now and then, to earn a *Good girl* even when the most desperate call of *What was that?* tickled her ears and crawled up her nose and stood the hair above her collar so tall and stiff that it tingled to a yammering itch.

Having been washed in Ford's pain nearly broke her heart. Whatever had happened had flung his hurt into the air in the hallway of that house. Tessa would have howled forever but for the intrusion of Tim. He pulled her back and asked her, *What?* What indeed? Others had been there with Ford: the man from the house, the woman from the park, the man from before, the one with the dogs. And then Tim had been able to smell something that she had not once she had lost the trail out there on the road. He had found

Ford's truck. She never understood what the people knew and what they did not. It didn't make any sense.

Now there was that same death again. It had saturated the hole behind the house, where the soil had drunk in the juice. A great deal more of it had been there on the tarp in the grass. Here was a little bit of it again. It was the deadest thing she had ever smelled. An old, strong death, wasted to the barest hint of whoever it had been and now boiling ripe with other life and process.

Ford had been close by and on his feet. She knew he'd gone into the trees straight across from where the truck was stopped. He was hurt. Tessa would find him. But a wish called out to her. She want-needed just a moment to load more of that fussy death drama into her brain. It was only a small detour. Tessa looked back to that gap between the two pines, to the door in the woods that Ford had used to go into the trees. She wanted him, but that want bumped into the part of herself ruled by her nose. The lone wolf needled the good girl into a dereliction of duty.

A shallow bowl of earth and leaves cradled a greasy, wonderful mess all pressed into a shirt with cookies in the pocket. Tim huffed and puffed up the hill after her, and he yowled at the smell of the dead-wet shirt, but was kind enough to run the light over it while she took it all in.

"Tessa!" He was getting good at making yells sound like whispers. "Get out of there!"

But he needn't have said anything. Her head had already been yanked up by her ears. She'd heard voices, even better than cookies right now, lilting in on the breeze from the south. And besides, she was ready to go. Good girl.

*

Tim kept to the dog's sensibilities and whisper-shouted to her from the edge of the hollow, even as he poured light onto the shirt wadded up there. The beam pooled in the rumpled fabric that was blackened with a dark crust, a rind of the now familiar stink. "Tessa! Get out of there!" It was too much. A shirt ripe with decomp in the woods after all the rest of the night's nonsense?

Tim had wisely gone to bed early, even before the late news, so as to rest untroubled; he remembered that his wife had snuggled up next to him, sighing happily. He'd been sleeping, warm and peaceful—he was sure of it, but, at this point, it was almost impossible to believe.

"What the hell?" he moaned out loud.

The dog's head jerked up from the slimy pile of ruined shirt, and she'd taken off through the trees. Bayard was relieved to whisk his light away from the stinking puzzle, and he watched Tessa plodding through the leaves at the fuzzy edge of the brightness. She weaved her way around the swells of underbrush along a track running deeper into the woods, still hunkered down, still stealthy. Tim heard a female's voice first. Not her words, but her tone: angry and afraid. He transferred the flashlight to free up his right hand, then drew his sidearm.

The closer he and Tessa came to the voices, the more he was certain the evening's players were lining up. The commotion sounded very much as if Jason Getty and Leah Tamblin were together, fussing, and not far ahead.

Tessa slowed to his side. Her caution radiated like heat into his leg. Bayard switched off the light, then hooked the ring and little fingers of his flashlight hand under her collar, allowing himself to be led forward like a blind man.

Tessa guided him tentatively at first, ramping up her speed only as his confidence in her night vision and his own footing grew. At a slow, bent-kneed trot in the woods on one of the oddest nights of his life, Tim Bayard became a true believer. Despite the suspense, he smiled in wonder, and it lit a swoon of affection for his helpmate. Tessa's wagging tail whipped the backs of his legs.

Tim felt the air of an open space against his cheek at the same instant that Tessa went utterly still. A light danced in the trees ahead. Rounding with her, silently, into the clearing, he saw two shadowed figures streaking to the right. Their flashlight swung wildly and he heard the voice that was almost positively Leah's cry out in pain. The light drew around to reveal Jason Getty curling his arm over her shoulder, a short-barreled pistol in his hand.

Tessa exploded from her pad of leaves, and Bayard crossed his wrists to point both his gun and his light at the pair. His left thumb lit the flashlight, while his right index finger settled against the trigger. The light dialed forward and back as he drew the slide.

"Put the gun down. Let her go, Jason."

Getty's face slid up a spectrum of confusions. He startled at the light in his face, gaped at Bayard, and, after quick-stepping away from Leah, he looked at the gun in his hand with all the goggling expected after a cry of *Abracadabra!*

"But I didn't—"

"He wasn't—"

"Ford!" yelled Bayard. He'd finally made sense of the commotion flickering at the edge of his field of vision. Tessa nuzzled Ford Watts, who lay slumped against a tree. A tiny adjustment of the light and Bayard saw that the front of his shirt was soaked dark with blood. He swung his full attention back to Jason, who stood stunned and pinned again by the light.

"Goddammit, Getty!" Fury trembled up through Bayard's shoulders, and down into his arms, but his training kept it north of his wrists. His aim held steady. At the speed of thought, he tallied up the hours of paperwork and the stress of trial preparation against the cost of a bullet divided by the time he had between now and when backup arrived. His trigger finger anxiously awaited the sum.

But Tessa, it seemed, also had a calculation in the works. Bayard watched Tessa spring at Jason, her paws landing on his chest, her face thrusting into his. Tim waited for the scream.

But Getty didn't scream. He didn't flail, only staggered back a step as Tessa's weight knocked him off-balance. She licked his face and wagged her tail like to shake her hindquarters loose.

"Tessa, get back!" Bayard locked his elbows again, bewilderment banging sparks against his outrage. "Getty, drop your weapon!" Jason did. Tessa still mauled him with kisses. "Tessa, for God's sake, get down!" Bayard shouted. It worked that time, or so he thought. Tessa wheeled around to his authority and cocked her head at him. Their eyes met, her pupils throwing back the blank, white reflection of his flashlight beam. She ran at him, leaping at the last second as she had with Jason. And as with her launch at Jason, it caused Bayard to lurch back. He braced, trying to nail his equilibrium down through his feet, but gravity yanked hard at his hips and kicked his knees loose. His finger twitched against the trigger and a shot roared into the trees.

Jason ran.

29

WITH NO TRUCK, no plan, and hours burned off his escape, Boyd realized he was hopelessly separated from his getaway, but not all that far from the stand of forest he'd cut through earlier that same evening. But the setback was far worse than just lost time. They'd seen him from the road and surely called the cops by now; the manhunt would be marshaling fast even as he pinned down his location in the forest. If Boyd was plain about the whole situation, it was probably going down exactly that way.

The first time he heard a voice droning under the sound of the leaves rearranging themselves underfoot, he'd held his breath until it felt like a hot cannonball in his chest. He placed the sound to his right, then it suddenly seemed slightly ahead of his path. He'd only turned his head just a little, but now the sound tilted far behind him, and down, fun-house wrong, as if the ground had sloped away, though no such hill was part of these woods. He shoved away the thought that his mind's compass might be off track.

Boyd tiptoed on and was stopped cold little more than a

mile later by more voices, seemingly dead ahead. He strained at the ears until the voices—surely at least two—faded out.

Now he was disoriented. Not about his place on the map, but as to where he could safely move ahead. Where were they? His confidence shrank back after every few yards he gained, and Boyd faced down the fear of wandering hesitant circles without a plan.

He sucked in a breath and dredged his middle for that hard will that always drove him forward, but for a chilling change all he came up with was the scraping, hollow notion of how hungry he was. His hands stung with scratches from fending off the looping vines and whipping branches. Something had taken a sip from his neck and left a hot, itching knot in his skin.

Boyd walked on, and the whispering trees had him snapping his head around to hear if there were words in the rustling. The pulse beating in his eyes rose up to loom clearer than the shapes of the trees ahead, fuzzing the whole picture to a dark, booming blur. He slid his feet over the rough ground, suddenly wary of roots that would grab and topple him. He swung his hands through empty air, reaching out, swatting great handfuls of nothing and more nothing. A horrible free-falling thrill swooped through his chest. His throat dialed down to a stingy straw. The air curdled and wouldn't pass through. A scampering in the brush spooked a yelp from him, which in turn dropped him to a crouch for fear of having been heard. Then he found his knees didn't want to unlock.

Boyd tried to stand, but his thighs pulled against it, grinding him smaller and smaller while a panic crowded the fight right out of him. He wanted Bart. The pining for his brother welled thick in his throat. He reached for the memory of Katielynn, but shrank back from the image of the hate burning in her eyes, a rich, red underscore widening across her chest.

Boyd's will had pulled him time and again ahead of his feelings, up over anything or anyone in his way. Eventually his will had run past it all, outrun even his own grasp, leaving him alone on a hill, gulping a cold breeze and sitting on a tremor that was trying hard to hatch into full-blown hysterics. He inched back until he butted up against a trunk and slid down, cornered in a cold sweat by the ghost of voices in the night that he could not make out for trying.

Tessa understood basic physics. She knew it innately and better than most high-school science students. Cause and effect and the nature of opposing forces were her specialty. But in her way of knowing things, there were fewer distinctions. It was all the same to her. Pressure was pressure, no matter if it was a hand against a door or just the vibe of fright and anger clacking off the people around her like a hard rubber ball off the table legs at home. Among this group huddled in the woods, the pressure yielded cracks as real and wide as any she could shove her nose into.

She left the pressure to itself, though. Ford was found! She pulled up from a gallop to a careful prance to duck down next to him once she drew close. He hadn't opened his hand to her. Most people rubbed her head or scratched her ears first, which was pleasant enough, but Ford always stroked her jaw, making her squint with delight and sag into his open palm. He with his hand held out at chin height was what she knew, what was right. He even did it in his sleep when she trotted in for a midnight check on her people.

The ruckus in the clearing pinched her attention away from Ford. They were barking and snarling and yelping like a trio of cornered foxes. Tessa whirled into the mix. The keystone strain was on Tim, and the air shook all around where he stood. His anger bore down on the man from the house, and she didn't know why. He was okay, the man from the house; someone you could love when he wasn't crumpling. She tried to show Tim that everything was all right, that the man just needed to hear a *Good girl*.

Then she went to Tim directly, but before she could convince him, a blast broke over the night.

And now the man from the house was running. Directly toward the hole.

Tessa's senses arced in a wide dome around wherever she was. Light and sound played in the vault of what she knew, showing her the edges and guiding her around the curves. The meager light was swallowed up everywhere by things, and it glimmered, uninterrupted, where things were not. Sound muffled over, under, and through the woods, and the notes of the wind murmured back to her the shape and distance of what was out there.

These woods were woolly in places—dense enough in spots to discourage even Tessa's curiosity—but tall and twiggy and dry in long stretches, and mulchy in the hollows, damp and compelling. The night noises were a sissing, clattering cascade. Up ahead and to the right was a gap. It was huge. Sound fell in, starlight fell in, and soon, if he didn't trip up, the man from the house would fall in, too.

Tessa chased him down, barking. She galloped to his right, herding him back away from where he'd meet the edge, but the forest's fingers tangled close in that space and their whip ends thrashed him. She hung back, giving him no reason to risk a double-around. She let him think he was just a touch faster. He ran a narrow margin between the brambles and the path to the pit that he couldn't feel, just yards ahead and three wide slide-steps to his right. The man from the house ran heedless, nibbling into his leeway, as he shrank from the grasping brush that crowded closer and closer and flogged his left side as he sped by. But Tessa knew she could be scarier than a bush. She found more speed and snarled and snapped at his right flank. He screamed and veered away from her. Almost safe. Tessa pulled alongside her herd of one as he came abreast of the hole. Dancing inches from the edge, she bared her fangs in an unparalleled performance of ferocity.

Nimble as she was, though, losing her back legs to crumbling earth was a daunting tax on her agility. The first displaced stones rattled down the sides of the drop. Tessa lunged for firmer ground, but the rim gave way under her push-off. She yelped and flexed her toes into the loose dirt. Her back legs cycled for purchase, but instead she kicked away more ground beneath her than the millimeters of advantage she bought.

Tessa understood gravity. She'd had blessedly little experience with pain in her life. Ford had always kept her safe. But she tensed for a lesson and fell.

Boyd hadn't completely lost it in nearly twenty years. Gunfire didn't always bother him, but every now and again, without warning, it would bring back the picture of his mother on her knees in the kitchen, cringing away from the .22's barrel, or the family dog cowering under the stock of the hunting rifle, or of Bart charging blindly past any good sense, flying in front of their father's rage and aim in the yard.

His father had never pulled the trigger, except to shoot at game, but the threat of it came down reliably three or four days each time before he'd take his leave again. The screaming clashes had left Boyd likely to wet the bed for weeks afterward. He'd stew, so bitter against his mother, his brother, and any danged dog who couldn't seem to keep clear of Daddy's temper. It was simple enough, wasn't it, not to get on Daddy's last nerve? It wasn't as if the man didn't offer up plenty of warnings. From these lessons, Boyd had lost patience with stupid people who couldn't do as they ought to protect the peace. But Boyd had never brandished a gun that he didn't fire. He was a better man than that. It was a cowardly thing to threaten if you weren't willing to see it through.

When the shot rang out as he hunkered against the tree, the bullet tore through the leaves and nicked bark somewhere close by. The seam it cut through the air split the strangling quiet from around him and catapulted Boyd Montgomery out of the last of his self-control.

He sprang from his crouch and vaulted the last landmark he'd managed to keep track of, a fallen tree he'd crossed once already on his way into this part of the forest. Some deep instinct of the landscape kept him more or less upright, but as soon as he felt a more open breeze, Boyd's speed came on. The wind of it, and of his own breath, roared through his ears, blessedly louder than the echo of the muzzle blast.

When the dog had jumped him, back in the clearing, Jason had thought for a moment that she was intent on ripping off his face; that she had somehow sniffed out everything he'd got away with. Her breath had streamed up his cheeks, but before he could even brace for the pain, her soft, wet tongue had stroked his chin. Her excited panting lapped over him, and he swayed with the happy waving of her tail that was rocking her paws against his chest.

Bayard's taking a shot at him had canceled out all the high-minded analysis of interspecies communion, and Jason had fled. Fled like he didn't know he had that brand of flee in him. The dog had gone primal and given chase, bearing down in an attack. Jason had felt a swell of almost pride that he'd been able to keep her mostly behind him. But he'd no more than thought it, and she was there, striding easily beside him and growling over the crash of his feet and the thundering of his pulse. The Neanderthal terror of having a wolf at his knee had blanked his mind, but then she'd disappeared with a yelp.

And by her fall, Jason now knew where he was. His breath burned bright tracks down his throat and caught full fire in his lungs. He bent over gasping, hands on knees, his shirt sticking, cold and wet, to his back. The blood pulled a tidal sound against his eardrums, so he didn't hear or see the man rushing up behind him.

Nor, apparently, did Boyd see much of anything, tearing down the gap in the trees as if all the bears in the woods were on him. He was lucky not to have fallen into the sinkhole himself. He barreled, full throttle, into Jason, who was hunched over in the middle of the lane, minding his own struggling heart.

The two men shouted their surprise, and both took the collision for a tactical maneuver. Jason thought Bayard had come to finish what his pistol shot hadn't. Boyd battled everyone he'd been expecting over his shoulder for the last three years. Whoever it might be was about to take a beating in Phil's place for not being where he'd always been, where he *should* have been, with his cars and his pills. That they were both wrong hardly mattered. Punching and tussling became a blaring red command, instantly washing both men clean of civility. Boyd's teeth itched to sink into raw meat, and Jason's knuckles couldn't get enough thrashing. That they couldn't see each other only blocked the last inhibition that would have pulled them back. So they wound around each other, clawing, clambering, twisting for advantage and protection, each raining blows on the other without knowing or caring where they landed.

Months of tension stoked strength into Jason's thin arms, and years of bottled frustration fed vengeance into Boyd. With the ebb of stamina, the two men reeled up the path they'd come. Then the flow of renewed purpose tottered them forward, deeper into uncharted territory. Uncharted for the two of them bound together, but Jason, at least, knew where he was.

The light of the next day had been seeping into the sky for the better part of an hour. The trees hoarded night at their roots, so the slow dawning was only clear at the verge of the crater.

The slate gray of the forest floor could no longer compete with the ink black of the dark well at their feet. Their tussle had marched them to the ledge of fickle dirt at the rim of the sinkhole. All the heat of the fight left Boyd as he flung out his arms and sucked in a great measure of terror in its place. He heard the patter of loosened soil and imagined that he felt little holes sieving open, tickling his feet through the soles of his boots. His prodigious will scrambled backward, but ran up against his frozen spine. He was poised like a diver, looking out over a great pool of shadow.

Where there should have been solid ground, there was nothing under all ten of Boyd's toes and five of Jason's. Jason was firmly on his back foot and just slightly behind the tightrope line where Boyd perched. Boyd shifted his weight to his heels and inched back the tips of his elbows, a trembling reversal from the irresistible drag of the yawning hole, but his back struck Jason's chest, and Jason did not yield.

He slid his leg through Boyd's wide stance, blocking the bettering of the other man's balance. He gripped the man's left arm for pull and his right shoulder for push. One hard twist from Jason and the detective, or so he thought, would drop headlong into the abyss.

Jason, once again at a crossroads, swallowed an ache in his throat. Time itself was nauseating, the seconds oozing over him, so slow and lucid compared to the last occasion he'd straddled a man's death. There had been no choice with Harris. The instant kicked and was over, bronco-wild and terrifying.

This was worse. The abandoned roadwork that branched back to the main thoroughfare was just a few yards away. He knew where he was now. It pulled at him like a magnet. But he wouldn't do it, no. Still, he couldn't unsee the last gap of opportunity. He might make it before the rest of the police arrived, if he could bring himself to . . .

Both men, chests heaving, looked to the rumble of running feet. Jason felt a tickle of hair brush his face. It set his eyes to watering as the two men turned their heads, automatically, together. Jason heard Leah, "Detective, wait!"—then Bayard's voice, from farther away than it should have been, demanding that Jason step back.

The last thing Jason needed was a puzzle. Suddenly, the man he'd latched onto was too tall and thin to be the policeman, but that was somehow not as disorienting as the desperate need to rub the itch from his nose and to figure out how Tim Bayard's hair had grown half a foot and turned yellow overnight.

"Get him off me," cried the man on the ledge, voice pitched phobia-high.

Bayard's flashlight lit his face. "Boyd Montgomery? What are you—"

"Get him off and I'll go with you. Whatever you think, I never laid a hand on Bart. I never would have. He did that hisself. Please! Just get him offa me. We're gonna fall," Boyd wailed.

"What the *hell*?!" Bayard yelled full into the trees.

"I only came back for Phil," Boyd babbled.

"Getty, back *up*!"

". . . Katielynn and that whore-hound, long-haired faggot . . . in my *bed*." A clump of dirt dislodged when Boyd, in spite of himself, ground his foot just the slightest for emphasis. It rattled a tiny avalanche over the side. Boyd shrieked. "I wasn't gonna hurt nobody!"

Jason had seen Leah in silhouette straighten at the mention of Katielynn, and she'd cringed as if she'd been slapped at the description of Reid. Jason, at the dawning of the end of his bid, heard the shower of dirt over the edge gain tempo. It was over and he was leaving this glen headfirst down the sinkhole or in handcuffs.

Boyd slipped forward and reached back for a hold. He found only Jason, who buckled under the fight between momentum and retreat. Clods of forest floor rained down the cliffside. Bayard ran forward with a cry of "No!" He swiped blindly in the gloom, snagged a flailing arm, and hauled back on it. A scream tumbled down the side of the rock wall, cut short midhowl with a sodden rip and a splintering clatter of dead wood.

30

THE LIGHT dialed the black a little bit bluer with every passing second. Tim Bayard sucked in a breath over the wicked cramp that knotted his side. His holstered cell phone had gone a fair piece toward digging all the way up under his ribs, and he couldn't help but wish he'd left the damned thing in the car. Jason Getty sprawled over Tim's lower legs and had more length of him over the lip of the sinkhole than out of it. This was especially worrisome the harder Getty clamped and clawed, climbing Tim's body.

"Jason!" Leah ran forward, but Bayard threw out a halting hand.

"Stop. Don't come any closer. Getty, stop! Hold on, but for God's sake, stop pulling." Tim and Jason lay still, locked in a jumble. Their breaths, ragged and halting, slipped into a rhythm until their shoulders rose and fell in time. "Getty, ease back this way. But slowly. Can you feel it slipping?"

Jason nodded and crept forward on his elbows, trying to kick away as little dirt as possible. A few inches at a time, they held their breath and pulled off the rim. Flat on his back on the packed earth, Tim sighed one last time, "What the hell?"

Back on his feet, he motioned for Leah's flashlight. His own had got dropped in the lunge and had been kicked away over the edge. His gun had also been knocked clear, but Tim didn't mention that just yet. He ran the light over the ground casually, checking the integrity of the footing around them and for any sign of his pistol. "You two just stay right there where I can see you," he said in the same voice he would have used if he'd been fully armed and heading up a posse.

He followed a solid-looking swath of ground to the edge and peered over the brink. Two stories down, Boyd Montgomery lay still, bristling all over with red-tipped spears from a tangle of roots jutting out from the side of the embankment.

Bayard rubbed at his eyes, as if he could soothe away the image. But it had already sunk in. "Oh, Christ."

"He hit me with the shovel."

Bayard's head snapped up, as did Jason's. "What?" Bayard asked.

Leah's ears were still ringing from the shot, and it didn't do anything kind for the pain pulsing hot-pink and green in her head. She stared at the two men, watching them watch her in the rising light, knowing that everything that lay ahead was all blame and tears and trying to explain something that was nearly impossible to make any sense of. She'd had to dig for her stupid truth just once too often.

All Leah wanted was to subtract herself from this night, to undo everything she'd changed, right or wrong, about what would have happened without her. If that meant leaving Jason to his fate, then so be it. Her fury filled her through to the fingertips. She wished she could catch his eye, so that he'd see her resolve, so that he'd know not to fight it. But she couldn't make him out any clearer than that he was the taller of the two outlines facing her.

"He hit me with the shovel," she repeated. "I went over to the house—just to see where Reid had died, that's all I was going to do, I swear. And then I caught him digging up the backyard." She drew in a shuddery breath.

Jason found more bitter pleasure in having called it right than he would have guessed. Given the first chance, just as he'd thought she would, she had turned away from his explanation. He knew his own fault in this night, and others. The reasons for what had happened didn't mean all that much in the end. But that she hadn't waited until he was at least out of earshot stung with an equal measure of surprise. The last chance at a mad dash for the road cast its vote, and Jason's blood fizzed into his legs, readying him to run, no matter if it ended with a bullet in his back. But the disappointment was deadweight and it slowed the trick.

Leah's anger carved the mist, drawing Bayard and Jason along on the brass hook of her story. "At first, I just assumed he was the man who lived there. I didn't know that he was Boyd Montgomery until I saw him up close. How could I have known?" She pointed an accusing finger at Bayard. "You told me he was dead." Her arm fell to dangle at her side, exhaustion sapping the strength from her. "He'd just dug up some hideous thing—Phil, I guess, from the sound of it—and then he hit me when he realized I saw him. But then Jason ran out of the house to help me. We got away, but Montgomery was chasing us all over the place. He stabbed Detective Watts. Oh, God, I think Mr. Watts only came out to the house because of me."

Leah sobbed out her very real regret, while Jason's fight

and flight went cold in his feet. He tried to play it back and translate at the same time.

"God Almighty! Ford!" Bayard quickly herded them together and steered them back toward what they'd all nearly forgotten in the clearing. He kept at a trot as best he could through the undergrowth in the rising dawn.

Jason caught her eye once they were close enough to see each other in the low light, and she drilled him straight through with a hard look. She sketched out her story on the way, calling it out to Bayard's back, but holding Jason silent with blazing eyes. She told them the story, true enough, of how Jason had helped her get to her car, their pursuit to rescue Detective Watts when the truck burned rubber down the road, and how they didn't know a thing about what Boyd Montgomery had been up to this night. Not one thing. Both men listened, but only Jason heard.

The morning had teased up a mist from the ground, but the faint river fog, as it grew, made the dark almost preferable for finding things. Big, fallen cop things, for instance. The lone flashlight had been more useful in total darkness. Now all the beam threw back was a glare of haze. Whatever her gamble back at the hole, Leah's thoughts for Ford Watts dropped an electric despair down through her stomach. They'd left him for far too long.

They walked three abreast, picking their way back as best they could. Leah heard a dragging behind her, she was almost sure. She spun to the source, replayed the sound in her mind, and overlaid it on the last image she had of him—slack against a tree, his long legs stretched out before him. In her imagination, he drew one leg up through the leaves and fallen twigs beneath him. The projection matched exactly the dredging scrape she'd heard. Leah grabbed Bayard's flashlight arm and pushed it around toward the rustle.

She found his ankle first, darker than all the dead wood that the light crawled over, and also, unlike the forest shrapnel, it was wrapped in a sock. They ran to Ford's side.

Bayard knelt to the business of it all, trying his cell phone and peering at Ford. Jason cast around in hopes of finding help or inspiration.

Only Leah wrapped her arms around the injured man. All that would come was a sobbing whisper: "Mr. Watts?"

She cleared her throat and forced down a fuller breath. "Mr. Watts?"

"Mr. Watts? Are—are you okay?" she whispered. She knew full well it was a ridiculous question but had nothing else in her head to offer him. She laid her hand against his chest, feeling for breath and heartbeat, but too afraid to press with any force. Her trembling canceled out anything she might have felt anyway. He didn't make a sound that Leah could hear over her own chattering teeth. "Please be okay. Oh, please, God, be okay . . ."

A warm spot knocked against her back, patting out of rhythm with her quaking. Ford was comforting her, stroking her shoulder blade with one weak hand.

Relief pulled her downward, and all of Leah's plan slid away. She tried to catch Jason's eye as she slipped into the smoky swoon that rushed up to cradle her. Jason knelt at her side and she whispered to him, *"Don't say anything wrong. Let that son of a bitch take it all."*

*

A keening wail reminded her of screaming, but it wasn't her. She wasn't frightened anymore. Just so tired. Ford was perfectly still next to her. The crying wore on, rising and falling, louder and more annoying. She wanted it to stop, but an electric *No!* snatched away her gauzy doze. It was sirens.

She beat on Ford's chest without thinking. "They're here! Mr. Watts, they're here!" She dashed bravely through the trees and into the growing light, right through the pounding in her head, toward the sound.

The pursuit of the girl in the park had become a black hole that Maggie kept tossing men and dogs into. Ford was hurt and Maggie could do nothing but wait. Tim hadn't called in forever. So she paced. She put on her shoes and set out her bag and keys on the table by the door. Then she moved them to the car, to be extra ready. She doubled back to leave the key poised in the ignition. Once she returned to the house, she realized she could save ten seconds by having the garage door already opened, and the round-trip took another half minute off the clock, leaving her stranded in the middle of the kitchen again.

"Margaret, you're going to make yourself sick," she said aloud.

She sat on her hands on the sofa until she felt pins and needles sparking in her palms. She took up dialing Ford's number again just to hear his voice, to feel close, as if she were sending her intent over the airwaves. It gave her fingers something to do. Maggie wanted a cigarette, a craving she hadn't jousted with in twenty years.

The last time had been when the final pregnancy test

had failed to yield that hateful, damned second pink line. The at-home tests had cost a fortune back then. She and Ford had spent hundreds of dollars they didn't have over the course of a few years, buying a test at a time, then sometimes one more, just in case it had been wrong that month. Joking, but not really, they'd issued a challenge to that last one—this was it, or else. She'd washed her hands and straightened the towels, forcing herself not to hold her breath. She wouldn't risk the jinx of looking for the pink parallel lines before the full two minutes had passed. She gave it an extra minute because her watch was digital and therefore not entirely trustworthy, since you could never know how much of that first minute you'd missed.

It turned out that a threat to a bit of plastic and chemical-laced padding is an empty one indeed. Maggie didn't cry that time, but, oh, how she'd ached for the taste of smoke sliding over her tongue and the golden nicotine zing rushing into her fingertips and filling her head like light. She'd quit for the baby. And she had honored that commitment in memoriam for the baby that never happened.

She and Ford had decided not to test for the reasons behind their childlessness. They both had a way of shrugging off what they could not change. They'd found it noble and resilient to accept things with dignity and to soldier on. They'd advised other people so often to do the same— to let it go, not to lather up over what you had no control over. She wondered now if that had been the right thing, to simply sigh in submission when the enemy was invisible, and seemingly impassable. She couldn't help but fear that the devil had upped the stakes to earn his due for all the times they'd denied him their fight in the past.

She dialed the phone again, but before the call could

go through, the call waiting sounded in her ear. It didn't have to pulse twice.

In the ambulance bay, Maggie was out of her car faster than the EMTs could unload their patient. She would have climbed in if they hadn't physically blocked her at the bumper. The sheet-covered feet were simply too big to belong to anyone else.

"Ford!"

"Ma'am, please step back."

"No! Ford! Oh my God."

She chased along beside the gurney. If the medics attempted to dissuade her, she didn't notice. She fumbled to untangle his hand from the cover before the whole party whisked up the ramp to the emergency suite.

"Ford," she called. "Don't you do this. Don't you go in there without looking at me."

A wince worked all his smile lines deeper into his pale face, and his eyelids slid open just enough to show a crescent of blue.

"Say something," Maggie demanded, but she stroked his face.

Ford's voice rasped through barely parted lips.

She leaned in just as a nurse gently pulled her back. "What?"

Ford swallowed and tried again, whispering, "I promise, Miss Margaret, it wasn't the chip dip."

The paramedics rushed him through the double doors, and the nurse guided Maggie away as they rolled Ford into the trauma room, but she didn't struggle. She played back his words, only slightly worried that they were brain-damaged nonsense, because she was almost positive it hadn't been a trick of the ugly sodium lights competing with the sunrise. Ford had winked at her.

The waiting-room chairs blanched under the too bright lights, and Maggie resented the vampires who apparently thought that bloodred upholstery was appropriate in an emergency room lounge. She tried to talk herself into some ease, but for once she couldn't find a voice in her throat or one in her head to keep her company. She reached for any sense of what might happen, not because she believed in it, but because that's just what she always did. But her mind felt as unfamiliar to her as this room, and strangely akin to it in theme, barren with only lurid splashes of alarm for decoration.

Through the window in the security doors, she watched doctors, nurses, and the occasional patient glide across her limited view. Then, between a pair of white-coated doctors, she saw Tim walk past to stand at a nurses'-station counter.

The lock on the doors clacked free and the pneumatic hinge whooshed them open. A young man in scrubs hustled out, intent over his clipboard, and Maggie took his distraction as opportunity. She sailed right in as the doors swept up behind her. Another man in one of the curtained alcoves looked up as she passed. An electric tingle brushed her scalp and disappeared into her braid. Maggie had never seen eyes so tired.

She didn't hear the young man in her head the way she heard her own voice; his glance didn't ring like Sister Patricia Ignatius's either, and Maggie didn't really know what exchange she had received in the passing glance until she stood at Tim's side.

"Did he tell you what happened to Tessa?" she asked.

She'd caught Tim off guard, as he'd been drifting away, far into a long-range stare. "Huh? Who? What happened to Tessa? What do you mean?"

Maggie opened, then shut, her mouth. "I just thought—I don't actually know." A nervous laugh slipped out before she could swallow it back. "Don't mind me. But, Tim, where *is* Tessa?"

He sighed. "She ran off into the woods, but I'm sure she's fine. I'll send someone out there to find her, okay?"

"Did you ask him?" Maggie tried to point discreetly at the man in the treatment bay, but he was already watching them. She dropped her hand quickly and pretended she'd been about to search her pocket. All that was in there was fuzz.

"Do you know Jason?" Tim asked.

"I don't think so." Maggie slid her eyes to take another quick look. "But he came in with you, right? He looks at least like he's been out in the woods all night."

Tim shook his head at her, an expression of disbelief wiped over the smile on his face. "Well, when Tessa ran off, it was after that very guy." They both looked back at Jason, who suddenly found the backs of his hands terribly interesting. "See? That's why Ford follows your nose," Tim said. "I'll be right back."

Maggie watched them, Tim's back eclipsing all but the subordinate slump of the other man. His hands twitched forceless gestures in his lap, while Tim raked his fingers through his hair. His mouth was set in a straight, grim line and he patted Maggie's arm as he went by her.

Bayard called to the firemen standing off to the side, waiting for their next orders. "You guys, can you get some climbing gear together and some rope and come with me?"

31

"THERE ARE a few things that don't seem to make all that much sense." Tim Bayard sipped at the ice water Leah had poured for him.

"I can imagine," she said.

"Our forensics guy isn't too keen on the age of that corpse. It was pounded all to hell and the plastic sort of messes with things—getting the timeline pinned down and all—but it could very well have been put there *after* Montgomery moved out of that house."

"I do wonder about the story behind that one." She took a drink from her own glass and sighed. All the lies that she'd kept to herself had been so easy, sitting as smooth and cool as river rocks below her thoughts. It had always been that way. But wrestling to get a load of half-truths out was like talking around a mouthful of dice. "It's so strange."

"It's all pretty strange," he agreed mildly.

"But at least I know what happened to Reid, now." She nodded almost but not quite in time to agree with herself, so she stopped offbeat. "That's all I wanted. So, something good came out of this whole mess, anyway." Leah huffed a little self-scorn through her nose. "I always *have* to know, don't I? That's why I went out there in the first place, even though Detective Watts didn't want me to. That'll teach me, huh?"

Leah watched Bayard fold his paper napkin into a precise triangle, and the feeling that he knew very well that she was watching prickled at the back of her neck. But she wasn't quite sure that she was taking on the lesson he'd hoped to broadcast. She already knew that he was fussy and smartly creased. The thought made her pull back on a smile.

"Hmmmm. Yep," he said. "All Ford can tell us is that he ran inside because you were screaming a blue streak through the house and then Boyd Montgomery tried to shish-kebab him. Next thing he knows, Montgomery's trying to fling him out of the back of his own truck, driving around like a maniac."

"That sounds about right. Lots of screaming. Lots of driving around like maniacs." She went ahead and smiled at him this time, then down at the tabletop.

It was the first solidly hot day they'd had. The still, gray morning had burned off into something brighter, but just as heavy. She heard a bee in the azaleas on the other side of the porch railing and marveled at how tactically quiet the detective could be in the middle of a conversation. It was his secret weapon.

Hers was that she was all done.

Bayard finally cleared his throat and sprang the follow-up he'd called to arrange. "Why didn't you guys call for help in the car?"

That one was easy, and true. Well, mostly true. Leah smiled. "I would have tried to make a call. But my phone hadn't been charged for days. It was a weird week, if you remember. I used up all the rest of the battery trying to get ahold of you earlier in the day."

"And Mr. Getty's?"

"He forgot, if you can believe it. I could have killed him." No dissembling there, and the break from dodge 'em words felt like a vacation. "He was an utter wreck." She remembered Jason, crushed and contrite, pleading with her over the hood of her car. "But he didn't leave me. As scared as he was, he probably saved my life three times that night." She left out that he'd almost taken it once, too.

Bayard didn't look particularly agitated, but the questions came faster, to see if she could juggle. But she wasn't even catching.

"How did Montgomery get there?"

"I don't know."

"What was he going to do with that body?"

"I don't know."

"Why did he bother to stow the lanterns?"

"I don't know. We didn't see him do any of that."

"How in the heck was he planning on getting away after digging up Phil in Mr. Getty's yard?"

"I don't know."

The rhythm that he'd worked up faltered, but very much on purpose, so that Leah leaned into the gap he'd left before she could help herself, another *I don't know* poised obviously on the tip of her tongue.

Bayard raised his eyebrows in mock surprise.

A small, impressed smile lit her eyes more than her lips and she waited, a study in patience, for him to continue.

Bayard leaned in, elbows on knees. "Why wouldn't Boyd Montgomery have written that crime into his staged confession?"

Leah matched his pose and met his eyes. "I don't know."

Bayard looked her through for an intense three count. "That's mostly Mr. Getty's best effort, too."

"Well, it *was* only the back of a telephone bill, right? That's not a lot of room."

Bayard laughed and nodded, then finished it off with a small shrug. He settled back against the chair and took another sip of his water.

Leah thought he looked okay for a tenacious investigator sitting on a pile of pointy nothings. It was the one thing she wished she could ask him. Why, with his doubts, wasn't he furious? How could he stand it?

"Look," she said. "It was a horrible night. Nothing was sane. And the little I've seen of Mr. Getty"—she made a quick sound that could have been a sad laugh or a sneer—"I have no problem believing he hasn't got a clue."

It sounded cruel, which was useful, but she winced to hurt him, even if he'd never know. She'd gotten a gift, unsigned, but clearly from the one person who knew she could now handle a night in the woods. A gold-foiled lion bared its teeth on the front of the card. Sealed inside it, she'd found a reservation to a night excursion hosted in the jungle exhibit of a major zoo—Snore n' Roar Overnights— paid in full. She'd laughed until she cried, but to keep Mr. Anonymous anonymous, she hadn't been able to say thank you.

"Doesn't it bother you not to know the truth?" Bayard asked.

It seemed a little too close to telepathy that he'd lobbed her unspoken question back at her, but Bayard had inadvertently released her into another opportunity to speak plainly.

"No. Not really."

"Really?"

Leah laughed. "I've come to realize that no matter what I think I may know, it's always half a lie, Detective. There's just too much margin of error in every story. Even if you think you know both sides." She clicked her tongue from the wry roof of her mouth. "Especially if you know both sides." She looked out over the porch railing. "I think I'm about done with the truth."

Whatever else she might say, the interview was essentially over. Bayard said that they were still looking into things, but if he'd had more, he would have pressed harder. When he didn't, she offered the truce of an authentic smile, and the whole exercise trailed into formalities and then finally into pleasantries.

If he was looking back on his walk out, she made sure he'd find her staring off into the middle distance, certainly somewhere he could not follow.

The veterinarian's bill had been remarkable. Ford would not allow anyone to call it outrageous. Thousands of dollars didn't raise an eyebrow for a child's treatment, and it wasn't every day that a child saved a parent's life. But her recovery was full with the exception of a slightly stiff gait, and everyone who knew her called it a miracle. It seemed Tessa was often hung with superlatives. As far as she knew, she was just a dog.

Tim had taken her from the firefighter who had rappelled down to get her. She'd been stopped, at the expense of a pair of broken legs and other assorted injuries, on a shallow shelf more than halfway down the ravine. He'd carried her out of the clearing, tears streaming without shame, in a circle of his colleagues. He'd been a regular fixture at the Wattses' home for weeks after that day, bearing more excuses of news and paperwork than he'd needed to bother with. While Tessa and Ford recuperated, life and crime in Stillwater returned to normal and eventually pulled Tim back to his old routine. And his old habits.

A Tuesday in December brought voice mails from Ford on Bayard's cell phone, his desk phone's voice mail, and a return number blinking on the caller-ID box that had been scooted out of easy view on Bayard's kitchen counter. It was an invitation to swing by when he could.

"Got something to show you." Ford led Tim to a new room built onto the Wattses' kitchen. A baby gate barred the doorway, and on the floor, Tessa wrangled with a German shepherd, barely out of puppyhood. Another one dozed on her paws on a plush mat in the corner.

Since his retirement, Ford had taken up the cause to get a K9 officer included on Mid-County's payroll, volunteering as a liaison for the program and boarding some of the recruits during their training.

"You remember Giles Myers over in West?" Ford asked.

"Yep. He's a prick."

"Nah, he's okay. He sent these two rejects back over to me. They both failed the selection. She gets carsick." Ford pointed at the dog in the corner and she flicked her eyes at them. "And this one? I swear to Goshen, I think he failed the test on purpose. 'Bout the smartest doggone thing I've ever seen, but he doesn't want to work. He just wants to play."

Tim nodded and stroked Tessa's ears, crooning to her. She'd cast off her playmate as soon as she'd seen him arrive.

"So which one?" Ford sucked his teeth and smiled sidelong at his sappy friend.

"Which one what?"

"Which one's yours? Which one's going home with you?"

Tessa picked for Tim. The male had broad russet marks for eyebrows, giving a lively mischief to his face. He trundled up to Tessa while she sat contentedly against the gate getting her dose of head-scratch. He wrapped his paws around her nose and wrestled her head from side to side. Tessa ducked out of his lock and turned to Tim, tongue dangling through a wide dog-smile. She and the youngster pressed jowl to jowl and looked to the men staring down on them, Tessa knowing, the other all wide-eyed openness.

"Are you sure, Ford?" Bayard asked. "You could probably sell these guys for a good chunk of change."

"The day I sell a dog is the day you need to cart me off. We're keeping the other one."

Tim laughed. "Okay then, I guess this one. Christine's going to kill me."

Ford swept the latch on the gate and all three dogs spilled out into the kitchen. "He's ornery. But you know how he loves Tessa. Always has, since we had him here as a pup. Loves her ears and her tail and her feet . . . that's why named him Tug."

"Tug." Bayard squatted down and gave him an experimental pat on the flank, and the dog immediately leapt up to rest his paws on Tim's shoulders. They each looked into the other's eyes. "Hello, Tug."

32

I T TOOK a discreetly hired investigator over four months to figure out, definitively, that there was never any such person as Gary Harris. The VIN number on the motorcycle had eventually yielded a lead. In the weeks after Harris's death, Jason had dismantled the bike and tossed it away, piece by piece, a task both satisfying and exhausting at turns. He felt a primate's triumph at each bit of bodywork that he peeled off the metal skeleton, and a winner's relief at every bolt that finally relented in the grip of his wrench. But Jason found himself scrubbing tears out of his eyes as often as he did grease from the whorls and lines in the palms of his hands.

Somewhere between a trophy and a headstone, he'd kept the last pieces closed up in a box in the spare room, but had never found the time to get rid of it. Or so he'd told himself. He felt fuzzy-headed and unable to concentrate knowing it was still there even after Harris was not.

It was a rare model, though it hadn't looked like all that much to Jason. The PI traced the registration to a collector in Canada, who had, oddly, never reported it stolen. The

anecdotal chain of *I heard/he told me/I think I saw it once*
pointed to its last rider as being a young man named Harris
Trumble, whom no one in his hometown had seen more
than once or twice in nearly a decade. Harris was the son
of Jolene and Gary Trumble, and he was banded directly,
or as a person of note, to a long police record of vandalism,
petty to not-so-petty larceny, and an after-school fight that
had left a boy in a coma until he awoke blind in one eye
and permanently forgetful.

Harris had been remanded, for his last years as a minor,
to a state-run farm designed to take in unruly boys and
turn out upstanding young men through the miracle of
stall-mucking and hay-baling. But the records of his time
there trailed off in an irritable summary at the back of a
confidential file. The bored clerk had exchanged a few
moments alone with the paperwork for nothing more than
the distraction of an interesting and utterly false tale of
intrigue from Jason's hired snoop.

Harris Trumble never completed his required time on the
farm. When he was sixteen, his father, Gary, had charmed
the administration into a flagrant breach of protocol. They
allowed him to take the boy out, just for a few hours, for a
motorcycle ride. It *was* Father's Day after all.

Gary Trumble died a handful of years later, a bruised
John Doe in a gutter on a winter's day in Minneapolis. He
was, eventually, identified by his fingerprints. None of his
notified kin bothered to claim his remains.

The investigator had delivered facts enough for Jason
to piece together the origins of the name Gary Harris.
The complications of the history between father and son
hinted at what might have ignited such a furious fight
over the reshuffling of his alias, but knowing the what of

it didn't do much for the why. Was it out of remembrance of his father? Was it simply to protect his privacy? Or was it really for the reasons he'd given—an affront to his offer of friendship, such as it was?

The newest and most improved why, though, no matter what Jason could learn of the facts, was the question of the pull and sway that Gary/Harris/Trumble still held over Jason Getty so long after he'd been bundled off the lawn and into the lab. Why was he still there in Jason's expectations when he raised his face to the mirror? And why was he so much more present, such a noisy ghost in Jason's memory, as the days went by? The answer, Jason knew, was woven into the last advice given by a friend he didn't really know.

He hadn't spoken to Leah since they'd met at the side door of the police station. They'd been released from the hospital within the same hour and had shared only one urgent glance in the hall as they were led away to separate interview rooms.

She was waiting at the curb for her ride, tearing at a hangnail with her teeth, when Jason was sprung from the precinct office to make his own way back home. He knew immediately that she also knew that they'd cleared the first hurdle if they were both uncuffed on the sidewalk in the painful midmorning sun.

"You okay?" he'd asked.

"Uh-huh." She laughed into the stupid pause. "What the hell do you say after all that?"

They watched the circle-headed crosswalk icon through a cycle of green, flashing, and then red.

"There's only one way this will work," she said. "Every answer to every question is the same: we don't know any-thing. No matter what they ask. No matter what they tell us that the other one had said. It's 'I don't know' and only that. Every time."

"Okay."

"Jason, it's everything. You have to swear. You have to be strong. This is all for nothing if we screw it up now. There's no statute of limitations on what you did, and I'm pretty sure I just aided and abetted."

"I don't know why you did that."

"Because it was the only thing to do. You can thank me, but it's what I wanted, too. I did it to end it. We're square." She looked straight into him to punctuate the point.

"But your head, I almost—"

"I'll be fine."

A patrol car whooped a short blat on its siren and streaked away from the motor-pool at the top of the street. Jason and Leah flinched in unison.

"We have to be smart," she said. "We can't talk about this. We can't talk about anything. We can't see each other. Not for a long time. Maybe forever."

"Yeah, I understand," Jason said to his shoes, red-faced.

"I doubt it," she said with a small smile. "Can you please at least believe there's no hard feelings?"

Jason's anchor pulled loose. His life was receding in a small spark of terror and an even smaller thrill of something else, something both finer and sadder.

"I wish I could take it all back," he said. "That's the truth."

"The truth." A shiver rocked her. "I don't know about truth, what it is, what it isn't. I just don't know. But maybe there's a scoreboard instead. You saved my life. Probably more than once. Maybe I saved yours, too. As far as first-line commandments go, could be that we're both plus one, minus one. Maybe it's good enough for a reset?"

A smoke-colored minivan pulled up, and Leah raised her hand to the woman inside.

She turned to him and the sun fought through the last of the morning haze to light up the bruised shadow that aged half her face so that Jason saw her now and saw her decades from now in one image.

"Be safe," she said, and craned to the farthest reach of her tiptoes to press a rough and too quick kiss into the bristle of his jaw. She dashed for the van before he'd felt it all the way through. "Or better yet," she called, "be the guy you want to be. It's not like anyone can tell the difference anyway."

It changes a man to discover his wants. Envy, especially of Harris's ease, had been a crowbar to pry the cover off Jason's hidden box of cogs. He had seen how his own heart worked and found a treasure trove of shiny, dexterous spare parts lying around. With all that had happened, it seemed he should have looked different. He kept being disappointed to search his reflection and see only Jason. Very only.

Jason lost his aversion to his own backyard. In fact, he stared out on it for hours. What wasn't there anymore drew his eyes over and over. Once he'd said "I don't know" to Bayard enough times to make it stick, it began to tickle, the truth of it, the not knowing if it was really finished. At some point, the police were bound to run out of missing persons named Phil to try to match to the slides they'd made from the muck in the grass.

The urge to run didn't leave. The town was spoiled for him. He'd wake up in the dark, sweating, gulping down lungfuls of air that tasted just the same as the stuff he'd heaved in when Harris was only newly dead. Every trip down the hallway outside his room was a tightrope line skirting the baseboard to keep from treading on the long-vanished luminol track in the rug. Each realization that he'd forgotten to remember to step here or not step there spurred back the dread from when Bayard had prowled, ready to pounce on Jason's smallest mistake. Sometimes a particular quality of light glowered in through the front windows on a stormy day that brought surges of goose bumps so rigid they stung. And at every sound of tires slowing down on Old Green Valley Road, the best his imagination would let him expect was Bayard back with a righteous clue and a new golf shirt.

Jason wanted to call Leah, to tear it all down to its parts as he had the motorcycle, so that at the least he'd actually know what he knew and not have to be left alone with it. But he wasn't allowed.

At the back of his yard, the hole full of dirt and no Harris taunted him almost as much as it had when it had been full of horror and secret. But the secret, at least, no longer required any tending. The grass growing over it, however, still did.

Jason huffed over the lawn-mower handle. Sweat slipped into the waistband of his shorts, and a mosquito whined in his ear. He'd ducked it twice, but the eye-watering yowl climbed up the musical scale again, right beside his cheek. He yanked off his hat and swatted the air around his head. When he was free of the bug, and feeling utterly foolish for his flap-dancing, he smiled up into the sunlight and found that a plan waited for him in the corner of his mind. He'd just tilted it loose.

He wanted a sunburn. Actually, he wanted lots of sunburns, cancer be damned. He wanted a new skin, thick and leathery, with lines that proved that he laughed and frowned and that he wasn't just a blank page or a canvas to accept what others painted there. He'd go south. But he'd stroll, not bolt in a fugitive scamper in the middle of the night.

The man in Harris's magic mirror wasn't real, but who could tell the difference anyway?

The spell of the lie's power became a worry, became a niggle, became part of who he was.

There is very little ease for a man who wears a stranger's name. Jason Getty had grown accustomed to stutter-starting his signature, his heart leaping into his throat when the pen looped a *J* automatically, instead of the *R* he'd adopted at the first stride away from Stillwater. He'd learned to keep his eyes steady and his excuses primed for when he failed to answer at the first call of the name that was not his. The new backstory was an ill-fitting coat, which was the only sort he'd ever worn anyway. So instead, he'd changed his posture to make it look like a better fit.

He sang karaoke on Friday nights and slapped on a little cologne every now and then. His dog went with him everywhere. His smile was infectious and he was known to flirt up the waitresses on occasion. He always made himself drive just a little too fast, and he played cards. Inexplicably, he often won at cards. The man he saw reflected in the bar mirror wouldn't know the man staring out of the glass over the bathroom vanity back home.

But strangely, it wasn't these things or even the jealous guarding of his dwindling stash of money that wore lines of worry into his forehead. Nor was it the eyestrain born of staring at the Spanish-to-English dictionary late into the night until his head ached and the words blurred together on the page as they did on his clumsy tongue. No. It was his preoccupation with wondering if the story had held, back there in Stillwater.

Was there any more than a passing interest in his disappearance? He had dotted the *i*'s and all that, then shed his habits and his name on a meandering westward feint. Jason had no way to check on any of it. He knew enough to be afraid of Internet tracking. Newspaper articles could be out there naming him a vicious thug on the run, sighing over his trail of senseless murder and mayhem, or local columns might have updates on the survivor's tearful tale of triumph.

But he'd never know, even if he risked a computer query. His hopes would always be pinned on the absence of a story. Knowing that nothing had happened—yet—wasn't even comfort's ghost. A simple phone call would damn him or put his mind at ease, but it was out of the question for a long time, though maybe not the forever that she'd suggested.

So he'd rolled what was left of his old life out of the real world and into his dreams. He'd had no choice—he wasn't a monster. In his own mind, he wasn't a liar either, but facts are facts.

Even if no one knows them.

Acknowledgments

So, here we are on the back pages together. Throughout these eighty-some-thousand words, I hope you and I have felt the same things. If I wrote it right, you and I, for a few hours, have ignored time and space, and the fundamental solitude of living alone in our own skulls. Thanks for being in here with me.

But I guarantee we feel very differently from one another now, way back here on page three-hundred-whatever. At "The End," I know I always look to the back pages of a book in the same way I sometimes linger in a littered theater as it clears out. The show's over, but I dunno, maybe there's still something to see that will bridge the gap from the spectacle back to my regular life. . . .

But me? This book? Back here, I'm just awash in gratitude. Whatever I got wrong in *Three Graves Full* was willful or I forgot to ask, because so many good people helped me get it right. My agent, Amy Moore-Benson, is one of my all-time favorites and the rekindler of snuffed enthusiasms. My editor, Karen Kosztolnyik at Gallery, is a lovely, wise, and patient person, and a rudder to steer with when I think

I'm out of ideas. Heather Hunt and the team at Gallery took what was always going to be an exciting time and made it manageable and fun. Their talents get labeled with "friendliness" and "competence" but that doesn't begin to cover how much they add to the publishing world. They've been wonderful to me. Steve Boldt is flat-out a prince among copyeditors.

For content, I owe a terrific debt to Special Agent Mike Breedlove of the Tennessee Bureau of Investigation. In helping me understand a detective's thoughts and deeds, he was invaluable. In friendship and support, he was just as priceless. Also, many thanks to Captain Terry L. Patterson of the Chesterfield County Police Department, a man so generous with his time and expertise, I could pick his brain for days. Again, if I got it wrong, no fault can be accorded to either of them.

The heart of the book, though, whatever is good about the storytelling, is obligated to a few people who held my hand, sometimes literally, sometimes cyber-ly, and sometimes just in spirit during the process:

My husband, Art, and my daughters, Julia and Rianne, are always the first line of defense. Nothing too awful gets past them, either incoming or outgoing. I love you more than I can write out. I hope you always feel that.

My friend and writing partner, Graeme Cameron, is nothing short of a genius, and also a man of extraordinary generosity. AuthorScoop's editor in chief, William Haskins, invited me onboard, putting me at least wrist-deep in the writing business every day, but I owe him even more for his humor, utterly brilliant poetry, and a friendship that has sustained me in all the hair-tearing times. The influence of these two extraordinary writers cannot be overstated.

Tana French, best-selling and award-winning author of incredible literary suspense, extended encouragement and friendship when she was too busy to do so. She treated a fan like a peer, and I don't know why she did it, but it's one of the finest things that's ever happened to me.

My fraternity of writers—Alex Adams, Chris Hyde, Sharon Maas, Rob McCreery, Nichola Feeney, Kim Michele Richardson, Butch Wilson, and Trish Stewart—thank you, thank you, and always be mine.

For steeping me in art, music, and laughter from the start, I love my first family: my mother, Jeanne-Miller Mason, and my sisters, Carmen Mason and Natalie Sherwood. Katie Delgado deserves my devotion threefold for friendship, bookishness, and web design. And for being the people I'd pack in my suitcase for the hypothetical desert island stranding: Jessica Coffey, Kelly Coffey Colvin, Lisa Fitchett, Kristi McCullough, Mary Rollins, and Patience Siegler.

Ursula Osterberg was always to be included in these acknowledgments, but my dear friend passed away before the book went to print. I will never plant anything in this hole you left in my heart, and I will miss you every day.

My nephew, Tommy Eccleston, caught a very menacing spider in exchange for a special mention here. What can I say? A promise is a promise and he's a lovely guy. Also very brave.

And Dr. David Arpin. Yes, I am acknowledging my chiropractor. He keeps me comfortably upright, which is no small feat. He loves books, too, which makes neck-cracking a social event I look forward to.

And thank you, Dear Reader, whoever and wherever you are. I hope we meet again on a page somewhere soon.